Robert Yelverton Tyrrell

The Troades of Euripides

Robert Yelverton Tyrrell

The Troades of Euripides

ISBN/EAN: 9783744734899

Printed in Europe, USA, Canada, Australia, Japan

Cover: Foto ©Andreas Hilbeck / pixelio.de

More available books at **www.hansebooks.com**

THE TROADES OF EURIPIDES.

Classical Series.

THE
TROADES OF EURIPIDES

WITH REVISED TEXT AND NOTES

BY

ROBERT YELVERTON TYRRELL, Litt.D.

FELLOW OF TRINITY COLLEGE, AND REGIUS PROFESSOR OF GREEK, DUBLIN;
HON. LITT.D. CAMBRIDGE, D.C.L. OXFORD, LL.D. EDINBURGH,
D.LIT. QUEEN'S UNIVERSITY IN IRELAND

London
MACMILLAN AND CO., Limited
NEW YORK: THE MACMILLAN COMPAN
1897

CONTENTS.

INTRODUCTION.

THE *Trojan Dames* is in many respects the best of the plays of Euripides for school reading. The four plays edited by Porson are in the hands of every schoolboy, yet they were chosen for annotation by that great scholar, not because they were the best instruments to the hand of the teacher, but because they are preserved in a great number of *codices*, and came first in those which he chiefly used. At least three of these four plays are less fitted than most of the works of Euripides to be put into the hands of schoolboys, and none of them, I think, are so suitable for this purpose as the *Troades*.

This play does not derive its interest from the evolution of a plot. Perhaps one might say that in this particular condition of dramatic excellence the *Troades* is the weakest, while the *Oedipus Tyrannus* of Sophocles is the strongest, of the extant Greek plays. The *Troades* can hardly be said to have a plot. It may be described in the fine phrase of Tennyson as

"A fiery scroll written over with lamentation and woe."

But it has many conspicuous merits. Its Choral Odes are of singular brilliancy and skill. The Ode beginning at verse 794 is a matchless piece of workmanship. In my note on that passage I have pointed out the splendid perfection of literary execution which Euripides has there achieved. I have also adverted in the notes to passages in which the poet shows his characteristic tenderness and subtle power of psychological analysis. The play abounds in displays of dialectic cunning and rhetorical ingenuity. It should be remembered that these ἐπιδείξεις had for the Athenians all the charms which a spectacle had for the Romans and has still for us.

The date of the play was the eventful year 415 B.C. It was the last play of its trilogy; hence, perhaps, the almost disproportionate development of the lyrical parts of the drama. The musical element seems to have been, as a rule, most prominent in the last play of a trilogy. The two other plays were the *Alexandrus* and the *Palamedes*, with the *Sisyphus* as the Satyric supplement. We read that the poet did not gain the prize, which was awarded to Xenocles with the *Oedipus, Lycaon, Bacchae*, and the Satyric *Athamas*.

In preparing this edition I have consulted throughout the recognized authorities. But very little has
been done for the *Troades*. The edition of G. Burges,
in which the play is virtually re-written, is of no
practical use. Bothe's edition of 1845 is the most
serviceable. I have taken as the basis of the text
that of Dindorf in his *Poetae Scenici Graeci*, 1870.
When I depart from the text of Dindorf in favour of
my own views or those of others, I point out the
divergence in the commentary.

The MSS. on which Dindorf has based his text are
V (Nauck's B), the *Codex Vaticanus* 909, of the 12th century, and P (Nauck's *B*), the *Codex Vaticanus Palatinus*
287, of the 14th century. Both these MSS. are now in
Rome, the latter, as its name imports, came originally
from the Palatinate. It is the same MS. on which we
have to depend solely for the last half of the *Bacchae*,
of which the first 754 lines are found also in C. It is
a singular thing that this C, which omits the last half
of the *Bacchae*, omits also the whole of the *Troades*,
though it contains all the other plays of Euripides.
It is strange too that Stobaeus, who quotes so copi-
ously from the other plays of Euripides, seems not to
have known the *Troades* at all. The other MSS. which
contain the *Troades* are the *Codices Harniensis* (C), *Har-
leianus* (*A*), and *Neapolitanus* (the last containing the
Scholia); but these *codices* are not valuable for critical

purposes, as they may be traced back to V c P, or *codices* closely resembling one or other of these : they are all of course much later than V and P, and abound in worthless conjectures.

The *Christus Patiens*, being a patchwork of phrases chiefly from the *Bacchae*, *Troades*, *Hippolytus*, and *Rhesus*, throws some light on the text. I have again toiled through this extremely dull drama, but I have not found it by any means so useful in the criticism of the *Troades* as in the criticism of the *Bacchae*. I have carefully read the *Troades* of Seneca, and have recorded in the notes such parallels as seemed instructive.

On grammatical points I have referred to Madvig's *Greek Syntax* and Goodwin's *Greek Moods and Tenses*. I have contented myself with a reference to Liddell and Scott, where it seemed that the *Lexicon* gave sufficient information. As it is possible that my edition of the *Bacchae* may be in the hands of some readers of this book, I have referred to it from time to time, to avoid a repetition of the same note. I have taken pains to preserve, so far as I could, in translating, the dignity of the original. A boy should not be encouraged to think that the Greek poets were bald and frigid. Translations of the Greek Tragic poets like those of Professor Jebb really inspire a learner with admiration for the works which he is studying—an admiration which rapturous eulogies of the Greek masterpieces often fail to awake. At the end of the volume will be found an Appendix on the metres of the lyrical parts of the play.

The notes enclosed within square brackets with the initials H. C. appended are by Mr. Hastings Crossley, M.A., of Dublin, and some time Professor of Greek in Queen's College, Belfast. Other more or less recent comments on the *Troades* have been drawn from the *Classical Review*, Bursian's *Jahresbericht*, and occasionally from monographs, as, for instance, that of Dr. J. Heinsch. It will be seen that I have received some very judicious and scholarly comments from Mr. Stanley, formerly a distinguished student of Trinity College, Dublin, a Scholar of the House and Senior Moderator, now Vice-Principal of the Campbell College near Belfast. I have also, with Mr. Way's permission, beautified my edition by frequent quotations from his scholarly and artistic *Euripides in English Verse* (Vol. II., Macmillan, 1896).

ΕΥΡΙΠΙΔΟΥ ΤΡΩΙΑΔΕΣ.

ΥΠΟΘΕΣΙΣ.

Μετὰ τὴν Ἰλίου πόρθησιν ἔδοξεν Ἀθανᾷ τε καὶ Ποσει-
δῶνι τὸ τῶν Ἀχαιῶν στράτευμα διαφθεῖραι, τοῦ μὲν
εὐνοοῦντος τῇ πόλει διὰ τὴν κτίσιν, τῆς δὲ μισησάσης
τοὺς Ἕλληνας διὰ τὴν Αἴαντος εἰς Κασάνδραν ὕβριν.
οἱ δὲ Ἕλληνες κληρωσάμενοι περὶ τῶν αἰχμαλώτων
γυναικῶν τὰς ἐν ἀξιώμασιν ἔδωκαν Ἀγαμέμνονι μὲν
Κασάνδραν, Ἀνδρομάχην δὲ Νεοπτολέμῳ, Πολυξένην
δὲ τῷ Ἀχιλλεῖ. ταύτην μὲν οὖν ἐπὶ τῆς τοῦ Ἀχιλλέως
ταφῆς ἔσφαξαν, Ἀστυάνακτα δὲ ἀπὸ τῶν τειχῶν ἔρρι-
ψαν, Ἑλένην δὲ ὡς ἀποκτενῶν Μενέλεως ἤγαγεν, Ἀγαμέμνων δὲ τὴν χρησμῳδὸν ἐνυμφαγώγησεν, Ἑκάβη δὲ
τῆς μὲν Ἑλένης κατηγορήσασα, τοὺς ἀναιρεθέντας δὲ
κατοδυραμένη καὶ τὸν Ἀστυάνακτα κηδεύσασα πρὸς τὰς
Ὀδυσσέως ἤχθη σκηνάς, τούτῳ λατρεύειν δοθεῖσα.

Aelianus, *V. H.* 2, 8. Κατὰ τὴν πρώτην καὶ ἐνενη-
κοστὴν ὀλυμπιάδα, καθ' ἣν ἐνίκα Ἐξαίνετος ὁ Ἀκρα-
γαντῖνος στάδιον, ἀντηγωνίσαντο ἀλλήλοις Ξενοκλῆς
καὶ Εὐριπίδης. καὶ πρῶτός γε ἦν Ξενοκλῆς—Οἰδίποδι
καὶ Λυκάονι καὶ Βάκχαις καὶ Ἀθάμαντι σατυρικῷ.
τούτου δεύτερος Εὐριπίδης ἦν Ἀλεξάνδρῳ καὶ Παλαμήδει
καὶ Τρῳάσι καὶ Σισύφῳ σατυρικῷ.

ΤΑ ΤΟΥ ΔΡΑΜΑΤΟΣ ΠΡΟΣΩΠΑ.

ΠΟΣΕΙΔΩΝ.
ΑΘΑΝΑ.
ΕΚΑΒΗ.
ΧΟΡΟΣ ΑΙΧΜΑΛΩΤΙΔΩΝ ΤΡΩΙΑΔΩΝ.
ΤΑΛΘΥΒΙΟΣ.
ΚΑΣΑΝΔΡΑ.
ΑΝΔΡΟΜΑΧΗ.
ΜΕΝΕΛΑΟΣ.
ΕΛΕΝΗ.

ΕΥΡΙΠΙΔΟΥ ΤΡΩΙΑΔΕΣ.

ΠΟΣΕΙΔΩΝ.

Ἥκω λιπὼν Αἴγαιον ἁλμυρὸν βάθος
πόντου Ποσειδῶν, ἔνθα Νηρήδων χοροὶ
κάλλιστον ἴχνος ἐξελίσσουσιν ποδός·
ἐξ οὗ γὰρ ἀμφὶ τήνδε Τρωικὴν χθόνα
Φοῖβός τε κἀγὼ λαΐνους πύργους πέριξ   5
ὀρθοῖσιν ἔθεμεν ᾽ ανόσιν, οὔποτ᾽ ἐκ φρενῶν
εὔνοι᾽ ἀπέστη τῶν ἐμῶν Φρυγῶν πόλει,
ἣ νῦν καπνοῦται καὶ πρὸς Ἀργείου δορὸς
ὄλωλε πορθηθεῖσ᾽· ὁ γὰρ Παρνάσιος
Φωκεὺς Ἐπειὸς μηχαναῖσι Παλλάδος   10
ἐγκύμον᾽ ἵππον τευχέων ξυναρμόσας
πύργων ἔπεμψεν ἐντός, ὀλέθριον βάρος·
ὅθεν πρὸς ἀνδρῶν ὑστέρων κεκλήσεται
δούρειος ἵππος, κρυπτὸν ἀμπισχὼν δόρυ.
ἔρημα δ᾽ ἄλση καὶ θεῶν ἀνάκτορα   15
φόνῳ καταρρεῖ· πρὸς δὲ κρηπίδων βάθροις
πέπτωκε Πρίαμος Ζηνὸς ἑρκείου θανών.
πολὺς δὲ χρυσὸς Φρύγιά τε σκυλεύματα

3

πρὸς ναῦς Ἀχαιῶν πέμπεται· μένουσι δὲ
πρύμνηθεν οὖρον, ὡς δεκασπόρῳ χρόνῳ   20
ἀλόχους τε καὶ τέκν' εἰσίδωσιν ἄσμενοι,
οἳ τήνδ' ἐπεστράτευσαν Ἕλληνες πόλιν.
ἐγὼ δέ, νικῶμαι γὰρ Ἀργείας θεοῦ
Ἥρας Ἀθάνας θ', αἳ ξυνεξεῖλον Φρύγας,
λείπω τὸ κλεινὸν Ἴλιον βωμούς τ' ἐμούς·   25
ἐρημία γὰρ πόλιν ὅταν λάβῃ κακή,
νοσεῖ τὰ τῶν θεῶν οὐδὲ τιμᾶσθαι θέλει.
πολλοῖς δὲ κωκυτοῖσιν αἰχμαλωτίδων
βοᾷ Σκάμανδρος δεσπότας κληρουμένων.
καὶ τὰς μὲν Ἀρκάς, τὰς δὲ Θεσσαλὸς λεὼς   30
εἴληχ' Ἀθηναίων τε Θησεῖδαι πρόμοι.
ὅσαι δ' ἄκληροι Τρῳάδων, ὑπὸ στέγαις
ταῖσδ' εἰσὶ τοῖς πρώτοισιν ἐξῃρημέναι
στρατοῦ, ξὺν αὐταῖς δ' ἡ Λάκαινα Τυνδαρὶς
Ἑλένη, νομισθεῖσ' αἰχμάλωτος ἐνδίκως.   35
τὴν δ' ἀθλίαν τήνδ' εἴ τις εἰσορᾶν θέλει,
πάρεστιν, Ἑκάβην κειμένην πυλῶν πάρος,
δάκρυα χέουσαν πολλὰ καὶ πολλῶν ὕπερ·
ἣ παῖς μὲν ἀμφὶ μνῆμ' Ἀχιλλείου τάφου
λάθρα τέθνηκε τλημόνως Πολυξένη,   40
φροῦδος δὲ Πρίαμος καὶ τέκν'· ἣν δὲ παρθένον
μεθῆκ' Ἀπόλλων δρομάδα Κασάνδραν ἄναξ,
τὸ τοῦ θεοῦ τε παραλιπὼν τό τ' εὐσεβὲς
γαμεῖ βιαίως σκότιον Ἀγαμέμνων λέχος.
ἀλλ', ὦ ποτ' εὐτυχοῦσα, χαῖρέ μοι, πόλις,   45
ξεστόν τε πύργωμ'· εἴ σε μὴ διώλεσε
Παλλὰς Διὸς παῖς, ἦσθ' ἂν ἐν βάθροις ἔτι.

ΑΘΑΝΑ.

ἔξεστι τὸν γένει μὲν ἄγχιστον πατρός,
μέγαν τε δαίμον᾽ ἐν θεοῖς τε τίμιον,
λύσασαν ἔχθραν τὴν πάρος, προσεννέπειν; 50

ΠΟ. ἔξεστιν· αἱ γὰρ ξυγγενεῖς ὁμιλίαι,
ἄνασσ᾽ Ἀθάνα, φίλτρον οὐ σμικρὸν φρενῶν.

ΑΘ. ἐπῄνεσ᾽ ὀργὰς ἠπίους· φέρω δὲ σοὶ
κοινοὺς ἐμαυτῇ τ᾽ ἐς μέσον λόγους, ἄναξ.

ΠΟ. μῶν ἐκ θεῶν του καινὸν ἀγγελεῖς ἔπος, 55
ἢ Ζηνός, ἢ καὶ δαιμόνων τινὸς πάρα;

ΑΘ. οὔκ, ἀλλὰ Τροίας οὕνεκ᾽, ἔνθα βαίνομεν,
πρὸς σὴν ἀφῖγμαι δύναμιν, ὡς κοινὴν λάβω.

ΠΟ. ἦ πού νιν ἔχθραν τὴν πρὶν ἐκβαλοῦσα νῦν
εἰς οἶκτον ἦλθες πυρὶ κατῃθαλωμένης; 60

ΑΘ. ἐκεῖσε πρῶτ᾽ ἄνελθε· κοινώσει λόγους
καὶ ξυνθελήσεις ἂν ἐγὼ πρᾶξαι θέλω;

ΠΟ. μάλιστ᾽· ἀτὰρ δὴ καὶ τὸ σὸν θέλω μαθεῖν,
πότερον Ἀχαιῶν ἦλθες οὕνεκ᾽ ἢ Φρυγῶν.

ΑΘ. τοὺς μὲν πρὶν ἐχθροὺς Τρῶας εὐφρᾶναι θέλω, 65
στρατῷ δ᾽ Ἀχαιῶν νόστον ἐμβαλεῖν πικρόν.

ΠΟ. τί δ᾽ ὧδε πηδᾷς ἄλλοτ᾽ εἰς ἄλλους τρόπους,
μισεῖς τε λίαν καὶ φιλεῖς ὃν ἂν τύχῃς;

ΑΘ. οὐκ οἶσθ᾽ ὑβρισθεῖσάν με καὶ ναοὺς ἐμούς;

ΠΟ. οἶδ᾽, ἡνίκ᾽ Αἴας εἷλκε Κασάνδραν βίᾳ. 70

ΑΘ. κοὐδέν γ᾽ Ἀχαιῶν ἔπαθεν οὐδ᾽ ἤκουσ᾽ ὕπο.

ΠΟ. καὶ μὴν ἔπερσάν γ᾽ Ἴλιον τῷ σῷ σθένει.

ΑΘ. τοιγάρ σφε σὺν σοὶ βούλομαι δρᾶσαι κακῶς.

ΠΟ. ἕτοιμ᾽ ἃ βούλει τἀπ᾽ ἐμοῦ. δράσεις δὲ τί;

ΑΘ. δύσνοστον αὐτοῖς νόστον ἐμβαλεῖν θέλω. 75

ΠΟ. ἐν γῇ μενόντων ἢ καθ' ἁλμυρὰν ἅλα ;
ΑΘ. ὅταν πρὸς οἴκους ναυστολῶσ' ἀπ' Ἰλίου.
   καὶ Ζεὺς μὲν ὄμβρον καὶ χάλαζαν ἄσπετον
   πέμψει δνοφώδη τ' αἰθέρος φυσήματα,
   ἐμοὶ δὲ δώσειν φησὶ πῦρ κεραύνιον,   80
   βάλλειν Ἀχαιοὺς ναῦς τε πιμπράναι πυρί.
   σὺ δ' αὖ τὸ σὸν παράσχες Αἴγαιον πόρον
   τρικυμίαις βρέμοντα καὶ δίναις ἁλός,
   πλῆσον δὲ νεκρῶν κοῖλον Εὐβοίας μυχόν,
   ὡς ἂν τὸ λοιπὸν τἀμ' ἀνάκτορ' εὐσεβεῖν   85
   εἰδῶσ' Ἀχαιοὶ θεούς τε τοὺς ἄλλους σέβειν.
ΠΟ. ἔσται τάδ'· ἡ χάρις γὰρ οὐ μακρῶν λόγων
   δεῖται· ταράξω πέλαγος Αἰγαίας ἁλός.
   ἀκταὶ δὲ Μυκόνου Δήλιοί τε χοιράδες
   Σκῦρός τε Λῆμνός θ' αἱ Καφήρειοί τ' ἄκραι 90
   πολλῶν θανόντων σώμαθ' ἕξουσιν νεκρῶν.
   ἀλλ' ἕρπ' Ὄλυμπον καὶ κεραυνίους βολὰς
   λαβοῦσα πατρὸς ἐκ χερῶν καραδόκει,
   ὅταν στράτευμ' Ἀργεῖον ἐξιῇ κάλως.
   μῶρος δὲ θνητῶν ὅστις ἐκπορθῶν πόλεις,   95
   ναούς τε τύμβους θ', ἱρὰ τῶν κεκμηκότων,
   ἐρημίᾳ δοὺς αὐτὸς ὤλεθ' ὕστερον.

ΕΚΑΒΗ.

ἄνα, δύσδαιμον, πεδόθεν κεφαλὴν   στρ. α'.
ἐπάειρε δέρην τ'· οὐκέτι Τροία
τάδε καὶ βασιλεῖς ἐσμεν Τροίας.   100
μεταβαλλομένου δαίμονος ἀνέχου.
πλεῖ κατὰ πορθμόν, πλεῖ κατὰ δαίμονα,

μηδὲ προσίστη πρῷραν βιότου
πρὸς κῦμα πλέουσα τύχαις· αἰαῖ.   105
τί γὰρ οὐ πάρα μοι μελέᾳ στενάχειν,
ᾗ πατρὶς ἔρρει καὶ τέκνα καὶ πόσις
ὦ πολὺς ὄγκος ξυστελλόμενος
προγόνων, ὡς οὐδὲν ἄρ' ἦσθα.
τί με χρὴ σιγᾶν, τί δὲ μὴ σιγᾶν ;   ἀντιστρ. α'.
[τί δὲ θρηνῆσαι ;]   111
δύστηνος ἐγὼ τῆς βαρυδαίμονος
ἄρθρων κλισίας, ὡς διάκειμαι
νῶτ' ἐν στερροῖς λέκτροισι ταθεῖσ'.
οἴμοι κεφαλῆς, οἴμοι κροτάφων   115
πλευρῶν θ', ὥς μοι πόθος εἱλίξαι
καὶ διαδοῦναι νῶτον ἄκανθάν τ'
εἰς ἀμφοτέρους τοίχους, μελέων
ἐπιοῦσ' ἀεὶ δακρύων ἐλέγους.
μοῦσα δὲ χαὔτη τοῖς δυστήνοις.   120
ἄτας κελαδεῖν ἀχορεύτους.
πρῷραι ναῶν, ὠκείαις   στρ. β'.
Ἴλιον ἱρὰν αἲ κώπαις ἅλα
διὰ πορφυροειδῆ καὶ λίμνας
Ἑλλάδος εὐόρμους   125
αὐλῶν παιᾶνι στυγνῷ
συρίγγων τ' εὐφθόγγῳ φωνᾷ
βαίνουσαι πλεκτάν, Αἰγύπτου
παίδευμ', ἐξηρτήσασθ', αἰαῖ,
Τροίας ἐν κόλποις,   130
τὰν Μενελάου μετανισσόμεναι
στυγνὰν ἄλοχον, Κάστορι λώβαν,

τῷ τ' Εὐρώτᾳ δυσκλείαν,
ἃ σφάζει μὲν τὸν πεντήκοντ'   135
ἀροτῆρα τέκνων, ἐμὲ τὰν μελέαν δ'
ἐς τάνδ' ἐξώκειλ' ἄταν.
ὤμοι θάκους οὓς θάσσω   ἀντιστρ. β'.
σκηναῖς ἐφέδρους Ἀγαμεμνονίαις.
δούλα δ' ἄγομαι γραῦς ἐξ οἴκων,   140
κουρᾷ πενθήρει
κρᾶτ' ἐκπορθηθεῖσ' οἰκτρῶς.
ἀλλ' ὦ τῶν χαλκεγχέων Τρώων
ἄλοχοι μέλεαι, μέλεαι κοῦραι
καὶ δύσνυμφοι, τύφεται Ἴλιον,   145
ἐξαιάζωμεν·
μάτηρ δ' ὡσεὶ πτανοῖς κλαγγὰν
ὄρνις ἐξάρξω 'γὼ μολπὰν
οὐ τὰν αὐτὰν οἵαν δὴ
σκήπτρῳ Πριάμου διερειδομένα   150
ποδὸς ἀρχεχόρου πλαγαῖς Φρυγίαις
εὐκόμποις ἐξῆρχον θεούς.

ΗΜΙΧΟΡΙΟΝ.

Ἑκάβη, τί θροεῖς ; τί δὲ θωΰσσεις ;   στρ. γ'.
ποῖ λόγος ἥκει ; διὰ γὰρ μελάθρων
ἄϊον οἴκτους οὓς οἰκτίζει,   155
διὰ δὲ στέρνων φόβος ᾄσσει
Τρωάσιν, αἳ τῶνδ' οἴκων εἴσω
δουλείαν αἰάζουσιν.
ΕΚ. ὦ τέκνον, Ἀργείων πρὸς ναυσὶν   160
κινεῖται κωπήρης χείρ.

ΗΜ. οἲ 'γώ, τί θέλουσ' ; ἦ πού μ' ἤδη
  ναυσθλώσουσιν πατρῴας ἐκ γᾶς ;
ΕΚ. οὐκ οἶδ', εἰκάζω δ' ἄταν.
ΗΜ. ἰώ ἰώ
  μέλεαι μόχθων ἐπακουσόμεναι   165
  " Τρῳάδες, ἔξω κομίσασθ' οἴκων·
  στέλλουσ' 'Αργεῖοι νόστον."
ΕΚ. αἰαῖ,
  μή νύν μοι τὰν βακχεύουσαν
  Κασάνδραν πέμψητ' ἔξω,   170
  αἰσχύναν 'Αργείοισιν,
  μαινάδ', ἐπ' ἄλγει δ' ἀλγυνθῶ.
  Τροία Τροία δύσταν', ἔρρεις
  δύστανοι δ' οἵ σ' ἐκλείποντες
  καὶ ζῶντες καὶ δμαθέντες   175
ΗΜ. οἴμοι. τρομερὰ σκηνὰς ἔλιπον   ἀντιστροφ. γ΄.
  τάσδ' 'Αγαμέμνονος ἐπακουσομένα,
  βασίλεια, σέθεν, μή με κτείνειν
  δόξ' 'Αργείων κεῖται μελέαν,
  ἦ κατὰ πρύμνας ἤδη ναῦται   180
  στέλλονται κινεῖν κώπας.
ΕΚ. ὦ τέκνον, ὀρθρεύουσαν ψυχὰν
  ἐκπληχθεῖσ' ἦλθον φρίκᾳ.
ΗΜ. ἤδη τις ἔβα Δαναῶν κῆρυξ ;
  τῷ πρόσκειμαι δούλα τλάμων ;   185
ΕΚ. ἐγγύς που κεῖσαι κλήρου.
ΗΜ. ἰὼ ἰώ.
  τίς μ' 'Αργείων ἢ Φθιωτᾶν
  ἢ νησαίαν ἄξει χώραν

δύστανον πόρσω Τροίας;
ΕΚ. φεῦ φεῦ.
τῷ δ᾿ ἁ τλάμων ποῦ ποῦ γαίας   190
δουλεύσω γραῦς, ὡς κηφήν,
δειλαία νεκροῦ μορφά,
νεκύων ἀμενηνὸν ἄγαλμ᾿, ἢ
τὰν παρὰ προθύροις φυλακὰν κατέχουσ᾿,
ἢ παίδων θρέπτειρ᾿, ἃ Τροίας   .195
ἀρχαγοὺς εἶχον τιμάς;
ΧΟ. αἰαῖ αἰαῖ.   ποίοις δ᾿ οἴκτοις   στρ. δ΄.
τὰν σὰν λύμαν ἐξαιάξεις;
οὐκ Ἰδαίοις ἱστοῖς κερκίδα
δινεύουσ᾿ ἐξαλλάξω.   200
νέατον τεκέων σώματα λεύσσω,
νέατον.   μόχθους ἔξω κρείσσους,
ἢ λέκτροις πλαθεῖσ᾿ Ἑλλάνων—
ἔρροι νὺξ αὕτα καὶ δαίμων—
ἢ Πειρήνας ὑδρευσομένα   205
πρόπολος σεμνῶν ὑδάτων ἔσομαι.
τὰν κλεινὰν εἴθ᾿ ἔλθοιμεν
Θησέως εὐδαίμονα χώραν·
μὴ γὰρ δὴ δίναν γ᾿ Εὐρώτα,
τὰν ἐχθίσταν θεράπναν Ἑλένας,
ἔνθ᾿ ἀντάσω Μενέλᾳ δούλα,
τῷ τᾶς Τροίας πορθητᾷ.
τὰν Πηνειοῦ σεμνὰν χώραν,   ἀντιστρ. δ΄.
κρηπῖδ᾿ Οὐλύμπου καλλίσταν,   215
ὄλβῳ βρίθειν φάμαν ἤκουσ᾿
εὐθαλεῖ τ᾿ εὐκαρπείᾳ·

τάδε δεύτερά μοι μετὰ τὰν ἱερὰν
Θησέως ζαθέαν ἐλθεῖν χώραν.
καὶ τὰν Αἰτναίαν Ἡφαίστου   220
Φοινίκας ἀντήρη χώραν
Σικελῶν, ὀρέων ματέρ', ἀκούω
καρύσσεσθαι στεφάνοις ἀρετᾶς·
τάν τ' ἀγχιστεύουσαν γᾶν
Ἰονίῳ ναίοιν πόντῳ,   225
ἃν ὑγραίνει καλλιστεύων
ὁ ξανθὰν χαίταν πυρσαίνων
Κρᾶθις, ζαθέαις παγαῖσι τρέφων
εὔανδρόν τ' ὀλβίζων γᾶν.

καὶ μὴν Δαναῶν ὅδ' ἀπὸ στρατιᾶς   230
κῆρυξ, νεοχμῶν μύθων ταμίας,
στείχει ταχύπουν ἴχνος ἐξανύων.
τί φέρει; τί λέγει; δοῦλαι γὰρ δὴ
Δωρίδος ἐσμὲν χθονὸς ἤδη.

ΤΑΛΘΥΒΙΟΣ.

Ἑκάβη, πυκνὰς γὰρ οἶσθά μ' ἐς Τροίαν ὁδοὺς
ἐλθόντα κήρυκ' ἐξ Ἀχαιικοῦ στρατοῦ,   236
ἐγνωσμένος δὲ καὶ πάροιθέ σοι, γύναι,
Ταλθύβιος ἥκω, καινὸν ἀγγέλλων λόγον.
ΕΚ. τόδε τόδ', ὦ φίλαι γυναῖκες, ⏑ — ὃ φόβος ἦν
πάλαι.
ΤΑ. ἤδη κεκλήρωσθ', εἰ τόδ' ἦν ὑμῖν φόβος.   240
ΕΚ. αἰαῖ. τίν' ἢ
Θεσσαλίας πόλιν Φθιάδος εἶπας ἢ Καδμείας
χθονός;

ΤΑ. κατ' ἄνδρ' ἑκάστῃ κοὐχ ὁμοῦ λελόγχατε.

ΕΚ. τίν' ἄρα τίς ἔλαχε; τίνα πότμος εὐτυχὴς
    Ἰλιάδων μένει;   245

ΤΑ. οἶδ'· ἀλλ' ἕκαστα πυνθάνου, μὴ πάνθ' ὁμοῦ.

ΕΚ. τοὐμὸν δὲ τίς ἄρ' ἔλαχε τέκος, ἔννεπε, τλάμονα
    Κασάνδραν;

ΤΑ. ἐξαίρετόν νιν ἔλαβεν Ἀγαμέμνων ἄναξ.

ΕΚ. ἦ τᾷ Λακεδαιμονίᾳ νύμφᾳ δούλαν; ἰώ μοί μοι

ΤΑ. οὔκ, ἀλλὰ λέκτρων σκότια νυμφευτήρια.   251

ΕΚ. ἦ τὰν τοῦ Φοίβου παρθένον, ᾇ γέρας ὁ
    χρυσοκόμας ἔδωκ' ἄλεκτρον ζόαν;   .

ΤΑ. ἔρως ἐτόξευσ' αὐτὸν ἐνθέου κόρης.   255

ΕΚ. ῥῖπτε, τέκνον, ζαθέους
    κλάδας καὶ ἀπὸ χροὸς ἐνδυτῶν στεφέων ἱεροὺς
    στολμούς.

ΤΑ. οὐ γὰρ μέγ' αὐτῇ βασιλικῶν λέκτρων τυχεῖν;

ΕΚ. τί δ', ὃ νεοχμὸν ἀπ' ἐμέθεν ἐλάβετε τέκος, 260

ΤΑ. Πολυξένην ἔλεξας, ἢ τίν' ἱστορεῖς;

ΕΚ. τῷ πάλος ἔζευξεν;

ΤΑ. τύμβῳ τέτακται προσπολεῖν Ἀχιλλέως.

ΕΚ. ὤμοι ἐγώ. τάφῳ πρόσπολον ἐτεκόμαν. 265
    ἀτὰρ τίς ὅδ' ἢ νόμος ἢ τί θέσμιον, ὦ φίλος,
    Ἑλλάνων;

ΤΑ. εὐδαιμόνιζε παῖδα σήν. ἔχει καλῶς.

ΕΚ. τί τόδ' ἔλακες; ἆρά μοι ἀέλιον λεύσσει;

ΤΑ. ἔχει πότμος νιν, ὥστ' ἀπηλλάχθαι πόνων. 270

ΕΚ. τί δ', ἁ τοῦ χαλκεομήστορος Ἕκτορος δάμαρ,
    Ἀνδρομάχα τάλαινα, τίν' ἔχει τύχαν;

ΤΑ. καὶ τήνδ' Ἀχιλλέως ἔλαβε παῖς ἐξαίρετον.

ΕΚ. ἐγὼ δὲ τῷ πρόσπολος, ἁ τριτοβάμονος χερὶ
 δευομένα βάκτρου γεραιῷ κάρᾳ ;   276
ΤΑ. Ἰθάκης Ὀδυσσεὺς ἔλαχ᾽ ἄναξ δούλην σ᾽ ἔχειν.
ΕΚ. ἐή,
 ἄρασσε κρᾶτα κούριμον,
 ἕλκ᾽ ὀνύχεσσι δίπτυχον παρειάν.   280
 ἰώ μοί μοι.
 μυσαρῷ δολίῳ τε λέλογχα φωτὶ δουλεύειν,
 πολεμίῳ δίκας, παρανόμῳ δάκει,
 ὃς πάντα τἀκεῖθεν ἐνθάδ᾽   285
 ἀντίπαλ᾽ αὖθις ἐκεῖσε διπτύχῳ γλώσσᾳ
 φίλα τὰ πρότερ᾽ ἄφιλα τιθέμενος πάντων—
 γοᾶσθέ μ᾽, ὦ Τρῳάδες· βέβακα
 δύσποτμος, οἴχομαι   290
 τάλαιν᾽, ἃ δυστυχεστάτῳ
 προσέπεσον κλήρῳ.
ΧΟ. τὸ μὲν σὸν οἶσθα, πότνια, τὰς δ᾽ ἐμὰς τύχας
 τίς ἆρ᾽ Ἀχαιῶν ἢ τίς Ἑλλήνων ἔχει ;
ΤΑ. ἴτ᾽, ἐκκομίζειν δεῦρο Κασάνδραν χρεὼν   295
 ὅσον τάχιστα, δμῶες, ὡς στρατηλάτῃ
 ἐς χεῖρα δούς νιν εἶτα τὰς εἰληγμένας
 καὶ τοῖσιν ἄλλοις αἰχμαλωτίδων ἄγω.
 ἔα, τί πεύκης ἔνδον ἵσταται σέλας ;
 πιμπρᾶσιν ἢ τί δρῶσι Τρῳάδες μυχούς,   300
 ὡς ἐξάγεσθαι τῆσδε μέλλουσαι χθονὸς
 πρὸς Ἄργος, αὑτῶν τ᾽ ἐκπυροῦσι σώματα,
 θανεῖν θέλουσαι ; κάρτα τοι τοὐλεύθερον
 ἐν τοῖς τοιούτοις δυσλόφως φέρει κακά.
 ἄνοιγ᾽ ἄνοιγε, μὴ τὸ ταῖσδε πρόσφορον,   305

ἐχθρὸν δ᾽ Ἀχαιοῖς, εἰς ἔμ᾽ αἰτίαν βάλῃ.
ΕΚ. οὐκ ἔστιν, οὐ πιμπρᾶσιν, ἀλλὰ παῖς ἐμὴ
     μαινὰς θοάζει δεῦρο Κασάνδρα δρόμῳ.

ΚΑΣΑΝΔΡΑ.

ἄνεχε πάρεχε, φῶς φέρε· σέβω, φλέγω,   στρ.
ἰδοὺ ἰδού,   310
λαμπάσι τόδ᾽ ἱερόν.
μακάριος μὲν ὁ γαμέτας,
́⏑⏑⏑⏑⏑
μακαρία δ᾽ ἐγὼ βασιλικοῖς λέκτροις
κατ᾽ Ἄργος ἀ γαμουμένα,
Ὑμήν, ὦ Ὑμέναι᾽ ἄναξ.
ἐπεὶ σύ, μᾶτερ, ἐπὶ δάκρυσι   315
γόοισι τὸν θανόντα πατέρα πατρίδα τε
φίλαν καταστένουσ᾽ ἔχεις,
ἐγὼ δέ γ᾽ ἐπὶ γάμοις ἐμοῖς
ἀναφλέγω πυρὸς φῶς   320
ἐς αὐγάν, ἐς αἴγλαν,
διδοῦσ᾽, ὦ Ὑμέναιε, σοί,
διδοῦσ᾽, ὦ Ἑκάτα, φάος,
παρθένων ἐπὶ λέκτροις ἃ νόμος ἔχει.
πάλλε πόδ᾽ αἰθέριον, ἄναγ᾽ ἄναγε χορόν,   ἀντ.
εὐὰν εὐοῖ,   326
ὡς ἐπὶ πατρὸς ἐμοῦ
μακαριωτάταις τύχαις.
ὁ χορὸς ὅσιος,
ἄγε σὺ Φοῖβέ νιν· κατὰ σὸν ἐν δάφναις
ἀνάκτορον θυηπολῶ,   330

Ὑμήν, ὦ Ὑμέναι', Ὑμήν.
χόρευε, μᾶτερ, ἀναγέλασον,
ἔλισσε τᾷδ' ἐκεῖσε μετ' ἐμέθεν ποδῶν
φέρουσα φιλτάταν βάσιν.
βοᾶτε τὸν Ὑμέναιον εὖ   335
μακαρίαις ἀοιδαῖς
ἰακχαῖς τε νύμφαν.
ἴτ', ὦ καλλίπεπλοι Φρυγῶν
κόραι, μέλπετ' ἐμῶν γάμων
τὸν πεπρωμένον εὐνᾷ πόσιν ἐμέθεν.   340

ΧΟ. βασίλεια, βακχεύουσαν οὐ λήψει κόρην,
μὴ κοῦφον αἴρῃ βῆμ' ἐς Ἀργείων στρατόν;

ΕΚ. Ἥφαιστε, δᾳδουχεῖς μὲν ἐν γάμοις βροτῶν,
ἀτὰρ λυγράν γε τήνδ' ἀναιθύσσεις φλόγα,
ἔξω τε μεγάλων ἐλπίδων. οἴμοι, τέκνον,   345
ὡς οὐχ ὑπ' αἰχμῆς σ' οὐδ' ὑπ' Ἀργείου δορὸς
γάμους γαμεῖσθαι τούσδ' ἐδόξαζόν ποτε.
παράδος ἐμοὶ φῶς· οὐ γὰρ ὀρθὰ πυρφορεῖς
μαινὰς θοάζουσ', οὐδέ σ' αἱ τύχαι, τέκνον,
σοφὴν ἔθηκαν, ἀλλ' ἔτ' ἐν ταὐτῷ μένεις.   350
ἐσφέρετε πεύκας, δάκρυά τ' ἀνταλλάσσετε
τοῖς τῆσδε μέλεσι, Τρωάδες, γαμηλίοις.

ΚΑ. μῆτερ, πύκαζε κρᾶτ' ἐμὸν νικηφόρον
καὶ χαῖρε τοῖς ἐμοῖσι βασιλικοῖς γάμοις
καὶ πέμπε, κἂν μὴ τἀμά σοι πρόθυμά γ' ᾖ, 355
ὤθει βιαίως· εἰ γὰρ ἔστι Λοξίας,
Ἑλένης γαμεῖ με δυσχερέστερον γάμον
ὁ τῶν Ἀχαιῶν κλεινὸς Ἀγαμέμνων ἄναξ.
κτενῶ γὰρ αὐτὸν κἀντιπορθήσω δόμους

ποινὰς ἀδελφῶν καὶ πατρὸς λαβοῦσ' ἐμοῦ· 360
ἀλλ' αὔτ' ἐάσω· πέλεκυν οὐχ ὑμνήσομεν,
ὃς ἐς τράχηλον τὸν ἐμὸν εἶσι χἀτέρων,
μητροκτόνους τ' ἀγῶνας, οὓς οὑμοὶ γάμοι
θήσουσιν, οἴκων τ' Ἀτρέως ἀνάστασιν·
πόλιν δὲ δείξω τήνδε μακαριωτέραν 365
ἢ τοὺς Ἀχαιούς,—ἔνθεος μέν, ἀλλ' ὅμως
τοσόνδε γ' ἔξω στήσομαι βακχευμάτων,—
οἳ διὰ μίαν γυναῖκα καὶ μίαν Κύπριν
θηρῶντες Ἑλένην μυρίους ἀπώλεσαν.
ὁ δὲ στρατηγὸς ὁ σοφὸς ἐχθίστων ὕπερ 370
τὰ φίλτατ' ὤλεσ', ἡδονὰς τὰς οἴκοθεν
τέκνων ἀδελφῷ δοὺς γυναικὸς οὕνεκα,
καὶ ταῦθ' ἑκούσης κοὐ βίᾳ λελῃσμένης.
ἐπεὶ δ' ἐπ' ἀκτὰς ἤλυθον Σκαμανδρίους,
ἔθνησκον, οὐ γῆς ὅρι' ἀποστερούμενοι, 375
οὐδ' ὑψιπύργου πατρίδος· οὓς δ' Ἄρης ἕλοι,
οὐ παῖδας εἶδον, οὐ δάμαρτος ἐν χεροῖν
πέπλοις ξυνεστάλησαν, ἐν ξένῃ δὲ γῇ
κεῖνται. τὰ δ' οἴκοι τοῖσδ' ὅμοι' ἐγίγνετο·
χῆραί τ' ἔθνησκον, οἱ δ' ἄπαιδες ἐν δόμοις, 380
ἄλλως τέκν' ἐκθρέψαντες, οὐδὲ πρὸς τάφους
ἔσθ' ὅστις αὐτοῖς αἷμα γῇ δωρήσεται.
ἦ τοῦδ' ἐπαίνου τὸ στράτευμ' ἐπάξιον.
σιγᾶν ἄμεινον τἀσχρά, μηδὲ μοῦσά μοι
γένοιτ' ἀοιδὸς ἥτις ὑμνήσει κακά. 385
Τρῶες δὲ πρῶτον μέν, τὸ κάλλιστον κλέος,
ὑπὲρ πάτρας ἔθνησκον· οὓς δ' Ἄρης ἕλοι,
νεκροί γ' ἐς οἴκους φερόμενοι φίλων ὕπο

ἐν γῇ πατρῴᾳ περιβολὰς εἶχον χθονός,
χερσὶν περισταλέντες ὧν ἐχρῆν ὕπο.   390
ὅσοι δὲ μὴ θάνοιεν ἐν μάχῃ Φρυγῶν,
ἀεὶ κατ᾽ ἦμαρ ξὺν δάμαρτι καὶ τέκνοις
ᾤκουν, Ἀχαιοῖς ὧν ἀπῆσαν ἡδοναί.
τὰ δ᾽ Ἕκτορός σοι λύπρ᾽ ἄκουσον ὡς ἔχει·
δόξας ἀνὴρ ἄριστος οἴχεται θανών·   395
καὶ ταῦτ᾽ Ἀχαιῶν ἵξις ἐξεργάζεται·
εἰ δ᾽ ἦσαν οἴκοι, χρηστὸς ὢν ἐλάνθαν᾽ ἄν·
Πάρις τ᾽ ἔγημε τὴν Διός, γήμας δὲ μή,
σιγώμενον τὸ κῆδος εἶχ᾽ ἂν ἐν δόμοις.   399
φεύγειν μὲν οὖν χρὴ πόλεμον, ὅστις εὖ φρονεῖ·
εἰ δ᾽ ἐς τόδ᾽ ἔλθοι, στέφανος οὐκ αἰσχρὸς πόλει
καλῶς ὀλέσθαι, μὴ καλῶς δὲ δυσκλεές.
ὧν οὕνεκ᾽ οὐ χρή, μῆτερ, οἰκτείρειν σε γῆν,
οὐ τἀμὰ λέκτρα· τοὺς γὰρ ἐχθίστους ἐμοὶ
καὶ σοὶ γάμοισι τοῖς ἐμοῖς διαφθερῶ.   405
ΧΟ. ὡς ἡδέως κακοῖσιν οἰκείοις γελᾷς,
     μέλπεις θ᾽, ἃ μέλπουσ᾽ οὐ σαφῆ δείξεις ἴσως.
ΤΑ. εἰ μή σ᾽ Ἀπόλλων ἐξεβάκχευσεν φρένας,
     οὔ τἂν ἀμισθὶ τοὺς ἐμοὺς στρατηλάτας
     τοιαῖσδε φήμαις ἐξέπεμπες ἂν χθονός.   410
     ἀτὰρ τὰ σεμνὰ καὶ δοκήμασιν σοφὰ
     οὐδέν τι κρείσσω τῶν τὸ μηδὲν ἦν ἄρα.
     ὁ γὰρ μέγιστος τῶν Πανελλήνων ἄναξ,
     Ἀτρέως φίλος παῖς, τῆσδ᾽ ἔρωτ᾽ ἐξαίρετον
     μαινάδος ὑπέστη· καὶ πένης μέν εἰμ᾽ ἐγώ, 415
     ἀτὰρ λέχος γε τῆσδ᾽ ἂν οὐκ ἐκτησάμην.
     καὶ σοῦ μέν, οὐ γὰρ ἀρτίας ἔχεις φρένας,

B

Ἀργεῖ' ὀνείδη καὶ Φρυγῶν ἐπαινέσεις
ἀνέμοις φέρεσθαι παραδίδωμ'. ἕπου δέ μοι
πρὸς ναῦς, καλὸν νύμφευμα,τῷ στρατηλάτῃ.
σὺ δ', ἡνίκ' ἄν σε Λαρτίου χρῄζῃ τόκος   421
ἄγειν, ἕπεσθαι· σώφρονος δ' ἔσει λάτρις
γυναικός, ὥς φασ' οἱ μολόντες Ἴλιον.

ΚΑ. ἦ δεινὸς ὁ λάτρις· τί ποτ' ἔχουσι τοὔνομα
κήρυκες, ἓν ἀπέχθημα πάγκοινον βροτοῖς,   425
οἱ περὶ τυράννους καὶ πόλεις ὑπηρέται ;
σὺ τὴν ἐμὴν φῂς μητέρ' εἰς Ὀδυσσέως
ἥξειν μέλαθρα ;   ποῦ δ' Ἀπόλλωνος λόγοι
οἵ φασιν αὐτὴν εἰς ἔμ' ἡρμηνευμένοι
αὐτοῦ θανεῖσθαι ;   τἄλλα δ' οὐκ ὀνειδιῶ.   430
δύστηνος, οὐκ οἶδ' οἷά νιν μένει παθεῖν·
ὡς χρυσὸς αὐτῷ τἀμὰ καὶ Φρυγῶν κακὰ
δόξει ποτ' εἶναι. δέκα γὰρ ἐκπλήσας ἔτη
πρὸς τοῖσιν ἐνθάδ' ἵξεται μόνος πάτραν
*   *   *   *   *   *
[οὗ δὴ στενὸν δίαυλον ᾤκισται πέτρας   435
δεινὴ Χάρυβδις, ὠμοβρώς τ' ὀρειβάτης
Κύκλωψ, Λιγυστίς θ' ἡ συῶν μορφώτρια,
Κίρκη, θαλάσσης θ' ἁλμυρᾶς ναυάγια,
λωτοῦ τ' ἔρωτες, ἡλίου θ' ἁγναὶ βόες,
αἱ σάρκα φωνήεσσαν ἥσουσίν ποτε,   440
πικρὰν Ὀδυσσεῖ γῆρυν. ὡς δὲ συντέμω,
ζῶν εἶσ' ἐς Ἅιδην, κἀκφυγὼν λίμνης ὕδωρ
κάκ' ἐν δόμοισι μυρί' εὑρήσει μολών.]
ἀλλὰ γὰρ τί τοὺς Ὀδυσσέως ἐξακοντίζω
πόνους ;

στεῖχ', ὅπως τάχιστ' ἐς Ἅιδου νυμφίῳ γημώμεθα.   445
ἢ κακὸς κακῶς ταφήσει νυκτός, οὐκ ἐν ἡμέρᾳ,
ὦ δοκῶν σεμνόν τι πράσσειν, Δαναϊδῶν ἀρχη-
        γέτα.
κἀμέ τοι νεκρὸν φάραγγες γυμνάδ' ἐκβεβλημένην
ὕδατι χειμάρρῳ ῥέουσαι νυμφίου πέλας τάφου
θηρσὶ δώσουσιν δάσασθαι, τὴν Ἀπόλλωνος
        λάτριν.   450
ὦ στέφη τοῦ φιλτάτου μοι θεῶν, ἀγάλματ' εὔια,
χαίρετ'· ἐκλέλοιφ' ἑορτάς, αἷς πάροιθ' ἠγαλ-
        λόμην.
ἴτ' ἀπ' ἐμοῦ χρωτὸς σπαραγμοῖς, ὡς ἔτ' οὖσ'
        ἁγνὴ χρόα
δῶ θοαῖς αὔραις φέρεσθαί σοι τάδ', ὦ μαντεῖ'
        ἄναξ.
ποῦ σκάφος τὸ τοῦ στρατηγοῦ; ποῖ ποτ'
        ἐμβαίνειν με χρή;   455
οὐκέτ' ἂν φθάνοις ἂν αὔραν ἱστίοις καραδοκῶν,
ὡς μίαν τριῶν Ἐρινῦν τῆσδέ μ' ἐξάξων χθονός.
χαῖρέ μοι, μῆτερ, δακρύσῃς μηδέν· ὦ φίλη πατρὶς
οἵ τε γῆς ἔνερθ' ἀδελφοὶ χὠ τεκὼν ἡμᾶς πατήρ,
οὐ μακρὰν δέξεσθέ μ'· ἥξω δ' ἐς νεκροὺς νικη-
        φόρος   460
καὶ δόμους πέρσατ' Ἀτρειδῶν, ὧν ἀπωλόμεσθ'
        ὕπο.
ΧΟ. Ἑκάβης γεραιᾶς φύλακες, οὐ δεδόρκατε
    δέσποιναν ὡς ἄναυδος ἐς πέδον πίτνει;
    οὐκ ἀντιλήψεσθ'; ἢ μεθήσετ', ὦ κακαί,

γραῖαν πεσοῦσαν ;   αἴρετ᾽ εἰς ὀρθὸν δέμας.   465

ΕΚ. ἐᾶτέ μ᾽, οὗτοι φίλα τὰ μὴ φίλ᾽, ὦ κόραι,
κεῖσθαι πεσοῦσαν· πτωμάτων γὰρ ἄξια
πάσχω τε καὶ πέπονθα κἄτι πείσομαι.
ὦ θεοί· κακοὺς μὲν ἀνακαλῶ τοὺς ξυμμάχους,
ὅμως δ᾽ ἔχει τι σχῆμα κικλήσκειν θεούς,   470
ὅταν τις ἡμῶν δυστυχῆ λάβῃ τύχην.
πρῶτον μὲν οὖν μοι τἀγάθ᾽ ἐξᾷσαι φίλον,
τοῖς γὰρ κακοῖσι πλείον᾽ οἶκτον ἐμβαλῶ.
ἦμεν τύραννοι κἀς τύρανν᾽ ἐγημάμην,
κἀνταῦθ᾽ ἀριστεύοντ᾽ ἐγεινάμην τέκνα,   475
οὐκ ἀριθμὸν ἄλλως, ἀλλ᾽ ὑπερτάτους Φρυγῶν,
οὓς Τρῳὰς οὐδ᾽ Ἑλληνὶς οὐδὲ βάρβαρος
γυνὴ τεκοῦσα κομπάσειεν ἄν ποτε,
κἀκεῖνά τ᾽ εἶδον δορὶ πεσόνθ᾽ Ἑλληνικῷ,   479
τρίχας τ᾽ ἐτμήθην τάσδε πρὸς τύμβοις νεκρῶν,
καὶ τὸν φυτουργὸν Πρίαμον οὐκ ἄλλων πάρα
κλύουσ᾽ ἔκλαυσα, τοῖσδε δ᾽ εἶδον ὄμμασιν
αὐτὴ κατασφαγέντ᾽ ἐφ᾽ ἑρκείῳ πυρᾷ,
πόλιν θ᾽ ἁλοῦσαν.   ἃς δ᾽ ἔθρεψα παρθένους
εἰς ἀξίωμα νυμφίων ἐξαίρετον,   485
ἄλλοισι θρέψασ᾽ ἐκ χερῶν ἀφῃρέθην,
κοὔτ᾽ ἐξ ἐκείνων ἐλπὶς ὡς ὀφθήσομαι,
αὐτή τ᾽ ἐκείνας οὐκέτ᾽ ὄψομαί ποτε.
τὸ λοίσθιον δὲ θριγκὸς ἀθλίων κακῶν,
δούλη γυνὴ γραῦς Ἑλλάδ᾽ εἰσαφίξομαι.   490
ἃ δ᾽ ἐστὶ γήρᾳ τῷδ᾽ ἀσυμφορώτατα,
τούτοις με προσθήσουσιν, ἢ θυρῶν λάτριν
κλῇδας φυλάσσειν, τὴν τεκοῦσαν Ἕκτορα,

ἢ σιτοποιεῖν κἀν πέδῳ κοίτας ἔχειν
ῥυσοῖσι νώτοις βασιλικῶν ἐκ δεμνίων,   495
τρυχηρὰ περὶ τρυχηρὸν εἱμένην χρόα
πέπλων λακίσματ', ἀδόκιμ' ὀλβίοις ἔχειν.
οἲ 'γὼ τάλαινα, διὰ γάμον μιᾶς ἕνα
γυναικὸς οἵων ἔτυχον, ὧν τε τεύξομαι.
ὦ τέκνον, ὦ ξύμβακχε Κασάνδρα θεοῖς,   500
οἵαις ἔλυσας ξυμφοραῖς ἅγνευμα σόν.
σύ τ', ὦ τάλαινα, ποῦ ποτ' εἶ, Πολυξένη;
ὡς οὔτε μ' ἄρσην οὔτε θήλεια σπορὰ
πολλῶν γενομένων τὴν τάλαιναν ὠφελεῖ.
τί δῆτά μ' ὀρθοῦτ'; ἐλπίδων ποίων ὕπο;   505
ἄγετε τὸν ἁβρὸν δήποτ' ἐν Τροίᾳ πόδα,
νῦν δ' ὄντα δοῦλον, στιβάδα πρὸς χαμαιπετῆ
πέτρινά τε κρήδεμν', ὡς πεσοῦσ' ἀποφθαρῶ
δακρύοις καταξανθεῖσα. τῶν δ' εὐδαιμόνων
μηδένα νομίζετ' εὐτυχεῖν πρὶν ἂν θάνῃ.   510
ΧΟ. ἀμφί μοι Ἴλιον, ὦ   σρτ.
Μοῦσα, καινῶν ὕμνων
ᾆσον ἐν δακρύοις
ᾠδὰν ἐπικήδειον·
νῦν γὰρ μέλος ἐς Τροίαν ἰακχήσω,   515
τετραβάμονος ὡς ὑπ' ἀπήνας
Ἀργείων ὀλόμαν τάλαινα δοριάλωτος,
ὅτ' ἔλιπον ἵππον οὐράνια
βρέμοντα, χρυσοφάλαρον ἔνοπλον ἐν πύλαις
      Ἀχαιοί·   520
ἀνὰ δ' ἐβόασεν λεὼς
Τρῳάδος ἀπὸ πέτρας σταθείς,

ἴτ', ὦ πεπαυμένοι πόνων,
τόδ' ἱερὸν ἀνάγετε ξόανον   525
Ἰλιάδι διογενεῖ κόρᾳ.
τίς οὐκ ἔβα νεανίδων,
τίς οὐ γεραιὸς ἐκ δόμων ;
κεχαρμένοι δ' ἀοιδαῖς
δόλιον ἔσχον ἄταν.   530
πᾶσα δὲ γέννα Φρυγῶν   ἀντιστρ.
πρὸς πύλας ὡρμάθη,
πεύκᾳ 'ν οὐρείᾳ
ξεστὸν λόχον Ἀργείων
καὶ Δαρδανίας ἄταν θεᾷ δώσων   535
χάριν ἄζυγος ἀμβροτοπώλου·
κλωστοῦ δ' ἀμφιβόλοις λίνοισι, ναὸς ὡσεὶ
σκάφος κελαινὸν εἰς ἕδρανα
λάϊνα δάπεδά τε φόνια πατρίδι Παλλάδος
        θέσαν θεᾶς.
ἐπὶ δὲ πόνῳ καὶ χαρᾷ   540
νύχιον ἐπὶ κνέφας παρῆν,
Λίβυς τε λωτὸς ἐκτύπει
Φρύγιά τε μέλεα, παρθένοι δ'
ἀέριον ἀνὰ κρότον ποδῶν
βοάν τ' ἔμελπον εὔφρον'· ἐν
δόμοις δὲ παμφαὲς σέλας
πυρὸς μέλαιναν αἴγλαν
⏑ ⏑ ἔδωκεν ὕπνῳ.   550
ἐγὼ δὲ τὰν ὀρεστέραν   ἐπῳδός.
τότ' ἀμφὶ μέλαθρα παρθένον
Διὸς κόραν ἐμελπόμαν

χοροῖσι· φοινία δ' ἀνὰ 555
πτόλιν βοὰ κατεῖχε περ-
γάμων ἕδρας· βρέφη δὲ φίλι-
α περὶ πέπλους ἔβαλλε μα-
τρὶ χεῖρας ἐπτοημένας·
λόχου δ' ἐξέβαιν' Ἄρης, 560
κόρας ἔργα Παλλάδος.
σφαγαὶ δ' ἀμφιβώμιοι
Φρυγῶν, ἔν τε δεμνίοις
καράτομος ἐρημία
νεανιῶν στέφανον ἔφερεν 565
Ἑλλάδι κουροτρόφῳ,
Φρυγῶν δὲ πατρίδι πένθος.
Ἑκάβη, λεύσσεις τήνδ' Ἀνδρομάχην
ξενικοῖς ἐπ' ὄχοις πορθμευομένην;
παρὰ δ' εἰρεσίᾳ μαστῶν ἕπεται 570
φίλος Ἀστυάναξ, Ἕκτορος ἶνις.
ποῖ ποτ' ἀπήνης νώτοισι φέρει,
δύστηνε γύναι, πάρεδρος χαλκέοις
Ἕκτορος ὅπλοις σκύλοις τε Φρυγῶν
δοριθηράτοις,
οἷσιν Ἀχιλλέως παῖς Φθιώτης 575
στέψει ναοὺς ἀπὸ Τροίας;

ΑΝΔΡΟΜΑΧΗ.

Ἀχαιοὶ δεσπόται μ' ἄγουσιν.　　στρ. α'.
ΕΚ. ὤμοι.　ΑΝ. τί παιᾶν' ἐμὸν στενάζεις
ΕΚ. αἰαῖ.　ΑΝ. τῶνδ' ἀλγέων
ΕΚ. ὦ Ζεῦ.　ΑΝ. καὶ ξυμφορᾶς;　　580

ΕΚ. τέκεα— ΑΝ. πρίν ποτ' ἦμεν.

ΕΚ. βέβακ' ὄλβος, βέβακε Τροία   ἀντιστρ. α'.

ΑΝ. τλάμων. ΕΚ. ἐμῶν τ' εὐγένεια παίδων.

ΑΝ. φεῦ φεῦ. ΕΚ. φεῦ δῆτ', ἐμᾶς τ'

ΑΝ. ὤμοι. ΕΚ. λαμπρὰ τύχα   585

ΑΝ. πόλεος ΕΚ. ἃ καπνοῦται.

ΑΝ. μόλοις, ὦ πόσις, μοι,   στρ. β'.

ΕΚ. βοᾷς τὸν παρ' "Αιδᾳ   587

     παῖδ' ἐμόν, ὦ μελέα.   587 a

ΑΝ. σᾶς δάμαρτος ἄλκαρ,   587 b

ΕΚ. σύ τοι, λῦμ' 'Αχαιῶν,   ἀντιστρ. β'.

     τέκνων δήποτ' ἀμῶν   588 a

     πρεσβυγενὲς Πριάμῳ,

     κοίμισαί μ' ἐς "Αιδου.   588 b

ΑΝ. οἵδε πόθοι μεγάλοι, σχέτλι' αἲ τάδε πάσχομεν

     ἄλγη,   στρ. γ'.

     οἰχομένας πόλεως, ἐπὶ δ' ἄλγεσιν ἄλγεα κεῖται,

     δυσφροσύναισι θεῶν· ὁ δὲ σὸς γόνος ἔκφυγεν

     "Αιδαν.   592

     ὃς λεχέων στυγερῶν χάριν ὤλεσε πέργαμα

     Τροίας.

     σώματα δ' αἱματόεντα θεᾷ παρὰ Παλλάδι

     νεκρῶν

     γυψὶ φέρειν τέταται, ζυγὰ δ' ἤνυσε δούλια Τροία.

     ἀντιστρ. γ'.

ΕΚ. ὦ πατρίς, ὦ μελέα, καταλειπομέναν σε δακρύω,

     νῦν τέλος οἰκτρὸν ὁρᾷς, καὶ ἐμὸν δόμον, ἔνθ'

     ἐλοχεύθην.   597

     ὦ τέκν', ἐρημόπολις μᾶτηο ἀπολείπεται ὑμῶν.

‿ ‿ ‿ ‿ ‿ ‿ οἷος ἰάλεμος, οἷά τε πένθη
δάκρυά τ᾽ ἐκ δακρύων καταλείβεται ἀμετέροισι
δώμασιν, οὐδ᾽ ὁ θανὼν ἀδάκρυτ᾽ ἐπιλάθεται
ἀλγέων.   603

ΧΟ. ὡς ἡδὺ δάκρυα τοῖς κακῶς πεπραγόσι,
θρήνων τ᾽ ὀδυρμοί, μοῦσά θ᾽, ἢ λύπας ἔχει. 605

ΑΝ. ὦ μῆτερ ἀνδρός, ὅς ποτ᾽ Ἀργείων δορὶ
πλείστους διώλεσ᾽, Ἕκτορος, τάδ᾽ εἰσορᾷς ;

ΕΚ. ὁρῶ τὰ τῶν θεῶν, ὡς τὰ μὲν πυργοῦσ᾽ ἄνω
τὸ μηδὲν ὄντα, τὰ δὲ δοκοῦντ᾽ ἀπώλεσαν.

ΑΝ. ἀγόμεθα λεία ξὺν τέκνῳ, τὸ δ᾽ εὐγενὲς   610
ἐς δοῦλον ἥκει, μεταβολὰς τοιάσδ᾽ ἔχον.

ΕΚ. τὸ τῆς ἀνάγκης δεινόν· ἄρτι κἀπ᾽ ἐμοῦ
βέβηκ᾽ ἀποσπασθεῖσα Κασάνδρα βίᾳ.

ΑΝ. φεῦ φεῦ.
ἄλλος τις Αἴας, ὡς ἔοικε, δεύτερος
παιδὸς πέφηνε σῆς· νοσεῖς δὲ χἄτερα.   615

ΕΚ. ὧν γ᾽ οὔτε μέτρον οὔτ᾽ ἀριθμός ἐστί μοι·
κακῷ κακὸν γὰρ εἰς ἅμιλλαν ἔρχεται.

ΑΝ. τέθνηκέ σοι παῖς πρὸς τάφῳ Πολυξένη
σφαγεῖσ᾽ Ἀχιλλέως, δῶρον ἀψύχῳ νεκρῷ.

ΕΚ. οἲ 'γὼ τάλαινα. τοῦτ᾽ ἐκεῖν᾽ ὅ μοι πάλαι   620
Ταλθύβιος αἴνιγμ᾽ οὐ σαφῶς εἶπεν σαφές.

ΑΝ. εἶδόν νιν αὐτὴ κἀποβᾶσα τῶνδ᾽ ὄχων
ἔκρυψα πέπλοις κἀπεκοψάμην νεκρόν.

ΕΚ. αἰαῖ, τέκνον, σῶν ἀνοσίων προσφαγμάτων.
αἰαῖ μάλ᾽ αὖθις, ὡς κακῶς διόλλυσαι.   625

ΑΝ. ὄλωλεν ὡς ὄλωλεν, ἀλλ᾽ ὅμως ἐμοῦ
ζώσης γ᾽ ὄλωλεν εὐτυχεστέρῳ πότμῳ.

ΕΚ. οὐ ταὐτόν, ὦ παῖ, τῷ βλέπειν τὸ κατθανεῖν·
　　τὸ μὲν γὰρ οὐδέν, τῷ δ᾽ ἔνεισιν ἐλπίδες.
ΑΝ. ὦ μῆτερ, ὦ τεκοῦσα, κάλλιστον λόγον
　　ἄκουσον, ὥς σοι τέρψιν ἐμβάλω φρενί.　　　630
　　τὸ μὴ γενέσθαι τῷ θανεῖν ἴσον λέγω,
　　τοῦ ζῆν δὲ λυπρῶς κρεῖσσόν ἐστι κατθανεῖν.
　　ἀλγεῖ γὰρ οὐδὲν τῶν κακῶν ᾐσθημένος·
　　ὁ δ᾽ εὐτυχήσας ἐς τὸ δυστυχὲς πεσὼν
　　ψυχὴν ἀλᾶται τῆς παροιθ᾽ εὐπραξίας.　　　635
　　κείνη δ᾽ ὁμοίως ὥσπερ οὐκ ἰδοῦσα φῶς
　　τέθνηκε, κοὐδὲν οἶδε τῶν αὑτῆς κακῶν.
　　ἐγὼ δὲ τοξεύσασα τῆς εὐδοξίας
　　λαχοῦσα πλεῖστον τῆς τύχης ἡμάρτανον.
　　ἃ γὰρ γυναιξὶ σώφρον᾽ ἔσθ᾽ ηὑρημένα,　　640
　　ταῦτ᾽ ἐξεμόχθουν Ἕκτορος κατὰ στέγας.
　　πρῶτον μέν, ἔνθα, κἂν προσῇ κἂν μὴ προσῇ
　　ψόγος γυναιξίν, αὐτὸ τοῦτ᾽ ἐφέλκεται
　　κακῶς ἀκούειν, ἥτις οὐκ ἔνδον μένει,
　　τούτου παρεῖσα πόθον ἔμιμνον ἐν δόμοις,　　645
　　εἴσω τε μελάθρων κομψὰ θηλειῶν ἔπη
　　οὐκ εἰσεφρούμην· τὸν δὲ νοῦν διδάσκαλον
　　οἴκοθεν ἔχουσα χρηστὸν ἐξήρκουν ἐμοί,
　　γλώσσης τε σιγὴν ὄμμα θ᾽ ἥσυχον πόσει
　　παρεῖχον· ᾔδη δ᾽ ἁμὲ χρῆν νικᾶν πόσιν,　　　650
　　κείνῳ τε νίκην ὧν μ᾽ ἐχρῆν παριέναι.
　　καὶ τῶνδε κληδὼν ἐς στράτευμ᾽ Ἀχαικὸν
　　ἐλθοῦσ᾽ ἀπώλεσέν μ᾽· ἐπεὶ γὰρ ᾑρέθην,
　　Ἀχιλλέως με παῖς ἐβουλήθη λαβεῖν
　　δάμαρτα· δουλεύσω δ᾽ ἐν αὐθεντῶν δόμοις,　　655

κεἰ μὲν παρώσασ' Ἕκτορος φίλον κάρα
πρὸς τὸν παρόντα πόσιν ἀναπτύξω φρένα,
κακὴ φανοῦμαι τῷ θανόντι· τόνδε δ' αὖ
στέργουσ', ἐμαυτῆς δεσπόταις μισήσομαι.
καίτοι λέγουσιν ὡς μί' εὐφρόνη χαλᾷ   660
τὸ δυσμενὲς γυναικὸς εἰς ἀνδρὸς λέχος·
ἀπέπτυσ' αὐτήν, ἥτις ἄνδρα τὸν πάρος
καινοῖσι λέκτροις ἀποβαλοῦσ' ἄλλον φιλεῖ.
ἀλλ' οὐδὲ πῶλος ἥτις ἂν διαζυγῇ
τῆς ξυντραφείσης ῥᾳδίως ἕλξει ζυγόν.   665
καίτοι τὸ θηριῶδες ἄφθογγόν τ' ἔφυ
ξυνέσει τ' ἄχρηστον τῇ φύσει τε λείπεται.
σὲ δ', ὦ φίλ' Ἕκτορ, εἶχον ἄνδρ' ἀρκοῦντά μοι
ξυνέσει, γένει, πλούτῳ τε κἀνδρείᾳ μέγαν·
ἀκήρατον δέ μ' ἐκ πατρὸς λαβὼν δόμων   670
πρῶτος τὸ παρθένειον ἐζεύξω λέχος.
καὶ νῦν ὄλωλας μὲν σύ, ναυσθλοῦμαι δ' ἐγὼ
πρὸς Ἑλλάδ' αἰχμάλωτος ἐς δοῦλον ζυγόν.
ἆρ' οὐκ ἐλάσσω τῶν ἐμῶν ἡγεῖ κακῶν
Πολυξένης ὄλεθρον, ἣν καταστένεις;   675
ἐμοὶ γὰρ οὐδ', ὃ πᾶσι λείπεται βροτοῖς,
ξύνεστιν ἐλπίς, οὐδὲ κλέπτομαι φρένας
πράξειν τι κεδνόν· ἡδὺ δ' ἐστὶ καὶ δοκεῖν.

ΧΟ. ἐς ταὐτὸν ἥκεις ξυμφορᾶς· θρηνοῦσα δὲ
τὸ σὸν διδάσκεις μ' ἔνθα πημάτων κυρῶ.   680

ΕΚ. αὐτὴ μὲν οὔπω ναὸς εἰσέβην σκάφος,
γραφῇ δ' ἰδοῦσα καὶ κλύουσ' ἐπίσταμαι.
ναύταις γὰρ ἢν μὲν μέτριος ᾖ χειμὼν φέρειν,
προθυμίαν ἔχουσι σωθῆναι πόνων,

ὁ μὲν παρ' οἴαχ', ὁ δ' ἐπὶ λαίφεσιν βεβώς, 685
ὁ δ' ἄντλον εἴργων ναός· ἢν δ' ὑπερβάλῃ
πολὺς ταραχθεὶς πόντος, ἐνδόντες τύχῃ
παρεῖσαν αὑτοὺς κυμάτων δρομήμασιν.
οὕτω δὲ κἀγὼ πόλλ' ἔχουσα πήματα
ἄφθογγός εἰμι καὶ παρεῖσ' ἐῶ στόμα· 690
νικᾷ γὰρ οὐκ θεῶν με δύστηνος κλύδων.
ἀλλ', ὦ φίλη παῖ, τὰς μὲν Ἕκτορος τύχας
ἔασον· οὐ γὰρ δάκρυά νιν σώσει τὰ σά·
τίμα δὲ τὸν παρόντα δεσπότην σέθεν,
φίλον διδοῦσα δέλεαρ ἀνδρὶ σῶν τρόπων. 695
κἂν δρᾷς τάδ', ἐς τὸ κοινὸν εὐφρανεῖς φίλους,
καὶ παῖδα τόνδε παιδὸς ἐκθρέψειας ἄν,
Τροίᾳ μέγιστον ὠφέλημ' εἶναί ποτε,
ἐξ οὗ γενόμενοι παῖδες ὕστερον πάλιν
κατοικίσειαν, καὶ πόλις γένοιτ' ἔτι.
ἀλλ', ἐκ λόγου γὰρ ἄλλος ἐκβαίνει λόγος, 701
τίν' αὖ δέδορκα τόνδ' Ἀχαιικὸν λάτριν
στείχοντα, καινῶν ἄγγελον βουλευμάτων;
ΤΑ. Φρυγῶν ἀρίστου πρίν ποθ' Ἕκτορος δάμαρ,
μή με στυγήσῃς· οὐχ ἑκὼν γὰρ ἀγγελῶ 705
Δαναῶν τε κοινὰ Πελοπιδῶν τ' ἀγγέλματα.
ΑΝ. τί δ' ἔστιν; ὥς μοι φροιμίων ἄρχει κακῶν.
ΤΑ. ἔδοξε τόνδε παῖδα, πῶς εἴπω λόγον;
ΑΝ. μῶν οὐ τὸν αὐτὸν δεσπότην ἡμῖν ἔχειν;
ΤΑ. οὐδεὶς Ἀχαιῶν τοῦδε δεσπόσει ποτέ. 710
ΑΝ. ἀλλ' ἐνθάδ' αὐτὸν λείψανον Φρυγῶν λιπεῖν;
ΤΑ. οὐκ οἶδ' ὅπως σοι ῥᾳδίως εἴπω κακά.
ΑΝ. ἐπῄνεσ' αἰδῶ, πλὴν ἐὰν λέγῃς καλά.

ΤΑ. κτενοῦσι σὸν παῖδ᾽, ὡς πύθῃ κακὸν μέγα.

ΑΝ. οἴμοι, γάμων τόδ᾽ ὡς κλύω μεῖζον κακόν. 715

ΤΑ. νικᾷ δ᾽ Ὀδυσσεὺς ἐν Πανέλλησιν λέγων.

ΑΝ. αἰαῖ μάλ᾽, οὐ γὰρ μέτρια πάσχομεν κακά.

ΤΑ. λέξας ἀρίστου παῖδα μὴ τρέφειν πατρός·

ΑΝ. τοιαῦτα νικήσειε τῶν αὑτοῦ πέρι.

ΤΛ. ῥῖψαι δὲ πύργων δεῖν σφε Τρωικῶν ἄπο. 720
ἀλλ᾽ ὣς γενέσθω, καὶ σοφωτέρα φανεῖ,
μήτ᾽ ἀντέχου τοῦδ᾽, εὐγενῶς δ᾽ ἄλγει κακοῖς,
μήτε σθένουσα μηδὲν ἰσχύειν δόκει.
ἔχεις γὰρ ἀλκὴν οὐδαμῆ· σκοπεῖν δὲ χρή·
πόλις τ᾽ ὄλωλε καὶ πόσις, κρατεῖ δὲ σύ, 725
ἡμεῖς τε πρὸς γυναῖκα μάρνασθαι μίαν
οἷοί τε· τούτων οὕνεκ᾽ οὐ μάχης ἐρᾶν,
οὐδ᾽ αἰσχρὸν οὐδὲν οὐδ᾽ ἐπίφθονόν σε δρᾶν,
οὔτ᾽ αὖ σ᾽ Ἀχαιοῖς βούλομαι ῥίπτειν ἀράς.
εἰ γάρ τι λέξεις ᾧ χολώσεται στρατός, 730
οὔτ᾽ ἂν ταφείη παῖς ὅδ᾽ οὔτ᾽ οἴκτου τύχοι.
σιγῶσα δ᾽ εὖ τε τὰς τύχας κεκτημένη
τὸν τοῦδε νεκρὸν οὐκ ἄθαπτον ἂν λίποις,
αὐτή τ᾽ Ἀχαιῶν πρευμενεστέρων τύχοις.

ΑΝ. ὦ φίλτατ᾽, ὦ περισσὰ τιμηθεὶς τέκνον, 735
θανεῖ πρὸς ἐχθρῶν, μητέρ᾽ ἀθλίαν λιπών.
ἡ τοῦ πατρὸς δέ σ᾽ εὐγένει᾽ ἀπώλεσεν,
ἢ τοῖσιν ἄλλοις γίγνεται σωτηρία,
τὸ δ᾽ ἐσθλὸν οὐκ ἐς καιρὸν ἦλθε σοὶ πατρός.
ὦ λέκτρα τἀμὰ δυστυχῆ τε καὶ γάμοι, 740
οἷς ἦλθον ἐς μέλαθρον Ἕκτορός ποτε,
[οὐχ ὡς σφαγεῖον Δαναΐδαις τέξουσ᾽ ἐμόν,

ἀλλ' ὡς τύραννον Ἀσιάδος πολυσπόρου.]
ὦ παῖ, δακρύεις ; αἰσθάνει κακῶν σέθεν ;
τί μου δέδραξαι χερσὶ κἀντέχει πέπλων,   745
νεοσσὸς ὡσεὶ πτέρυγας ἐσπίτνων ἐμάς ;
οὐκ εἶσιν Ἕκτωρ κλεινὸν ἁρπάσας δόρυ,
γῆς ἐξανελθών, σοὶ φέρων σωτηρίαν,
οὐ ξυγγένεια πατρός, οὐκ ἰσχὺς Φρυγῶν·
λυγρὸν δὲ πήδημ' ἐς τράχηλον ὑψόθεν   750
πεσὼν ἀνοίκτως πνεῦμ' ἀπορρήξεις σέθεν.
ὦ νέον ὑπαγκάλισμα μητρὶ φίλτατον,
ὦ χρωτὸς ἡδὺ πνεῦμα· διὰ κενῆς ἄρα
ἐν σπαργάνοις σε μαστὸς ἐξέθρεψ' ὅδε,
μάτην δ' ἐμόχθουν καὶ κατεξάνθην πόνοις.   755   —
νῦν, οὔποτ' αὖθις, μητέρ' ἀσπάζου σέθεν,
πρόσπιτνε τὴν τεκοῦσαν, ἀμφὶ δ' ὠλένας
ἕλισσ' ἐμοῖς νώτοισι καὶ στόμ' ἅρμοσον.
ὦ βάρβαρ' ἐξευρόντες Ἕλληνες κακά,
τί τόνδε παῖδα κτείνετ' οὐδὲν αἴτιον ;   760
ὦ Τυνδάρειον ἔρνος, οὔποτ' εἶ Διός,
πολλῶν δὲ πατέρων φημί σ' ἐκπεφυκέναι,
Ἀλάστορος μὲν πρῶτον, εἶτα δὲ Φθόνου,
Φόνου τε Θανάτου θ', ὅσα τε γῆ τρέφει κακά.
οὐ γάρ ποτ' αὐχῶ Ζῆνά γ' ἐκφῦσαί σ' ἐγώ, 765
πολλοῖσι κῆρα βαρβάροις Ἕλλησί τε.
ὄλοιο· καλλίστων γὰρ ὀμμάτων ἄπο
αἰσχρῶς τὰ κλεινὰ πεδί' ἀπώλεσας Φρυγῶν.
ἀλλ' ἄγετε, φέρετε, ῥίπτετ', εἰ ῥίπτειν δοκεῖ·
δαίνυσθε τοῦδε σάρκας. ἔκ τε γὰρ θεῶν   770
διολλύμεσθα, παιδί τ' οὐ δυναίμεθ' ἂν

θάνατον ἀρῆξαι. κρύπτετ᾽ ἄθλιον δέμας
καὶ ῥίπτετ᾽ ἐς ναῦν. ἐπὶ καλὸν γὰρ ἔρχομαι
ὑμέναιον, ἀπολέσασα τοὐμαυτῆς τέκνον.

ΧΟ. τάλαινα Τροία, μυρίους ἀπώλεσας   775
μιᾶς γυναικὸς καὶ λέχους στυγνοῦ χάριν.

ΤΑ. ἄγε, παῖ, φίλιον πρόσπτυγμα μεθεὶς
μητρὸς μογερᾶς βαῖνε πατρῴων
πύργων ἐπ᾽ ἄκρας στεφάνας, ὅθι σοι
πνεῦμα μεθεῖναι ψῆφος ἐκράνθη.   780
λαμβάνετ᾽ αὐτόν. τὰ δὲ τοιάδε χρὴ
κηρυκεύειν, ὅστις ἄνοικτος
καὶ ἀναιδείᾳ τῆς ἡμετέρας
γνώμης μᾶλλον φίλος ἐστίν.

ΕΚ. ὦ τέκνον, ὦ παῖ παιδὸς μογεροῦ,   785
συλώμεθα σὴν ψυχὴν ἀδίκως
μήτηρ κἀγώ. τί πάθω; τί σ᾽ ἐγώ,
δύσμορε, δράσω; τάδε σοι δίδομεν
πλήγματα κρατὸς στέρνων τε κόπους·
τῶνδε γὰρ ἄρχομεν· οἲ ᾽γὼ πόλεως,   790
οἴμοι δὲ σέθεν· τί γὰρ οὐκ ἔχομεν,
τίνος ἐνδέομεν μὴ οὐ πανσυδίᾳ
χωρεῖν ὀλέθρου διὰ παντός ;

στρ. α΄.

ΧΟ. μελισσοτρόφου Σαλαμῖνος ὦ βασιλεῦ Τελαμών,
νάσου περικύμονος οἰκήσας ἕδραν   795
τᾶς ἐπικεκλιμένας ὄχθοις ἱεροῖς, ἵν᾽ ἐλάας
πρῶτον ἔδειξε κλάδον γλαυκᾶς Ἀθάνα,
οὐράνιον στέφανον λιπαραῖσί τε κόσμον Ἀθή-
ναις,

ἔβας τῷ τοξοφόρῳ ξυναριστεύων ποτ᾽ Ἀλκμή-
νας γόνῳ,
Ἴλιον Ἴλιον ἐκπέρσων πόλιν   805
ἀμετέραν τὸ πάροιθεν ⏑ — ⏑ — —

                                                 ἀντιστρ. α'.

ὅθ᾽ Ἑλλάδος ἄγαγε πρῶτον ἄνθος ἀτυζόμενος
πώλων, Σιμόεντι δ᾽ ἐπ᾽ εὐρείτᾳ πλάταν   809
ἔσχασε ποντοπόρον καὶ ναύδετ᾽ ἀνήψατο
    πρυμνᾶν,
καὶ χερὸς εὐστοχίαν ἐξεῖλε ναῶν,   811
Λαομέδοντι φόνον· κανόνων δὲ τυκίσματα
    Φοίβου
πυρὸς φοίνικι πνοᾷ καθελὼν Τροίας ἐπόρθησεν
    χθόνα,
δὶς δὲ δυοῖν πιτύλοιν τείχη περὶ
Δαρδανίας φονία κατέλυσεν αἰχμά.

                                                 στρ. β'.

μάταν ἄρ᾽, ὦ χρυσέαις ἐν οἰνοχόαις ἁβρὰ
    βαίνων,   820
Λαομεδόντιε παῖ,
Ζανὸς ἔχεις κυλίκων
πλήρωμα, καλλίσταν λατρείαν·
ἁ δέ σε γειναμένα πυρὶ δαίεται.   825
ἠϊόνες δ᾽ ἅλιαι
ἰαχοῦσ᾽· οἷον δ᾽ ὑπὲρ
οἰωνὸς τεκέων βοᾷ,   830
αἱ μὲν εὐνάτορας, αἱ δὲ παῖδας,
αἱ δὲ ματέρας γεραιάς.
τὰ δὲ σὰ δροσόεντα λουτρὰ

γυμνασίων τε δρόμοι
βεβᾶσι· σὺ δὲ πρόσωπα νεαρὰ χάρισι παρὰ
   Διὸς θρόνοις
καλλιγάλανα τρέφεις· Πριάμοιο δὲ γαῖαν
Ἑλλὰς ὤλεσ᾽ αἰχμά.   838

ἀντιστρ. β'.

Ἔρως Ἔρως, ὃς τὰ Δαρδάνεια μέλαθρά ποτ᾽
   ἦλθες
Οὐρανίδαισι μέλων,
ὡς τότε μὲν μεγάλως
Τροίαν ἐπύργωσας, θεοῖσιν
κῆδος ἀναψάμενος. τὸ μὲν οὖν Διὸς   845
οὐκέτ᾽ ὄνειδος ἐρῶ·
τὸ δὲ τᾶς λευκοπτέρου
Ἀμέρας φίλιον βροτοῖς
φέγγος ὀλοὸν ὀλοὸν εἶδε γαίας,   850
εἶδε περγάμων ὄλεθρον,
τεκνοποιὸν ἔχουσα τᾷδε
γᾷ πόσιν ἐν θαλάμοις,
ὃν ἀστέρων τέθριππος ἔλαβε χρύσεος ὄχος
   ἀναρπάσας,   855
ἐλπίδα γᾷ πατρίᾳ μεγάλαν· τὰ θεῶν δὲ
φίλτρα φροῦδα Τροίᾳ.

ΜΕΝΕΛΑΟΣ.

ὦ καλλιφεγγὲς ἡλίου σέλας τόδε,   860
ἐν ᾧ δάμαρτα τὴν ἐμὴν χειρώσομαι
Ἑλένην· ὁ γὰρ δὴ πολλὰ μοχθήσας ἐγὼ
Μενέλαός εἰμι, καὶ στράτευμ᾽ Ἀχαιικόν.

c

ἦλθον δὲ Τροίαν οὐχ ὅσον δοκοῦσί με
γυναικὸς οὕνεκ᾽, ἀλλ᾽ ἐπ᾽ ἄνδρ᾽ ὃς ἐξ ἐμῶν   865
δόμων δάμαρτα ξεναπάτης ἐλήσατο.
κεῖνος μὲν οὖν δέδωκε σὺν θεοῖς δίκην
αὐτός τε καὶ γῆ δορὶ πεσοῦσ᾽ Ἑλληνικῷ.
ἥκω δὲ τὴν Λάκαιναν, οὐ γὰρ ἡδέως
ὄνομα δάμαρτος ἥ ποτ᾽ ἦν ἐμὴ λέγω,   870
ἄξων· δόμοις γὰρ τοῖσδ᾽ ἐν αἰχμαλωτικοῖς
κατηρίθμηται Τρωάδων ἄλλων μέτα.
οἵπερ γὰρ αὐτὴν ἐξεμόχθησαν δορί,
κτανεῖν ἐμοί νιν ἔδοσαν, εἴτε μὴ κτανὼν
θέλοιμ᾽ ἄγεσθαι πάλιν ἐς Ἀργείαν χθόνα.   875
ἐμοὶ δ᾽ ἔδοξε τὸν μὲν ἐν Τροίᾳ μόρον
Ἑλένης ἐᾶσαι, ναυπόρῳ δ᾽ ἄγειν πλάτῃ
Ἑλληνίδ᾽ ἐς γῆν, κᾆτ᾽ ἐκεῖ δοῦναι κτανεῖν,
ποινὰς ὅσων τεθνᾶσ᾽ ἐν Ἰλίῳ φίλοι.
ἀλλ᾽ εἶα χωρεῖτ᾽ ἐς δόμους, ὀπάονες,   880
κομίζετ᾽ αὐτήν, τῆς μιαιφονωτάτης
κόμης ἐπισπάσαντες· οὔριοι δ᾽ ὅταν
πνοαὶ μόλωσι, πέμψομέν νιν Ἑλλάδα.
ΕΚ. ὦ γῆς ὄχημα, κἀπὶ γῆς ἔχων ἕδραν,
ὅστις ποτ᾽ εἶ σύ, δυστόπαστος εἰδέναι,   885
Ζεύς, εἴτ᾽ ἀνάγκη φύσεος εἴτε νοῦς βροτῶν,
προσηυξάμην σε· πάντα γὰρ δι᾽ ἀψόφου
βαίνων κελεύθου κατὰ δίκην τὰ θνήτ᾽ ἄγεις.
ΜΕ. τί δ᾽ ἔστιν; εὐχὰς ὡς ἐκαίνισας θεῶν.
ΕΚ. αἰνῶ σε, Μενέλα᾽, εἰ κτενεῖς δάμαρτα σήν.   890
ὁρῶν δὲ τήνδε φεῦγε, μή σ᾽ ἕλῃ πόθῳ.
αἱρεῖ γὰρ ἀνδρῶν ὄμματ᾽, ἐξαιρεῖ πόλεις,

πίμπρησι δ' οἴκους· ὧδ' ἔχει κηλήματα.
ἐγώ νιν οἶδα καὶ σὺ χοἰ πεπονθότες.

ΕΛΕΝΗ.

Μενέλαε, φροίμιον μὲν ἄξιον φόβου   895
τόδ' ἐστίν· ἐν γὰρ χερσὶ προσπόλων σέθεν
βίᾳ πρὸ τῶνδε δωμάτων ἐκπέμπομαι.
ἀτὰρ σχεδὸν μὲν οἶδά σοι στυγουμένη,
ὅμως δ' ἐρέσθαι βούλομαι γνῶμαι τίνες
Ἕλλησι καὶ σοὶ τῆς ἐμῆς ψυχῆς πέρι.   900

ΜΕ. οὐκ εἰς ἀκριβὲς ἦλθες, ἀλλ' ἅπας στρατὸς
κτανεῖν ἐμοί σ' ἔδωκεν, ὅνπερ ἠδίκεις.

ΕΛ. ἔξεστιν οὖν πρὸς ταῦτ' ἀμείψασθαι λόγῳ,
ὡς οὐ δικαίως, ἢν θάνω, θανούμεθα ;

ΜΕ. οὐκ ἐς λόγους ἐλήλυθ', ἀλλά σε κτενῶν.   905

ΕΚ. ἄκουσον αὐτῆς, μὴ θάνῃ τοῦδ' ἐνδεής,
Μενέλαε, καὶ δὸς τοὺς ἐναντίους λόγους
ἡμῖν κατ' αὐτῆς· τῶν γὰρ ἐν Τροίᾳ κακῶν
οὐδὲν κάτοισθα. συντεθεὶς δ' ὁ πᾶς λόγος
κτενεῖ νιν οὕτως ὥστε μηδαμῆ φυγεῖν.   910

ΜΕ. σχολῆς τὸ δῶρον· εἰ δὲ βούλεται λέγειν,
ἔξεστι. τῶν σῶν δ' οὕνεχ', ὡς μάθῃ, λόγων
δώσω τόδ' αὐτῇ, τῆσδε δ' οὐ δώσω χάριν.

ΕΛ. ἴσως με, κἂν εὖ κἂν κακῶς δόξω λέγειν,
οὐκ ἀνταμείψει, πολεμίαν ἡγούμενος.   915
ἐγὼ δ', ἅ σ' οἶμαι διὰ λόγων ἰόντ' ἐμοῦ
κατηγορήσειν, ἀντιθεῖσ' ἀμείψομαι
τοῖς σοῖσι τἀμὰ καὶ τὰ σ' αἰτιάματα.
πρῶτον μὲν ἀρχὰς ἔτεκεν ἥδε τῶν κακῶν

Πάριν τεκοῦσα· δεύτερον δ' ἀπώλεσε   920
Τροίαν τε κἄμ' ὁ πρέσβυς οὐ κτανὼν βρέφος,
δαλοῦ πικρὸν μίμημ', Ἀλέξανδρόν ποτε.
ἐνθένδε τἀπίλοιπ' ἄκουσον ὡς ἔχει·
ἔκρινε τρισσὸν ζεῦγος ὅδε τρισσῶν θεῶν.
καὶ Παλλάδος μὲν ἦν Ἀλεξάνδρῳ δόσις   925
Φρυξὶ στρατηγοῦνθ' Ἑλλάδ' ἐξανιστάναι,
Ἥρα δ' ὑπέσχετ' Ἀσιάδ' Εὐρώπης θ' ὅρους
τυραννίδ' ἕξειν, εἴ σφε κρίνειεν Πάρις,
Κύπρις δὲ τοὐμὸν εἶδος ἐκπαγλουμένη
δώσειν ὑπέσχετ', εἰ θεὰς ὑπερδράμοι   930
κάλλει· τὸν ἔνθεν δ' ὡς ἔχει σκέψαι λόγον·
νικᾷ Κύπρις θεάς, καὶ τοσόνδ' οὑμοὶ γάμοι
ὤνησαν Ἑλλάδ', οὐ κρατεῖσθ' ἐκ βαρβάρων.
οὔτ' ἐς δόρυ σταθέντες, οὐ τυραννίδι.
ἃ δ' ηὐτύχησεν Ἑλλάς, ὠλόμην ἐγὼ   935
εὐμορφίᾳ πραθεῖσα, κὠνειδίζομαι
ἐξ ὧν ἐχρῆν με στέφανον ἐπὶ κάρᾳ λαβεῖν.
οὔπω με φήσεις αὐτὰ τἀν ποσὶν λέγειν,
ὅπως ἀφώρμησ' ἐκ δόμων τῶν σῶν λάθρα.
ἦλθ' οὐχὶ μικρὰν θεὸν ἔχων αὐτοῦ μέτα   940
ὁ τῆσδ' ἀλάστωρ, εἴτ' Ἀλέξανδρον θέλεις
ὀνόματι προσφωνεῖν νιν εἴτε καὶ Πάριν·
ὅν, ὦ κάκιστε, σοῖσιν ἐν δόμοις λιπὼν
Σπάρτης ἀπῆρας νηῒ Κρησίαν χθόνα.
εἶεν.
οὐ σ', ἀλλ' ἐμαυτὴν τοὐπὶ τῷδ' ἐρήσομαι,   945
τί δὴ φρονήσασ' ἐκ δόμων ἅμ' ἑσπόμην
ξένῳ, προδοῦσα πατρίδα καὶ δόμους ἐμούς;

τὴν θεὸν κόλαζε καὶ Διὸς κρείσσων γενοῦ,
ὃς τῶν μὲν ἄλλων δαιμόνων ἔχει κράτος,
κείνης δὲ δοῦλός ἐστι· συγγνώμη δ' ἐμοί.   950
ἔνθεν δ' ἔχοις ἂν εἰς ἔμ' εὐπρεπῆ λόγον,
ἐπεὶ θανὼν γῆς ἦλθ' Ἀλέξανδρος μυχούς,
χρῆν μ', ἡνίκ' οὐκ ἦν θεοπόνητά μου λέχη,
λιποῦσαν οἴκους ναῦς ἐπ' Ἀργείων μολεῖν.
ἔσπευδον αὐτὸ τοῦτο· μάρτυρες δέ μοι   955
πύργων πυλωροὶ κἀπὸ τειχέων σκοποί,
οἵ πολλάκις μ' ἐφηῦρον ἐξ ἐπάλξεων
πλεκταῖσιν ἐς γῆν σῶμα κλέπτουσαν τόδε.
βίᾳ δ' ὁ καινός μ' οὗτος ἁρπάσας πόσις
Δηίφοβος ἄλοχον εἶχεν ἀκόντων Φρυγῶν.   960
πῶς οὖν ἔτ' ἂν θνήσκοιμ' ἂν ἐνδίκως, πόσι,
πρὸς σοῦ† δικαίως,† ἢν ὁ μὲν βίᾳ γαμεῖ,
τὰ δ' οἴκοθεν κεῖν' ἀντὶ νικητηρίων
πικρῶς ἐδούλευσ'; εἰ δὲ τῶν θεῶν κρατεῖν
βούλει, τὸ χρήζειν ἀμαθές ἐστί σοι τόδε.   965
ΧΟ. βασίλει', ἄμυνον σοῖς τέκνοισι καὶ πάτρᾳ,
πειθὼ διαφθείρουσα τῆσδ', ἐπεὶ λέγει
καλῶς, κακοῦργος οὖσα· δεινὸν οὖν τόδε.
ΕΚ. ταῖς θεαῖσι πρῶτα σύμμαχος γενήσομαι,
καὶ τήνδε δείξω μὴ λέγουσαν ἔνδικα.   970
ἐγὼ γὰρ Ἥραν παρθένον τε Παλλάδα
οὐκ ἐς τοσοῦτον ἀμαθίας ἐλθεῖν δοκῶ
ὥσθ' ἡ μὲν Ἄργος βαρβάροις ἀπημπόλα,
Παλλὰς δ' Ἀθήνας Φρυξὶ δουλεύειν ποτέ,
αἳ παιδιαῖσι καὶ χλιδῇ μορφῆς πέρι   975
ἦλθον πρὸς Ἴδην. τοῦ γὰρ οὕνεκ' ἂν θεὰ

Ηρα τοσοῦτον ἔσχ' ἔρωτα καλλονῆς;
πότερον ἀμείνον· ὡς λάβοι Διὸς πόσιν,
ἢ γάμον 'Αθάνα θεῶν τινος θηρωμένη,
ἢ παρθενείαν πατρὸς ἐξῃτήσατο,   980
φεύγουσα λέκτρα; μὰμαθεῖς ποίει θεὰς
τὸ σὸν κακὸν κοσμοῦσα· μὴ οὐ πείσῃς σοφούς.
Κύπριν δ' ἔλεξας, ταῦτα γὰρ γέλως πολύς,
ἐλθεῖν ἐμῷ ξὺν παιδὶ Μενέλεω δόμους.
οὐκ ἂν μένουσ' ἂν ἥσυχός γ' ἐν οὐρανῷ   985
αὐταῖς 'Αμύκλαις σ' ἤγαγεν πρὸς Ἴλιον
ἦν οὑμὸς υἱὸς κάλλος ἐκπρεπέστατος,
ὁ σὸς δ' ἰδών νιν νοῦς ἐποιήθη Κύπρις·
τὰ μῶρα γὰρ πάντ' ἐστὶν 'Αφροδίτη βροτοῖς,
καὶ τοὔνομ' ὀρθῶς ἀφροσύνης ἄρχει θεᾶς·   990
ὃν εἰσιδοῦσα βαρβάροις ἐσθήμασι
χρυσῷ τε λαμπρὸν ἐξεμαργώθης φρένας.
ἐν μὲν γὰρ Ἄργει μίκρ' ἔχουσ' ἀνεστρέφου,
Σπάρτης δ' ἀπαλλαχθεῖσα τὴν Φρυγῶν πόλιν
χρυσῷ ῥέουσαν ἤλπισας κατακλύσειν   995
δαπάναισιν· οὐδ' ἦν ἱκανά σοι τὰ Μενέλεω
μέλαθρα ταῖς σαῖς ἐγκαθυβρίζειν τρυφαῖς.
εἶεν, βίᾳ γὰρ παῖδα φῂς σ' ἄγειν ἐμόν·
τίς Σπαρτιατῶν ᾔσθετ', ἢ ποίαν βοὴν
ἀνωλόλυξας, Κάστορος νεανίου   1000
τοῦ ξυζύγου τ' ἔτ' ὄντος οὐ κατ' ἄστρα πω;
ἐπεὶ δὲ Τροίαν ἦλθες 'Αργεῖοί τέ σου
κατ' ἴχνος, ἦν δὲ δοριπετὴς ἀγωνία,
εἰ μὲν τὰ τοῦδε κρείσσον' ἀγγέλλοιτό σοι,
Μενέλαον ᾔνεις, παῖς ὅπως λυποῖτ' ἐμός,   1005

ἔχων ἔρωτος ἀνταγωνιστὴν μέγαν·
εἰ δ' εὐτυχοῖεν Τρῶες, οὐδὲν ἦν ὅδε·
ἐς τὴν τύχην δ' ὁρῶσα τοῦτ' ἤσκεις, ὅπως
ἕποι' ἅμ' αὐτῇ, τἀρετῇ δ' οὐκ ἤθελες.
κἄπειτα πλεκταῖς σῶμα σὸν κλέπτειν λέγεις
πύργων καθιεῖσ', ὡς μένουσ' ἀκουσίως ;   1011
ποῦ δῆτ' ἐλήφθης ἢ βρόχους ἀρτωμένη,
ἢ φάσγανον θήγουσ', ἃ γενναία γυνὴ
δράσειεν ἂν ποθοῦσα τὸν πάρος πόσιν ;
καίτοι σ' ἐνουθέτουν γε πολλὰ πολλάκις,   1015
ὦ θύγατερ, ἔξελθ', οἱ δ' ἐμοὶ παῖδες γάμους
ἄλλους γαμοῦσι, σὲ δ' ἐπὶ ναῦς Ἀχαικὰς
πέμψω ξυνεκκλέψασα, καὶ παῦσον μάχης
Ἕλληνας ἡμᾶς τ'.   ἀλλὰ σοὶ τόδ' ἦν πικρόν.
ἐν τοῖς Ἀλεξάνδρου γὰρ ὕβριζες δόμοις,   1020
καὶ προσκυνεῖσθαι βαρβάρων ἀνδρῶν ὕπο
ἀρεστὸν ἦν σοι· κἀπὶ τοῖσδε σὸν δέμας
ἐξῆλθες ἀσκήσασα, κἄβλεψας πόσει
τὸν αὐτὸν αἰθέρ', ὦ κατάπτυστον κάρα·
ἣν χρῆν ταπεινὴν ἐν πέπλων ἐρειπίοις   1025
φρίκῃ τρέμουσαν, κρᾶτ' ἀπεσκυθισμένην
ἐλθεῖν, τὸ σῶφρον τῆς ἀναιδείας πλέον
ἔχουσαν ἐπὶ τοῖς πρόσθεν ἡμαρτημένοις.
Μενέλα', ἵν' εἰδῇς οἷ τελευτήσω λόγον,
στεφάνωσον Ἑλλάδ', ἀξίως τήνδε κτανὼν   1030
σαυτοῦ, νόμον δὲ τόνδε ταῖς ἄλλαισι θὲς
γυναιξί, θνήσκειν ἥτις ἂν προδῷ πόσιν.
ΧΟ. Μενέλαε, προγόνων ἀξίως δόμων τε σῶν
τῖσαι δάμαρτα, κἀφελοῦ πρὸς Ἑλλάδος

ψόγον τὸ θῆλύ τ᾽, εὐγενὴς ἐχθροῖς φανείς. 1035

ΜΕ. ἐμοὶ σὺ συμπέπτωκας ἐς ταὐτὸν λόγου,
ἑκουσίως τήνδ᾽ ἐκ δόμων ἐλθεῖν ἐμῶν
ξένας ἐς εὐνάς, χἠ Κύπρις κόμπου χάριν
λόγοις ἔνεστι. βαῖνε λευστήρων πέλας,
πόνους τ᾽ Ἀχαιῶν ἀπόδος ἐν μικρῷ μακροὺς
θανοῦσ᾽, ἵν᾽ εἰδῇς μὴ καταισχύνειν ἐμέ. 1041

ΕΛ. μή, πρός σε γονάτων, τὴν νόσον τὴν τῶν θεῶν
προσθεὶς ἐμοὶ κτάνῃς με, συγγίγνωσκε δέ.

ΕΚ. μηδ᾽ οὓς ἀπέκτειν᾽ ἥδε συμμάχους προδῷς·
ἐγὼ πρὸ κείνων καὶ τέκνων σε λίσσομαι, 1045

ΜΕ. παῦσαι, γεραιά· τῆσδε δ᾽ οὐκ ἐφρόντισα.
λέγω δὲ προσπόλοισι πρὸς πρύμνας νεῶν
τήνδ᾽ ἐκκομίζειν, ἔνθα ναυστολήσεται.

ΕΚ. μή νυν νεὼς σοὶ ταὐτὸν ἐσβήτω σκάφος.

ΜΕ. τί δ᾽ ἔστι; μεῖζον βρῖθος ἢ πάροιθ᾽ ἔχει; 1050

ΕΚ. οὐκ ἔστ᾽ ἐραστὴς ὅστις οὐκ ἀεὶ φιλεῖ. .

ΜΕ. ὅπως ἂν ἐκβῇ τῶν ἐρωμένων ὁ νοῦς.
ἔσται δ᾽ ἃ βούλει· ναῦν γὰρ οὐκ ἐσβήσεται
εἰς ἥνπερ ἡμεῖς· καὶ γὰρ οὐ κακῶς λέγεις·
ἐλθοῦσα δ᾽ Ἄργος ὥσπερ ἀξία κακῶς 1055
κακὴ θανεῖται καὶ γυναιξὶ σωφρονεῖν
πάσαισι θήσει. ῥᾴδιον μὲν οὐ τόδε·
ὅμως δ᾽ ὁ τῆσδ᾽ ὄλεθρος ἐς φόβον βαλεῖ
τὸ μῶρον αὐτῶν, κἂν ἔτ᾽ ὦσ᾽ ἐχθίονες.

ΧΟ. οὕτω δὴ τὸν ἐν Ἰλίῳ   στρ. α′.
ναὸν καὶ θυόεντα βω-   1061
μὸν προὔδωκας Ἀχαιοῖς,
ὦ Ζεῦ, καὶ πελάνων φλόγα,

σμύρνης αἰθερίας τε κα-
πνὸν καὶ Πέργαμον ἱράν,   1065
Ἰδαῖά τ' Ἰδαῖα κισσοφόρα νάπη
χιόνι κατάρυτα ποταμία
τέρμονά τε πρωτόβολον ἁλίῳ
τὰν καταλαμπομέναν ζαθέαν θεράπναν.   1070
φροῦδαί σοι θυσίαι χορῶν τ'   ἀντιστρ. α'.
εὔφαμοι κέλαδοι κατ' ὄρ-
φναν τε παννυχίδες θεῶν,
χρυσέων τε ξοάνων τύποι,
Φρυγῶν τε ζάθεοι σελᾶ-   1075
ναι ξυνδώδεκα πλήθει.
μέλει μέλει μοι τάδ' εἰ φρονεῖς, ἄναξ,
οὐράνιον ἕδρανον ἐπιβεβὼς
αἰθέρα τ', ἐμᾶς πόλεος ὀλομένας,
ἃν πυρὸς αἰθομένα κατέλυσεν ὁρμά.   1080
ὦ φίλος ὦ πόσι μοι,   στρ. β'.
σὺ μὲν φθίμενος ἀλαίνεις
ἄθαπτος, ἄνυδρος, ἐμὲ δὲ πόντιον σκάφος 1085
ἀΐσσον πτεροῖσι πορεύσει
ἱππόβοτον Ἄργος, ἵνα τε τείχη
λάϊνα Κυκλώπι' οὐράνια νέμονται.
τέκνων δὲ πλῆθος ἐν πύλαις
δάκρυσι κατάορα στένει, βοᾷ βοᾷ,   1090
μᾶτερ, ὤμοι, μόναν δή μ' Ἀχαιοὶ κομίζουσι
        σέθεν ἀπ' ὀμμάτων
κυανέαν ἐπὶ ναῦν
εἰναλίαισι πλάταις   1095
ἢ Σαλαμῖν' ἱεράν,

ἢ δίπορον κορυφὰν
Ἴσθμιον, ἔνθα πύλας
Πέλοπος ἔχουσιν ἕδραι.
εἶθ' ἀκάτου Μενέλα   ἀντιστρ. β'.
μέσον πέλαγος ἰούσας,   1101
δίπαλτον ἱερὸν ἀνὰ μέσον πλατᾶν πέσοι
Αἰγαίου κεραυνοφαὲς πῦρ,
Ἰλιόθεν ὅτε με πολυδάκρυτον
Ἑλλάδι λάτρευμα γᾶθεν ἐξορίζει,   1105
χρύσεα δ' ἔνοπτρα, παρθένων
χάριτας, ἔχουσα τυγχάνει Διὸς κόρα·
μηδὲ γαῖάν ποτ' ἔλθοι Λάκαιναν πατρῷόν
     τε θάλαμον ἑστίας,   1110
μηδὲ πόλιν Πιτάνας,
χαλκόπυλόν τε θεάν,
δύσγαμον αἶσχος ἑλὼν
Ἑλλάδι τᾷ μεγάλᾳ·   1115
καὶ Σιμοεντιάσιν
μέλεα πάθεα ῥοαῖσιν.

ἰὼ ἰώ,
καιναὶ καινῶν μεταβάλλουσαι
χθονὶ συντυχίαι. λεύσσετε Τρώων
τόνδ' Ἀστυάνακτ' ἄλοχοι μέλεαι   1120
νεκρὸν ὃν πύργων δίσκημα πικρὸν
Δαναοὶ κτείναντες ἔχουσιν.
ΤΑ. Ἑκάβη, νεὼς μὲν πίτυλος εἷς λελειμμένος
λάφυρα τἀπίλοιπ' Ἀχιλλείου τόκου·
μέλλει πρὸς ἀκτὰς ναυστολεῖν Φθιώτιδας· 1125

αυτος δ' ἀνῆκται Νεοπτόλεμος, καινάς τινας
Πηλέως ἀκούσας ξυμφοράς, ὥς νιν χθονὸς
Ἄκαστος ἐκβέβληκεν ὁ Πελίου γόνος.
οὗ θᾶσσον οὕνεκ' ἢ χάριν μονῆς ἔχων   1129
φροῦδος, μετ' αὐτοῦ δ' Ἀνδρομάχη, πολλῶν ἐμοὶ
δακρύων ἀγωγός, ἡνίκ' ἐξώρμα χθονὸς
πάτραν τ' ἀναστένουσα καὶ τὸν Ἕκτορος
τύμβον προσεννέπουσα. καί σφ' ᾐτήσατο
θάψαι νεκρὸν τόνδ', ὃς πεσὼν ἐκ τειχέων
ψυχὴν ἀφῆκεν Ἕκτορος τοῦ σοῦ γόνος·   1135
φόβον τ' Ἀχαιῶν, χαλκόνωτον ἀσπίδα
τήνδ', ἣν πατὴρ τοῦδ' ἀμφὶ πλεύρ' ἐβάλλετο,
μή νιν πορεῦσαι Πηλέως ἐφ' ἑστίαν,
μηδ' ἐς τὸν αὐτὸν θάλαμον, οὗ νυμφεύσεται
μήτηρ νεκροῦ τοῦδ' Ἀνδρομάχη, λύπας ὁρᾶν,
ἀλλ' ἀντὶ κέδρου περιβόλων τε λαΐνων   1141
ἐν τῇδε θάψαι παῖδα· σὰς δ' εἰς ὠλένας
δοῦναι, πέπλοισιν ὡς περιστείλῃς νεκρὸν
στεφάνοις θ', ὅση σοι δύναμις, ὡς ἔχει τὰ σα,
ἐπεὶ βέβηκε καὶ τὸ δεσπότου τάχος   1145
ἀφείλετ' αὐτὴν παῖδα μὴ δοῦναι τάφῳ.
ἡμεῖς μὲν οὖν, ὅταν σὺ κοσμήσῃς νέκυν,
γῆν τῷδ' ἐπαμπισχόντες ἀροῦμεν δόρυ·
σὺ δ' ὡς τάχιστα πρᾶσσε τἀπεσταλμένα.
ἑνὸς μὲν οὖν μόχθου σ' ἀπαλλάξας ἔχω·   1150
Σκαμανδρίους γὰρ τάσδε διαπερῶν ῥοὰς
ἔλουσα νεκρὸν κἀπένιψα τραύματα.
ἀλλ' εἶμ' ὀρυκτὸν τῷδ' ἀναρρήξων τάφον,
ὡς ξύντομ' ἡμῖν τἀπ' ἐμοῦ τε κἀπὸ σοῦ

εἰς ἓν ξυνελθόντ᾽ οἴκαδ᾽ ὁρμήσῃ πλάτην. 1155

ΕΚ. θέσθ᾽ ἀμφίτορνον ἀσπίδ᾽ Ἕκτορος πέδῳ,
λυπρὸν θέαμα κοὐ φίλον λεύσσειν ἐμοί.
ὦ μεῖζον᾽ ὄγκον δορὸς ἔχοντες ἢ φρενῶν,
τί τόνδ᾽, Ἀχαιοί, παῖδα δείσαντες φόνον
καινὸν διειργάσασθε; μὴ Τροίαν ποτὲ 1160
πεσοῦσαν ὀρθώσειεν; οὐδὲν ἦτ᾽ ἄρα,
ὅθ᾽ Ἕκτορος μὲν εὐτυχοῦντος ἐς δόρυ
διωλλύμεσθα μυρίου τ᾽ ἄλλης χερός,
πόλεως δ᾽ ἁλούσης καὶ Φρυγῶν ἐφθαρμένων
βρέφος τοσόνδ᾽ ἐδείσατ᾽. οὐκ αἰνῶ φόβον, 1165
ὅστις φοβεῖται μὴ διεξελθὼν λόγῳ.
ὦ φίλταθ᾽, ὥς σοι θάνατος ἦλθε δυστυχής.
εἰ μὲν γὰρ ἔθανες πρὸ πόλεως, ἥβης τυχὼν
γάμων τε καὶ τῆς ἰσοθέου τυραννίδος,
μακάριος ἦσθ᾽ ἄν, εἴ τι τῶνδε μακάριον. 1170
νῦν δ᾽ αὔτ᾽ ἰδὼν μὲν γνούς τε σῇ ψυχῇ, τέκνον,
οὐκ οἶσθ᾽, ἐχρήσω δ᾽ οὐδὲν ἐν δόμοις ἔχων.
δύστηνε, κρατὸς ὥς σ᾽ ἔκειρεν ἀθλίως
τείχη πατρῷα, Λοξίου πυργώματα,
ὃν πόλλ᾽ ἐκήπευσ᾽ ἡ τεκοῦσα βόστρυχον 1175
φιλήμασίν τ᾽ ἔδωκεν, ἔνθεν ἐκγελᾷ
ὀστέων ῥαγέντων φόνος, ἵν᾽ αἰσχρὰ μὴ λέγω.
ὦ χεῖρες, ὡς εἰκοὺς μὲν ἡδείας πατρὸς
κέκτησθ᾽, ἐν ἄρθροις δ᾽ ἔκλυτοι πρόκεισθε νῦν.
ὦ πολλὰ κόμπους ἐκβαλὸν φίλον στόμα, 1180
ὄλωλας, ἐψεύσω μ᾽, ὅτ᾽ ἐσπίπτων λέχος,
ὦ μῆτερ, ηὔδας, ἦ πολύν σοι βοστρύχων
πλόκαμον κεροῦμαι, πρὸς τάφον θ᾽ ὁμηλίκων

κώμους ἐπάξω, φίλα διδοὺς προσφθέγματα.
σὺ δ' οὐκ ἔμ', ἀλλ' ἐγώ σε τὸν νεώτερον,   1185
γραῦς, ἄπολις, ἄτεκνος, ἄθλιον θάπτω νεκρόν.
οἴμοι, τὰ πόλλ' ἀσπάσμαθ', αἵ τ' ἐμαὶ τροφαί,
ἄϋπνοί τε κλῖναι, φροῦδά μοι.   τί καί ποτε
γράψειεν ἄν σε μουσοποιὸς ἐν τάφῳ;
τὸν παῖδα τόνδ' ἔκτειναν Ἀργεῖοί ποτε   1190
δείσαντες ;   αἰσχρὸν τοὐπίγραμμά γ' Ἑλ-
          λάδι.
ἀλλ' οὖν πατρῴων οὐ λαχὼν ἕξεις ὅμως
ἐν ᾗ ταφήσει χαλκόνωτον ἰτέαν.
ὦ καλλίπηχυν Ἕκτορος βραχίονα
σώζουσ', ἄριστον φύλακ' ἀπώλεσας σέθεν.   1195
ὡς ἡδὺς ἐν πόρπακι σῷ κεῖται τύπος,
ἴτυός τ' ἐν εὐτόρνοισι περιδρόμοις ἱδρώς,   ·
ὃν ἐκ μετώπου πολλάκις πόνους ἔχων
ἔσταζεν Ἕκτωρ, προστιθεὶς γενειάδι.
φέρετε, κομίζετ' ἀθλίῳ κόσμον νεκρῷ   1200
ἐκ τῶν παρόντων· οὐ γὰρ ἐς κάλλος τύχας
δαίμων δίδωσιν· ὧν δ' ἔχω, λήψει τάδε.
θνητῶν δὲ μῶρος ὅστις εὖ πράσσειν δοκῶν
βέβαια χαίρει· τοῖς τρόποις γὰρ αἱ τύχαι
ἔμπληκτος ὡς ἄνθρωπος ἄλλοτ' ἄλλοσε   1205
πηδῶσι, κοὐδεὶς αὐτὸς εὐτυχεῖ ποτε.
ΧΟ. καὶ μὴν πρὸ χειρῶν αἵδε σοι σκυλευμάτων
     Φρυγίων φέρουσι κόσμον ἐξάπτειν νεκρῷ.
ΕΚ. ὦ τέκνον, οὐχ ἵπποισι νικήσαντά σε
     οὐδ' ἥλικας τόξοισιν, οὓς Φρύγες νόμους   1210
     τιμῶσιν, οὐκ ἐς πλησμονὰς θηρώμενοι,

μήτηρ πατρός σοι προστίθησ' ἀγάλματα
τῶν σῶν ποτ' ὄντων, νῦν δέ σ' ἡ θεοστυγὴς
ἀφείλεθ' Ἑλένη, πρὸς δὲ καὶ ψυχὴν σέθεν
ἔκτεινε, καὶ πάντ' οἶκον ἐξαπώλεσεν.   1215

ΧΟ. ἐή, φρενῶν
    ἔθιγες ἔθιγες, ὦ μέγας ἐμοί ποτ' ὢν ἀνάκτωρ
    πόλεως.

ΕΚ. ἃ δ' ἐν γάμοις ἐχρῆν σε προσθέσθαι χροΐ,
    Ἀσιατίδων γήμαντα τὴν ὑπερτάτην,
    Φρύγια πέπλων ἀγάλματ' ἐξάπτω χροός.   1220
    σύ τ', ὦ ποτ' οὖσα καλλίνικε μυρίων
    μῆτερ τροπαίων, Ἕκτορος φίλον σάκος,
    στεφανοῦ· θανεῖ γὰρ οὐ θανοῦσα σὺν νεκρῷ,
    ἐπεὶ σὲ πολλῷ μᾶλλον ἢ τὰ τοῦ σοφοῦ
    κακοῦ τ' Ὀδυσσέως ἄξιον τιμᾶν ὅπλα.   1225

ΧΟ. αἰαῖ, πικρὸν
    ὄδυρμα γαῖά σ', ὦ τέκνον, δέξεται.
    στέναξε, μᾶτερ,   ΕΚ. αἰαῖ.

ΧΟ. νεκρῶν ἴακχον.   ΕΚ. οἴμοι.   1229

ΧΟ. οἴμοι δῆτα σῶν ἀλάστων κακῶν.

ΕΚ. τελαμῶσιν ἕλκη τὰ μὲν ἐγώ σ' ἰάσομαι
    τλήμων ἰατρὸς ὄνομ' ἔχουσα, τἄργα δ' οὔ·
    τὰ δ' ἐν νεκροῖσι φροντιεῖ πατὴρ σέθεν.

ΧΟ. ἄρασσ' ἄρασσε κρᾶτα   1235
    πιτύλους διδοῦσα χειρός.

ΕΚ. ὤμοι μοι
    ὦ φίλταται γυναῖκες.

ΧΟ. _ _ σασ' ἔνεπε τίνα θροεῖς αὐδάν.

ΕΚ. οὐκ ἦν ἄρ' ἐν θεοῖσι πλὴν ἐμοὶ πόνοι   1240

Τροίᾳ τε πόλεων ἔκκριτον μισουμένῃ,
μάτην δ᾽ ἐβουθυτοῦμεν. εἰ δ᾽ ἡμᾶς θεὸς
‿ ‾ ‿ ‿ ‒ ‒ περιβαλὼν κάτω χθονός,
ἀφανεῖς ἂν ὄντες οὐκ ἂν ὑμνηθεῖμεν ἂν
μούσαις, ἀοιδὰς δόντες ὑστέροις βροτῶν. 1245
χωρεῖτε, θάπτετ᾽ ἀθλίῳ τύμβῳ νεκρόν·
ἔχει γὰρ οἷα δεῖ γε νερτέρων στέφη.
δοκῶ δὲ τοῖς θανοῦσι διαφέρειν βραχύ,
εἰ πλουσίων τις τεύξεται κτερισμάτων.
κενὸν δὲ γαύρωμ᾽ ἐστὶ τῶν ζώντων τόδε. 1250

ΧΟ. ἰὼ ἰώ·
μελέα μῆτηρ, ἣ τὰς μεγάλας
ἐλπίδας ἐν σοὶ κατέκναψε βίου.
μέγα δ᾽ ὀλβισθεὶς ὡς ἐκ πατέρων
ἀγαθῶν ἐγένου
δεινῷ θανάτῳ διόλωλας. 1255

ΕΚ. ἔα ἔα·
τίνας Ἰλιάσιν ταῖσδ᾽ ἐν κορυφαῖς
λεύσσω φλογέας δαλοῖσι χέρας
διερέσσοντας. μέλλει Τροίᾳ
καινόν τι κακὸν προσέσεσθαι.

ΤΑ. αὐδῶ λοχαγοῖς, οἳ τέταχθ᾽ ἐμπιμπράναι 1260
Πριάμου τόδ᾽ ἄστυ, μηκέτ᾽ ἀργοῦσαν φλόγα
ἐν χερσὶ σώζειν, ἀλλὰ πῦρ ἐνιέναι,
ὡς ἂν κατασκάψαντες Ἰλίου πόλιν
στελλώμεθ᾽ οἴκαδ᾽ ἄσμενοι Τροίας ἄπο.
ὑμεῖς δ᾽, ἵν᾽ αὑτὸς λόγος ἔχῃ μορφὰς δύο, 1265
χωρεῖτε, Τρώων παῖδες, ὀρθίαν ὅταν
σάλπιγγος ἠχὼ δῶσιν ἀρχηγοὶ στρατοῦ,

πρὸς ναῦς 'Αχαιῶν, ὡς ἀποστέλλησθε γῆς.
σύ τ', ὦ γεραιὰ δυστυχεστάτη γύναι,
ἔπου. μεθήκουσίν σ' 'Οδυσσέως πάρα   1270
οἶδ', ᾧ σε δούλην κλῆρος ἐκπέμπει χθονός.

ΕΚ. οἲ 'γὼ τάλαινα· τοῦτο δὴ τὸ λοίσθιον
καὶ τέρμα πάντων τῶν ἐμῶν ἤδη κακῶν·
ἔξειμι πατρίδος, πόλις ὑφάπτεται πυρί·
ἀλλ', ὦ γεραιὲ πούς, ἐπίσπευσον μόλις,   1275
ὡς ἀσπάσωμαι τὴν ταλαίπωρον πόλιν.
ὦ μεγάλα δήποτ' ἐμπνέουσ' ἐν βαρβάροις
Τροία, τὸ κλεινὸν ὄνομ' ἀφαιρήσει τάχα.
πιμπρᾶσί σ', ἡμᾶς δ' ἐξάγουσ' ἤδη χθονὸς
δούλας· ἰὼ θεοί. καὶ τί τοὺς θεοὺς καλῶ;   1280
καὶ πρὶν γὰρ οὐκ ἤκουσαν ἀνακαλούμενοι.
φέρ' ἐς πυρὰν δράμωμεν, ὡς κάλλιστά μοι
ξὺν τῇδε πατρίδι κατθανεῖν πυρουμένῃ.

ΤΑ. ἐνθουσιᾷς, δύστηνε, τοῖς σαυτῆς κακοῖς·
ἀλλ' ἄγετε, μὴ φείδεσθ'· 'Οδυσσέως δὲ χρὴ   1285
ἐς χεῖρα δοῦναι τήνδε καὶ πέμπειν γέρας.

ΕΚ. ὀτοτοτοτοτοτοῖ.   στρ. α'.

╰─╵─╵─╵─╵─

Κρόνιε, πρυτάνι Φρύγιε, γενέτα πάτερ,
ἀνάξια τᾶς   1290
Δαρδάνου γονᾶς τάδ' οἷα
πάσχομεν δέδορκας;

ΧΟ. δέδορκεν, ἀ δὲ μεγαλόπολις
ἄπολις ὄλωλεν οὐδ' ἔτ' ἔστι Τροία.

ΕΚ. ὀτοτοτοτοτοτοῖ.   ἀντιστρ. α'.
λέλαμπεν Ἴλιος,   1295

περγάμων τε πυρὶ καταίθεται τέραμνα καὶ
πόλις
ἄκρα τε τειχέων.
μαλερὰ μέλαθρα πυρὶ κατάδρομα
δαΐῳ τε λόγχᾳ.
ΧΟ. πτέρυγι δὲ καπνὸς ὥς τις οὐ-
ράνια πεσοῦσα δορὶ καταφθίνει γᾶ.　　1301
ΕΚ. ἰὼ γᾶ τρόφιμε τῶν ἐμῶν τέκνων　　στρ. β'.
ΧΟ. ἐή.
ΕΚ. ὦ τέκνα, κλύετε, μάθετε ματρὸς αὐδάν.
ΧΟ. ἰαλέμῳ τοὺς θανόντας ἀπύεις.
ΕΚ. γεραιά γ' ἐς πέδον τιθεῖσα μέλε' ἐμὰ　　1305
καὶ χερσὶ γαῖαν κτυποῦσα δισσαῖς.
ΧΟ. διάδοχά σοι γόνυ τίθημι γαίᾳ
τοὺς ἐμοὺς καλοῦσα νέρθεν
ἀθλίους ἀκοίτας.
ΕΚ. ἀγόμεθα, φερόμεθ'　ΧΟ. ἄλγος ἄλγος βοᾷς.
ΕΚ. δούλειον ὑπὸ μέλαθρον ἐκ πάτρας ἐμᾶς.
ἰώ.
Πρίαμε Πρίαμε, σὺ μὲν ὀλόμενος ἄταφος ἄφιλος
ἄτας ἐμᾶς ἄϊστος εἶ.
ΧΟ. μέλας γὰρ ὄσσε κατεκάλυψε
θάνατος ὅσιον ἀνοσίαις σφαγαῖσιν.　　1315
ΕΚ. ἰὼ θεῶν μέλαθρα καὶ πόλις φίλα.　　ἀντιστρ. β'.
ΧΟ. ἐή.
ΕΚ. τὰν φόνιον ἔχετε φλόγα δορός τε λόγχαν.
ΚΟ. τάχ' ἐς φίλαν γᾶν πεσεῖσθ' ἀνώνυμοι.
ΕΚ. κόνις δ' ἴσα καπνῷ πτέρυγι πρὸς αἰθέρα　　1320
ἄϊστον οἴκων ἐμῶν με θήσει.

D

ΧΟ. ὄνομα δὲ γᾶς ἀφανὲς εἰσιν· ἄλλα δ'
    ἄλλο φροῦδον, οὐδ' ἔτ' ἔστιν
    ἁ τάλαινα Τροία.
ΕΚ. ἐμάθετ', ἐκλύετε ; ΧΟ. Περγάμων γε κτύπον.
ΕΚ. ἔνοσις ἄπασαν ἔνοσις ἐπικλύσει πόλιν.   1326
    ἰώ.
    τρομερὰ τρομερὰ μέλεα φέρετ' ἐμὸν ἴχνος·
      ἴτ' ἐπὶ
    δούλειον ἀμέραν βίου.   1330
ΧΟ. ἰὼ τάλαινα πόλις· ὅμως δὲ
    πρόφερε πόδα σὸν ἐπὶ πλάτας Ἀχαιῶν.

NOTES.

3. **ἐξελίσσουσιν.** This word properly means *to unroll*, as in *Hipp.* 864 ; so also ἐξ. λόγον, '*unfold* a tale,' in *Ion* 397. But ἐξελίσσειν often has the same meaning as ἑλίσσειν, 'to cause to revolve, roll, whirl'; the prep. merely indicating a more complicated evolution, as in *H. F.* 977, ἐξελίσσων παῖδα κίονος κύκλῳ, where the child is described as being chased round and round the στῦλος ποδήρης, or pillar which supported the roof of the house. Xenophon uses ἐξελίσσειν τὴν φάλαγγα in the sense 'to deploy '; cp. Lat. *explicare.* Hesychius has ἐξελίσσουσι, κινοῦσι, probably referring to this passage. We might translate 'weave of their beauteous paces mazy circles'; cp. Tennyson, *Vivien*, "a charm Of *woven paces* and of waving hands."

4. **ἀμφὶ ... πέριξ**, a common pleonasm, so κύκλῳ πέριξ, ἀμφὶ περί.

6. **κανόσιν** = στάθμῃ, as often used by Homer in the phrase ἐπὶ στάθμη. Though κανών and στάθμη are both enumerated in the list of carpenters' stock in trade in Plat. *Phil.* 56 B, yet they cannot be said to be expressly distinguished, as στάθμη, '-chalked line,' and κανών, 'rule' (as L. and S. say, *s.v.* στάθμη). On the contrary, the κανών, as well as the στάθμη was 'a red chalked line' (*rubrica* rather than *amussis*), as we see from *H. F.* 945, φοίνικι κανόνι .. ἡρμοσμένα. So the schol. on ἐπὶ στάθμην ἴθυνε has στάθμην, κανόνα, ὑπομεμιλτωμένον σχοινίον : and Lucian, *Icaromenipp.* 14 has ἐπεὶ καὶ τοὺς τέκτονας πολλάκις ἑωρακέναι μοι δοκῶ θατέρῳ τῶν ὀφθαλμῶν ἄμεινον πρὸς τοὺς κανόνας ἀπευθύνοντας τὰ ξύλα, with which cp. *Pers.* i. 66, "oculo *rubricam* dirigat uno." From this usage of getting a straight direction by dropping a ruddled line comes the proverb found in Plat. *Charm.* 154 B, ἀτεχνῶς λευκὴ στάθμη εἰμὶ πρὸς τοὺς καλούς, 'I have absolutely no power of measuring,' *i.e.* 'I am

51

as useless as would be a στάθμη without μίλτος on it.' So
Soph. Frag. 306 :

> τοῖς μὲν λόγοις τοῖς σοῖσιν οὐ τεκμαίρομαι,
> οὐ μᾶλλον ἢ λευκῷ λίθῳ λευκὴ στάθμη.

7. εὔνοια. Constr. εὔνοια Φρυγῶν πόλει, 'good-will to Troy.'
ἀπέστη cannot be taken with πόλει, as it would require to be
followed by a genitive : εὔνοιᾶ, else the final a could not be
elided ; yet we have ἀνοιᾶ in *Andr.* 520.

9. Παρνάσιος = Φωκεύς.

12. ὀλέθριον βάρος :

"Fashioned the horse whose womb was fraught with arms,
And sent within your town its ruin-load."—W.

14. δούρειος. This word is here used in a different sense
from ἵππος δουράτεος in the *Odyssey*, and "durateus ecus,"
Lucr. i. 477 ; the latter words mean ' wooden,' but here, as is
plain from the context, δούρειος is not 'wooden,' but = ἐγκύμων
τευχέων, *fetus armis.* Cp. Val. Flac. ii. 573, "duria nox."

16. φονῷ καταρρεῖ, 'with blood are dripping.' This is
perhaps a more probable rendering than ' are ruining 'mid the
slaughter,' though the latter would be a better expression
and would involve the far more normal use of καταρρεῖ : but
the slaughter was over, and the ruin was consummated.

κρηπίδων. κρηπίς, Lat. *crepido*, is the *basis* or *pedestal* of
a building, especially of a temple or altar, as here. Hence,
below 215, the plains of Thessaly are called 'the lovely
pedestal (κρηπῖδα) of Olympus.'

23. νικῶμαι. Verbs which imply the idea of a comparison
take the genitive ; hence *e.g.* νικᾶσθαι, λείπεσθαι, περιγίγνεσθαι,
διαφέρειν τινος : cp. ἐκαλλιστεύετο πασῶν γυ‥‥‥‥‥‥ Η‥‥‥ ‥‥‥
' was most beautiful (as compared with) a. ·
τῆς μάχης, Xen. *An.* i. 7. 12, ' was after as regai‥‥·; ὑστέρησε,
i.e. 'was late for the battle.' ;battle,

26. ἐρημία. This word often means 'depopulation,'
lation,' sometimes 'unprotectedness '; both are included in
Milton's 'ruin bare '; see below, 97, 565, and Frag. 825 :

> αἱ γὰρ πόλεις εἰσ' ἄνδρες, οὐκ ἐρημία.

27. νοσεῖ, 'ill fare the gods without their wonted
honours.' Eur. nearly always uses νοσεῖν in a metaphorical
sense. For θέλει = φιλεῖ = *solet*, cp. Thuc. ii. 89, ἡσσημένων δ'
ἀνδρῶν οὐκ ἐθέλουσιν αἱ γνῶμαι … ὁμοῖαι εἶναι. This verb is
also often used to express a future event, like our *will* or
shall as the sign of the future, as ταὐτὸν τἀναντία ποιεῖν ἢ
πάσχειν ‥ οὐκ ἐθελήσει, Plat. *Rep.* 436 B. The gods of a de-

serted city were supposed to leave it, as no longer receiving sacrifices; Aesch. *Sept.* 207, θεοὺς | τοὺς τῆς ἀλούσης πόλεος ἐκλείπειν λόγος.

29. βοᾷ, 're-echoes,' as in P. 265, ἠϊόνες βοόωσι. So βοᾶσθαι in *Hel.* 1434.

31. Θησείδαι. Acamas and Demophon.

32. ἄκληροι. Not ' unallotted ' (as L. and S.), for we see *inf.* 249, that they were already allotted; but ' unballoted for,' as having been set aside each as the γέρας ἐξαίρετον of some leading Greek chieftain. Matthiae quotes from a grammarian in Becker's *Anecdota*, ἄκληροι ἔξω τοῦ κεκληρῶσθαι, Εὐριπίδης, a gloss which probably refers to this passage. The usual meaning is ' without lot,' ' destitute,' or (with gen.) ' without share of,' ' destitute of.'

33. ἐξῃρημέναι, ' reserved as a γέρας ἐξαίρετον.'

37. πάρεστιν. For the unnatural position of this word, cp. note on *Bacch.* 860, where I have quoted instances of the figure called *hyperbaton* in Eur.

40. λάθρα. Hec. did not yet know of the sacrifice of Polyxena ; see 260 ff. Many edd. prefer οἰκτρὰ of P to λάθρα of V. The latter is the much less likely word to have been introduced by conjecture, and is probably right. The use of the word absolutely in the sense of ' without her knowledge ' is very unusual. The change of ᾗ to ῆς in the foregoing verse would obviate this objection, but is not absolutely necessary.

42. μεθῆκ', ' permitted to remain a virgin,' ' spared her maidenhood.' So *inf.* 253, ᾇ γέρας ἔδωκ' ἄλεκτρον ζόαν. Cp. ἐλευθέραν μεθέντες, *Hec.* 550 ; and μεθίημ' Ἑρμιόνην ἀπὸ σφαγῆς, *Or.* sub fin.

δρομάδα, ' frantic,' ' frenzied ' ; the Eumenides are called δρομάδες in *Or.* 837, (cp. φοιτὰς νόσος), and λύσσα is called ἐλαφρὰ in *Bacch.* 851.

44. σκότιον, ' as a concubine ' ; cp. 252, and Z. 24 ; the word is applied to concubinage, ἀδραδούχητοι γάμοι, as a schol. on Homer calls them. Though γαμεῖ might for its form be future, yet it is probably present, as the present is used throughout, and Poseidon would not foretell this fact, and this only. For the present used for the future, to express *likelihood, intention,* see Goodwin, § 10, note 7.

45. εὐτυχοῦσα. The present participle, like the present infinitive, is also used as an imperfect. (See Goodwin, § 16, 2.)

50. λύσασαν. λυσάσῃ would also be good Greek, but it is much more usual to use the construction of the accusative before the infinitive, ἔξεστι (ἐμοί), λύσασαν (ἐμὲ) τὴν πάρος ἐχθραν, προσεννέπειν τὸν γένει μὲν ἀγχιστον πατρός, μέγαν τε δαίμον' ἐν θεοῖς τε τίμιον. The difference between the two constructions might be thus indicated by translation: ἔξεστί μοι λυσάσῃ κ.τ.λ. might be literally rendered, 'Is it permitted to me, having put aside our feud, to address,' etc. ἔξεστί μοι λύσασαν would be literally, 'Is it permitted for me, having put aside our feud, to address,' etc. It is to be observed that the construction of the accusative before the infinitive is preferred, not only when the dative after ἔξεστι is suppressed, as here, but even when the dative after ἔξεστι is expressed: ἔξεστί μοι λύσασαν προσεννέπειν, would be more regular than ἔξεστί μοι λυσάσῃ προσεννέπειν, yet the exact reverse of this construction is found, Soph. *O. R.* 350, ἐννέπω σε ... ἀφ' ἡμέρας | τῆς νῦν προσαυδᾶν μήτε τούσδε μήτ' ἐμέ, | ὡς ὄντι γῆς τῆσδ' ἀνοσίῳ μιάστορι, where the construction is as if he had first said ἐννέπω σοι, 'I command thee,' not ἐννέπω σε, 'I command that thou.'

53. ἐπήνεσ'. The aorist is sometimes used, especially by the dramatists, when a momentary action which is just taking place is to be expressed as if it had already happened, Goodwin, § 19, note 5; Madv. *Syn.* § 111 *b*. ᾔνεσα, ἐπήνεσα, ᾔσθην, ἀπέπτυσα are the most common examples of this usage, but we also find ἐφρόντισα, below 1046; ᾤμωξα, *Med.* 791; κατεδάκρυσα, *Hel.* 673; κατῴκτειρα, *Iph. A.* 469; ἐδεξάμην, Soph. *El.* 668; ἐχάρην, Ar. *Av.* 743; ἐγέλασα, Ar. *Eq.* 686. Thus here the aorist gives the sense of prompt and hearty acquiescence, as in *Or.* 1670. καὶ λέκτρ' ἐπήνεσ' ἡνίκ' ἂν διδῷ πατήρ, 'I at once accept her as my wife'; and *Med.* 707, οὐδὲ ταῦτ' ἐπήνεσα, 'I at once declare my disapproval'; τῆσδε δ' οὐκ ἐφρόντισα, *Tro.* 1046, 'I at once declare my indifference to her.' We also find in this idiom the periphrasis of the aorist part. with ἔχω, *e.g.* αἰνέσας ἔχω. The aorists ᾔνεσα, ἐπήνεσα, closely following present αἰνῶ, are found in *Alc.* 1093 ff., *Ion* 1609. Sometimes this idiom expresses, with a slightly altered shade of meaning, *impatience* rather than *promptitude*, as in *Iph. A.* 440, ἐπήνεσ' ἀλλὰ στεῖχε δωμάτων ἔσω, '' Tis well: enough: go in.' To this idiom also may be referred a kindred usage of the strong aorist in εἶπον, *Med.* 273, and the reply, ἔμαθον, or οὐκ ἔμαθον, in Plato.

56. τινός, 'any of the gods,' for 'any other one of the gods,' by a common idiom; conversely, we find phrases like γίγας ὅδ' ἄλλος, which does not mean 'here is another γίγας' (like the former), but 'here is another, who (unlike the former) is a γίγας.' The conjunction καὶ when placed between εἴτε and the second alternative in disjunctive hypotheses has a special force noticed by Dissen. It always implies that the speaker himself decidedly prefers the *first* alternative. *De Cor.* 244. 57, εἴτε ἀληθῆ περὶ ἐμοῦ γέγραπται εἴτε καὶ μή. So here, 'from Zeus or (which is less probable) from one of the other gods'; δαίμονες is here, as often, equivalent to θεοί. It is not likely that Athenè should be regarded by Poseidon as the possible bearer of a message from one of the 'lower deities' especially distinguished from the θεοί as δαίμονες. It is to be noticed that *inf.* 942 seems not to bear out Dissen's rule, which is perhaps a reason for accepting Nauck's view of the reading there; see note on 941.

58. κοινήν, 'that I may unite it with mine.'

59. νιν. When a phrase or periphrase contains absolutely only one idea, so that it is really equivalent to a single verb, as here εἰς οἶκτον ἦλθες is quite equivalent to ᾤκτειρας, then the phrase, just as if it were a single verb, can govern an accusative, which is sometimes called the accusative *remotioris objecti*. Thus νιν is here the accusative *remotioris objecti*, governed by εἰς οἶκτον ἦλθες = ᾤκτειρας: so in Soph. *El.* 123, τάκεις οἰμωγὰν 'Αγαμέμνονα. the phrase τάκεις οἰμωγὰν = οἰμώξεις, and governs 'Αγαμέμνονα in the accusative; and in Aesch. *Suppl.* 528, γένος νέωσον ... αἶνον = γένος ἐκ νέας αἰνει, 'recall the legend of *our race*.' We meet the same idiom in Eur. below, 152, 335, and in ἄχεα ... βοᾷ τὸν προδόταν, *Med.* 205; βοὴν ἔστησας ἄγγελον, *Heracl.* 656; στένω σε μέλος, *Or.* 1383; ἐπευφημήσατε παιᾶνα "Αρτεμιν, *Iph. A.* 1468; τόνδε ... δίκην μέτειμι, *Bacch.* 345. See other instances of this usage quoted on *Bacch.* 1289; and see note on 239.

The phrase, ποῖ μ' ὑπεξάγεις πόδα, *Hec.* 812, which is usually classed with the above, really rests on a different principle; the Greek poets add to the object-accusative of a person the accusative of the part of the body (including φρένας ψυχὴν and such words) to which the action refers; cp. μέθες με, πρὸς θεῶν, χεῖρα, Soph. *Phil.* 1301. Madv. *Greek Syntax*, § 31, Rem. 2. See *inf.* 408.

60. κατῃθαλωμένης. Supply Τροίας from verse 57. This use of the genitive absolute is common enough, especially in Aeschylus; see Aesch. *Suppl.* 115, 437, *Prom.* 880, *Theb.* 236, 263, *Ag.* 937, *Eum.* 742. A very strong case of this genitive is usually recognized in *Med.* 910, where (as in Aesch. *Suppl.* 437, if sound) the participle comes between the verb and the dependent case; but *Med.* 910 is a rather

suspicious passage (see Verrall's note), and Aesch. *Suppl.* 437 may be construed differently, as he suggests. Cp. 76.

61. ἐκεῖσε, *illuc primum praevertere*, 'first go back to my request for aid.'

68. ὃν ἂν τύχῃς, 'at random.'

70. εἷλκε, a *vox propria* for offering violence to a woman; cp. Λητὼ γὰρ ἕλκησε (from the collat. form ἑλκέω), λ. 580.

71. κοὐδέν γ'. The ellipse of κακῶς is unusual with πάσχειν, still more so with ἀκούειν. Nauck conjectures κοὐ δεῖν' for κοὐδέν' γ', as γ' is omitted in the best MSS.

72. ἔπερσάν γ'. ἐπέρσαντ', MSS. This certain correction is due to Victorius. There is a frequent confusion between Γ and Τ.

75. δύσνοστον νόστον. Eur. seems to affect this sort of expression; cp. γάμους δυσγάμους, *Phoen.* 1062; δυσθρηνήτοις θρήνοις, *Iph. T.* 143; δυσφήμους φήμας, *Hec.* 193. We have in Eur. very many adjectives of this form, *e.g.* δυσέρως, δυστράπεζος, δυσαίων, δυσθάνατος, δυσκέλαδος, δύσνυμφος, δύσχορτος, so also δυσλόφως, below 303. We find a rare subst. so formed in δυσχλαινία, *Hec.* 240, and a very strange formation in δυσελένα, 'ill-starred Helen,' *Or.* 1388; cp. δύσπαρις, Γ. 39, also αἰνόπαρις, *Hec.* 944. For μενόντων in v. 76, see note on 60.

82. τὸ σόν, sc. μέρος, 'for your part,' accus. in apposition to the sentence; see on 386.

84. μυχόν, the part of the coast between Caphareus and Geraestus, as Blakesley shows on Hdt. viii. 14, τὰ κοῖλα τῆς Εὐβοίας.

85. εὐσεβεῖν. This verb is found with accusative again in Aesch. *Ag.* 338, *Eum.* 260, 973, *Phoen.* 1320, etc., but in all these places Porson would write εὖ σέβειν, "*videntur tragici dixisse εὖ σέβειν θεοὺς et εὐσεβεῖν εἰς θεούς.*" Against this distinction it is urged (1) that we find εὐσεβεῖσθαι passive in Antipho 123. 42, and Plat. *Axioch.* 364: (2) that ἀσεβεῖν is found with accusative (which is very doubtful); and (3) that it would be awkward here to read εὖ σέβειν on account of the recurrence of σέβειν in next line; this consideration, however, is not of much weight, for in *Hec.* 526 ff. χεροῖν, χεροῖν, χειρὶ occur in three consecutive lines, in *El.* 411 γαίας and γῆς are found in the same line, πόδα is twice in *Bacch.* 647, πόνου and πόνος are the final words of lines 127, 128, of Aesch. *Eum.* For ὡς followed by ἂν with conjunctive in final clauses, cp. 1263 below: see Goodwin, § 44, note 2.

87. ἡ χάρις, 'the favour you ask of me requires but few words' (to express my assent to it), viz. ἔσται τάδ'.

94. ἐξιῇ κάλως. Used metaphorically in *Med.* 278, ἐξιᾶσι πάντα δὴ κάλων, 'are letting out every inch of rope,' *i.e.* 'are straining every nerve,' so φόνιον ἐξίει κάλων, *H. F.* 837, a very fine expression. Blakesley on Hdt. ii. 36, holds that this phrase means 'to shake out the reefs' in fine settled weather. Cp. *Med.* 770.

95–98. Mr. Way well preserves the thought:

"Fool, that in sack of towns lays temples waste,
And tombs the sanctuaries of the dead!
He sowing desolation reaps destruction."

98–152. I agree with Mr. Way, who imagines Hecuba to be lying asleep on the stage during the dialogue between Poseidon and Athenè. Some such supposition seems to be absolutely required. She could hardly come on after their departure, lie down, and forthwith call upon herself to get up. The words οὐκέτι ... Τροίας suggest the dazed condition of one who, waking under unaccustomed circumstances, finds a difficulty in realizing at first where she is. Assuming that she is there, it follows that she is asleep, or apparently so, since the proprieties of the Greek stage would forbid any movement on her part distracting the attention of the spectators from the dialogue between the gods. In no case, however, would her presence create any difficulty, gods being neither visible nor audible to mortals except at their own pleasure. This wail of Hecuba is given in the old editions without any division into strophe and antistrophe. Nauck regards the ode as beginning to be antistrophic at 153 ; Dind. recognizes its antistrophic character from 122 ; but I think there can be little doubt that it is antistrophic throughout. By writing αἰαῖ for αἰαῖ αἰαῖ in 105, and by omitting τί δὲ θρηνῆσαι, as very probably a gloss on τί δὲ μὴ σιγᾶν in 110, we have an antistrophic correspondence through-out. If we regard the ode up to 122 as non-antistrophic, it must be allowed that we meet a very strange phenomenon in so close an approach to antistrophic correspondence in a mono-strophic piece. The metre is all anapaestic, chiefly consisting of two measures or four feet (anapaests being scanned by dipodies), each strophe and antistrophe of course ending with a paroemiac : but presenting in the second strophe and anti-strophe some instances of anap. monom. hypermeter, as Ἑλλάδος εὐόρμους, as well as spondaic paroemiacs, as ἐς τάνδ' ἐξώκειλ' ἄταν, which are not allowed in more elaborate ana-paestic systems. Other liberties are the neglect of caesura after the first two feet, and the admission of dactyls followed by anapaests. In 122 the first verse of strophe β', a license has been overlooked by the edd. which would violate that *synapheia* (or mutual connection of all the verses in a system, so that the whole system is one verse) which is the leading feature of anapaestic systems. By the very slight change of ὠκεῖαι to ὠκείαις I have remedied this defect ; ὠκείαις would naturally have been assimilated to the case of πρῶραι, with which, at first sight, it would seem to agree ; but it really agrees with κώπαις in the next verse.

98. ἄνα = ἀνάστηθι, as frequently. There is no warrant for making ἄνα = ἀνάειρε. In 544 ἀνά is separated by *tmesis* from ἔμελπον. The verb ἀναμέλπω is found in Theocr. xvii. 113 ; ἄνα, of course, could not stand for ἄνασσα, as has been suggested. The τ' after δέρην was rightly added by Musgr.

100. τάδε, 'no Troy have we here any more, no more are we lords of Troy.' This is a common idiom, best illustrated by οὐχ "Εκτωρ τάδε, *Andr.* 108 ; see L. and S. ὅδε III.

101-104. Metaphors from ships prevail in this ode (see especially 117, 118): κατὰ πορθμὸν is *secundo flumine*, πρὸς κῦμα, *adverso flumine ;* hence κατὰ δαίμονα is 'as fate ordains.'

104. τύχαις, ''tis disaster that impels thy bark.' τύχαι sometimes means 'chance,' as in Thuc. i. 78. But in the plural this word generally = 'mishaps,' as *inf.* 349, *Or.* 4, *Andr.* 973, and perhaps in 1204 below ; πλεῖν τύχαις is an expression like πλεῖν βορέῃ ἀνέμῳ, πλεῖν αὔρᾳ κ.τ.λ. Mr. Way well renders :

"Breast not with thy prow the surges of life, who on waves of disaster, alas ! art tost."

108. ξυστελλόμενος, another nautical expression.

113. κλισίας, 'bed,' 'resting-place'; for the genitives in this passage, see Madv. *Greek Syntax*, § 61, Rems. 1 and 2 ; also *Bacch.* 263 note, 693 note.

116-119. ὡς ... ἐλέγους. 'How I crave to roll round my back, yea my spine, and to toss it to this side and that (as a rocking ship sways her keel now to larboard now to starboard) as I ever take up the burden of my piteous wailing.' The aged queen, swaying her body in time to her keening, figures herself as an old bark rocking on the heaving sea. The metaphor is so powerful as to strike modern ears at first as grotesque ; but the passage rightly considered is pathetic and artistic in the highest degree. Seidler first detected the nautical metaphor in ἀμφότεροι τοῖχοι, a phrase often applied to the sides of a ship, *e.g.* in Theocr. xxii. 12, ἀνέρρηξαν δ' ἄρα τοίχους | ἀμφοτέρους. So also the schol. on Ar. *Ran.* 536, quotes from the Ἀλκμήνη of Eur. these verses :

οὐ γὰρ ποτ' εἴων Σθένελον ἐπὶ τὸν εὐτυχῆ
χωροῦντα τοῖχον τῆς τύχης σ' ἀποστερεῖν,

adding this explanation, εἴρηται δὲ ἐκ μεταφορᾶς τῶν ἐπιβατῶν τῆς νεώς, οἵ, θατέρου μέρους αὐτοῖς κατακλυζομένου, πρὸς τὸ ἕτερον μεθίστανται. For διαδοῦναι, cp. *Or.* 1267, where Dind. rightly reads κόρας διάδοτε, 'roll round your eyes'; and so διατρέχειν, 'to run hither and thither.' I take μελέων as an adj., and punctuate after τοίχους. Mr. Way's version is very spirited :

"I yearn to rock me and sway—as a bark whose bulwarks
    roll in the trough of the sea—
To my keening, the while I wail my chant of sorrow and
    weeping unceasingly,
The ruin-song never link'd with the dance, the jangled
    music of misery."

119. ἐπιοῦσ'. This is the admirable conjecture of Musgrave for ἐπὶ τούς, which would really give no meaning, for it could not mean, as Hermann renders, *ad indulgendum perpetuo fletui*, but rather, as Paley points out, 'whatever songs of woe happen to present themselves,' like ὁ ἀεὶ ἄρχων, 'the archon for the time being.' But Musgrave's conjecture has in it all the elements of a certain emendation, for (1) it is a thoroughly appropriate word in itself; cp. τοὺς ἀναπαίστους ἐπίωμεν, Ar. *Ach.* 626; τίνα μοῦσαν ἐπέλθω, *Hel.* 165; (2) the construction would have puzzled the copyist, and made him write ἐπὶ τούς for ἐπιοῦσ' : for the construction is πρὸς τὸ σημαινόμενον, the participle ἐπιοῦσα agreeing with ποθῶ implied in μοι πόθος (ἐστί) according to a very frequent Attic usage; cp. διασκοπῶν οὖν τοῦτον ... ἔδοξέ μοι, Plat. *Apol.* vi. ; ὑπάρχει αὐτῇ ... διάγουσα, *Phaed.* xix. ; αἰδώς μ' ἔχει (αἰδοῦμαι) ... τυγχάνουσα, *Hec.* 970. For further examples see Madv. *Greek Syntax,* § 216. This construction occurs several times in this play, and will be noticed on each occurrence; see 531, 735, 852, 1090, 1209, 1223.

120. μοῦσα. Cp. 605 ; the wretched are denied that enjoyment of song which in *Med.* 192 ff. Eur. places so high among the pleasures and solaces of life : their only strain must be the recital of their woes; yet even this is some solace. χαύτη = καὶ αὕτη : Kirch. and Nauck give καύτὴ = καὶ αὐτή.

122. ὠκείαις. See note on 98 *sub fin.* The ships of the Greeks are apostrophized.

124. λίμνας is Hartung's conjecture accepted by Dind. for λιμένας, which was explained by a reference to the fact that the ancients rarely trusted themselves into the open sea, always coasting except in very favourable weather. It seems nearly certain that Eur. wrote λίμνας, a word which he often uses for 'the sea,' as in *Hec.* 446, *Hipp.* 147. Of course, if λιμένας were read, there should be a further remodelling of the passage, for λιμένας is a tribrach, and not admissible into anap. verse.

126. αὐλῶν. The αὐλός, generally rendered 'a flute,' was more like the *oboe* or *clarionet ;* στυγνός does not here mean 'ill-omened.' στυγνὸς παιὰν αὐλῶν is the 'horrid call of the clarionets,' for παιὰν was the 'war-song' which announced the beginning of the war, and it is called στυγνὸς from its sinister consequences. To perceive what the αὐλός really was, we must consider μοῦσα βαρύβρομος αὐλῶν, Ar. *Nub.* 313; δέξατο δ' εἰς χέρας βαρύβρομον αὐλὸν τερφθεῖσ' ἀλαλαγμῷ, *Hel.* 1351 ; so *barbaraque horribili stridebat tibia cantu,* Catull. xliv. 264.

127. εὐφθόγγῳ, 'the loud scream of the fifes,' not to be rendered 'auspicious.' From a fancied incompatibility between these two epithets (εὔφθογγος and στυγνός), edd. have conjectured ἀφθόγγῳ for εὐφθόγγῳ, and have even supposed εὐφθόγγῳ to be ironical.

128. βαίνουσαι. This word Hermann, followed by Paley, omits as a gloss. But it is vindicated by the strophic correspondence which these editors ignore, and it is absolutely required by the construction. The only reason for doubting the soundness of βαίνουσαι here is the rarity of the construction, βαίνουσαι Ἴλιον, 'wending to Ilios.' But this is actually a *characteristic* construction of Eur., which even attracted the notice of Aristophanes, and was parodied by him in the line, ἀτὰρ τί χρέος ἔβα με μετὰ τὸν Πασιάν ; as we are told by the schol. on Arist. on that passage (Ar. *Nub.* 30): the same construction is found again in *Hipp.* 1371, *Bacch.* 527, etc. Compare the Miltonic construction, 'arrive the isle,' and translate the Aristophanic passage, 'But stay, what debt *arrived me* after Pasias?'

πλεκτὰν ... ἐξηρτήσασθε. Edd. commonly read παιδείαν with the MSS., and render 'fastened (rather 'hung out from your sterns') the twisted handiwork of Egypt (your byblus cables) in the bay of Troy.' But who will commit himself to the doctrine that πλεκτὰν Αἰγύπτου παιδείαν could mean 'the twisted handiwork (or 'growth') of Egypt,' *i.e.* cables made of byblus. Surely in this sense παίδευμα would be absolutely required. Such a use of παιδεία is not to be paralleled in Eur. or elsewhere. Without doubt πλεκτὰν means 'a cable' (a frequent use in Eur.). For παιδείαν we must read παίδευμα, which probably owed its corruption into παιδείαν to the fact that some very ancient copyist did not know the substantive πλεκτάν, and changed παίδευμα to παιδείαν to make it agree with the supposed adjective πλεκτάν. The word παίδευμα excellently expresses the idea. An Egyptian product or manufacture, as that of cables out of byblus, may well be called in poetry 'a nurseling of Egypt,' just as sheep are called in *Andr.* 1100, φυλλάδος Παρνησσίας παιδεύματα. But παιδείαν could only mean something abstract, a process, and it would be stretching its meaning to an impossible degree to take it (as I have done in my former edition) as 'a lesson learnt from Egypt.' But even if it could bear that meaning, Eur. would hardly describe the simple man-œuvre of riding at anchor instead of beaching the ship as a lesson learnt from Egypt, since riding at anchor was familiar to the Greeks from the time of Homer, who often mentions it (*e.g.* δ. 782, κ. 92-96). Besides, Hecuba would be far more likely to refer to the fact that byblus cables came from Egypt than to the theory that a well-known nautical practice had its origin there. We cannot, therefore, by any means explain παιδείαν. But I have already suggested a theory to account for its having superseded the true reading, παίδευμα. Moreover, in reading παίδευμ' (and ἐξαιάζωμεν in 198, the corresponding verse) we make room for αἰαῖ in this verse, which the edd. usually omit. For instances of sing. πλεκτάν, 'ye hung out (each) your cable,' see on *Bacch.* 724. I add Mr. Way's ingenious and vigorous version of the strophe:

> "O ship-prows rushing
> To Ilium, brushing
> The purple-flushing sea with swift oars,
> Till flutes loud-ringing,
> Till fifes dread-singing,
> Proclaimed you swinging off Phrygian shores
> On hawsers plaited
> By Nile—ships fated
> To hunt the hated, the Spartan wife,
> Castor's defaming,
> Eurotas' shaming,
> A Fury claiming King Priam's life!
> Though sons he cherished
> Fifty, he perished,
> His murderess she : and, the misery-rife,
> Even me hath she wrecked on the rocks of strife."

133. **δυσκλείαν.** Cp. εὐκλείᾶν, Aesch. *Theb.* 682: but δύσκλειᾶν in *Med.* 218.

135. **σφάζει,** 'is the murderess of,' *i.e.* 'caused the death of'; for the use of the present, cp. ἥδε τίκτει σε, 'she is thy mother,' *Ion* 1560, and see Goodwin, § 10, note 4. It is coordinated with aor. ἐξώκειλε. μέν is here balanced by τε, so below 642. It is balanced by ἀτάρ, below 343, 415; by καί, *Hipp.* 288; by ἀλλά, *Or.* 553, etc., frequently in the phrase μέν, ἀλλ' ὅμως, *e.g.* in 366 below.

137. **ἐξώκειλ'.** The nautical metaphor is again taken up.

146. **ἐξαιάζωμεν.** By reading ἐξαιάζωμεν (cp. 198) for αἰάζωμεν and inserting ἐν in the corresponding verse 130, we get rid of the only monometers occurring in the whole of this anapaestic system, and thus make it more symmetrical and more expressive of the state of feeling which it represents.

148. **ὄρνις.** ὄρνισιν ὅπως is the reading of the MSS., which, however, Dindorf on metrical grounds rejects. It would, if sound, be quite parallel to *Hec.* 398, ὁποῖα κισσὸς δρυὸς ὅπως τῆσδ' ἕξομαι, 'I, like the ivy, will cling to her as an oak'; so here 'I, as the mother bird, for you as the fledgelings, will raise the strain.' The metre would be equally well preserved by reading ὄρνισιν ὅπως ἄρξω μολπάν.

151. **πλαγαῖς.** The loud stamp (*pedis supplosio*, Cic.) by which the aged queen gave the signal for the dances in honour of the gods to begin.

152. **ἐξῆρχον θεούς** = 'raised-in-honour-of the gods'; ἐξῆρχον θεοὺς governs οἵαν : see on 59 above : similarly in Soph. *El.* 557, εἰ δέ μ' ὧδ' ἀεὶ λόγους ἐξῆρχες, the phrase λόγους ἐξῆρχες = προσεφώνεις, and governs μ' in the accusative.

154. **ποῖ λόγος ἥκει,** '*quo spectat oratio*'; 'what mean the words which have reached us?'

156. **ἀΐσσει.** The first syllable is generally short in Eur., hence Seidler would read τάρβος for φόβος, but there are undoubted instances of ἀΐσσω in Eur. with ᾱ, *e.g. inf.* 1086.

163. **πατρῴας.** Many edd. change the reading to πατρίας, doubting whether the ῳ in πατρῴας can be short, and whether the MSS. have not given the word in mistake for πατρίας in the half-dozen places in which it appears with ῳ short in Eur. We have, however, Τρῳάδος in 521; and the diphthong is short in παλαιός, *El.* 497; Βοιωτός, *Iph. A.* 245; γεραιός, *Herc. Fur.* 446; Τροία, Soph. *Aj.* 424; οἰωνός, Soph. *El.* 1058; φιλαθήναιος, Ar. *Vesp.* 282. So it seems rash to change this

word to πατρίας whenever the ω is to be short, merely because in the case of this word an alternative resembling it in form and meaning is ready to our hand.

165. **μόχθων**, 'to hear the words of doom, *Out, dames of Troy, from your homesteads; the Argives betake them home,*' cp. μόχθων κλύειν, *Hel.* 665. μόχθων is of course lit. 'your woe,' 'your disastrous fate,' which is presented to them in the summons of the conquerors, and might depend on μέλεαι, 'wretched for your woes.'

171. **αἰσχύναν**, '*scortum Graecorum futuram, licet vates sit,*' Brodaeus; cp. 1114, and δύσγαμον αἰσχύναν, *Hel.* 687.

172. **ἀλγυνθῶ**, sc. μή, 'let me not by the sight of her re-double my pain.' The force of μή is carried on; so in 100 above καὶ = οὔτε, so also in 633 below οὐδὲν negatives the whole sentence. See on 1171.

175. **δμαθέντες**, 'the dead,' cp. τὸν νεόδμητον νεκρόν, *Rhes.* 887; δμαθέντας γὰρ ἀνίστη, *Alc.* 127. Mr. Stanley would take δμαθέντας as 'conquered,' the whole phrase referring, I suppose, to the Trojans who have 'survived their defeat'; but such a sentiment would have been expressed differently.

178. **μή**, 'whether,' with the indicative marks that the speaker believes that the thing about which he is asking (or expressing anxiety) is true, as προύξερευνήσω ... μή τις ... ἐν τρίβῳ φαντάζεται, *Phoen.* 93.

181. **στέλλονται**, 'are preparing to ply their oars' (κατὰ πρύμνας, 'by unloosing the cables at the stern ').

186. **κλήρου.** κλῆρος is not only 'the lots,' but 'the drawing of lots' = both *sortes* and *sortitio.*

188. **τίς ... χώραν.** The construction is τίς Ἀργείων ἢ Φθιωτᾶν (ἄξει με), ἢ (τίς) εἰς νησαίαν χώραν ἄξει με δύστανον πόρσω Τροίας.

191. **κηφήν.** Hec. compares herself to a 'drone,' as being about to live supported by others as a slave: Pliny speaks of the drones as slaves to the bees; so also Tzetzes, καὶ ταῖς μελίσσαις ὑπουργεῖ, ταύταις ὑδρηφοροῦντα (Brodaeus). There is no authority for making κηφήν ever mean an 'aged bird' (as Paley translates it both here and at *Bacch.* 1364), or for making it mean anything else but a 'drone.' See *Bacch.* 1364, where the MS. reading ὄρνις is rejected for ὄρνιν by some edd., who apparently believe in this signification of κηφῆνα.

194. **τὰν παρὰ προθύροις.** She fears that she will be forced to serve as portress or as children's attendant, she who once held royal state in Troy.

200. **ἐξαλλάξω,** ' no more shall I ply (shift) the nimble shuttle in Trojan looms ' ; so in *Hec.* 1060, ὁδὸν ἐξαλλάσσειν is 'to shift one's course,' taking now this way, now that.

201. **νέατον,** used as an adverb, ' for the last time ' ; this is the elegant conjecture of Seidler, for νέα τοι of the MSS.

204. **δαίμων,** ' cursed be that night and that lot ' ; δαίμων is ' fate,' ' lot,' as in Soph. *O. C.* 76, πλὴν τοῦ δαίμονος.

205. **ἢ ... ἔσομαι,** ' or I shall be kept as a servant to draw of the holy water of Pirenè ' ; ὑδάτων is partitive genitive, see Madv. *Greek Syntax,* § 51 d. Drawing water was the typical employment of slaves ; see the passage from Tzetzes quoted on 192, and Z. 457, καί κεν ὕδωρ φορέοις κ.τ.λ. Readers will at once think of ' hewers of wood and drawers of water ' in the Bible.

207–213. This is a characteristic passage ; the chorus pays a compliment to Athens and Theseus (the ideal hero of Eur.), and deprecates a banishment to the hated land of the Eurotas, and the meeting, as a slave, with Menelaus, who brought Troy to nought. Corinth, Athens, Sparta, Thessaly, and Sicily are in turn referred to.

211. **θεράπναν,** ' abode.' I cannot understand in what way of construing the passage Paley makes θεράπναν ' handmaid ' here. It is highly doubtful that θεράπνα ever means ' handmaid ' in Eur. or any Attic poet. The only place in Eur. where it could possibly mean ' handmaid ' is *Hec.* 482, and there it is not so taken by Paley (though it is by L. and S.). θεράπνη is a contracted form of θεράπαινα in *Hymn to Apollo,* 157, and Ap. *Rhod.* i. 786, but in those places it is a distinct epicism, and does not afford any ground for belief in the existence of such a meaning in an Attic poet. There is no place in Attic poetry where it may not bear the meaning of ' station,' ' abode,' and Hesych. explains θεράπνας by αὐλῶνας, σταθμούς. Paley in his latest ed. gave up the interpretation of θεράπναν as ' handmaid,' and of κηφὴν as ' an aged bird.'

212. **Μενέλᾳ,** from Μενέλας, so 863, 1100. So we have Λαέρτιος beside Λάρτιος, Ἰφιγόνη and Ἰφιγένεια, Σθενέλας and Σθενέλαος, Ἐτεοκλέης and Ἐτεοκλῆς, and, in Homer, Πάτροκλος, Πατροκλῆς, Πατρόκλευς, Μελάνθιος, Μελάνθευς.

215. **κρηπῖδ'.** See on 16 *supr.*

217. **εὐθāλεῖ.** Dor. for εὐθηλεῖ : we also find εὐθăλής (fr. εὖ, θάλλω).

218. τάδε δεύτερα. The construction is τάδε μοι δεύτερα (ἐστι), ἐλθεῖν ζαθέαν χώραν (τὰν Πηνειοῦ), δεύτερα μετὰ τὰν ἱερὰν Θησέως, 'next to (going to) the sacred land of Theseus, my next best lot were to go to the country of the Peneūs.' The poet says 'next to the land of Theseus,' meaning 'next to (going to) the land of Theseus,' just as Ar. *Nub.* 30 says, τί χρέος ἔβα με μετὰ τὸν Πασίαν, 'after Pasias,' meaning 'after (my debt to) Pasias.' For the use of δεύτερα cp. Frag. 252, τυραννίδ' ἢ θεῶν δευτέρα νομίζεται, *i.e.* 'next to the gods'; so πολὺ δεύτερον, Soph. *O.C.* 1226; and πολὺ δευτέρα, 'easily second,' *Thuc.* ii. 97.

221. ἀντήρη, 'over against Phoenice' (*i.e.* the Phoenician settlement of Carthage), a vague geographical description of Sicily. I have removed the comma from χώραν to Σικελῶν. The whole periphrasis is: 'the Aetnaean land of the Sicilians, sacred to Hephaestus (in reference to its volcanoes), over against Phoenice, and mother of mountains' (a poetical expression for ὀρεινήν).

223. καρύσσεσθαι. In reference to Sicilian successes (especially those of Hiero) in the public games, for which see Pindar *passim.*

224. τάν τ' ἀγχιστεύουσαν γᾶν. Probably Thurii, between the rivers Crathis and Sybaris.

225. ναίοιν is the conjecture of Dind. for ναῦται, ναῦτα of the MSS. It is perhaps the best attempt which has been made to restore the corrupted word, but is by no means certain. As to the form ναίοιν for ναίοιμι, cp. Frag. 895, ἄφρων ἂν εἴην εἰ τρέφοιν τὰ τῶν πέλας, where τρέφοιν is explained by the grammarian as ἀπὸ τοῦ τρεφοίην κατὰ συγκοπὴν τοῦ η. This appears to recognize οιν as a termination of the optative, but it is strange that it does not oftener occur.

227. ξανθὰν πυρσαίνων. Proleptic, like εὔανδρον ὀλβίζων, see *Bacch.* 1055 note. That the waters of the Crathis dyed the hair auburn, we have the evidence of several scholiasts and grammarians cited by Brodaeus and Barnes, and that of Ovid, *Met.* xv. 315, *Crathis et hinc Sybaris nostris conterminus arvis | electro similes faciunt auroque capillos.*

232. ἐξανύων, 'to bring to an end,' 'finish,' often applied to words like δρόμον, πόρον, and so to ἴχνος, here ' to bring his quick step to its journey's end.' More daring is πόλον ἐξανύσας, *Or.* 1685, where ἐξ = 'to arrive at a place,' with *accus. loci*; so also *Suppl.* 1142, and ζυγὰ δ' ἤνυσεν, below 595.

239. This verse consists of three dochmii ⏑ ⏑ ⏑ | —⏑ | — | ⏑— | —⏑ | — || ⏑ ⏑ ⏑ | —⏑ | —. A word has dropped out, perhaps πάρεσθ', as Dind. suggests. In ὅ φόβος ἦν, the phrase φόβος ἦν is treated as = ἐφοβούμην, and governs δ in the accus. This rests on the same principle as the cases quoted on 59 above, but I treat it separately, because in the case of pronouns the true construction is often mistaken ; for instance, here many editors would explain δ as nom. in apposition to φόβος : but in that case it should be ὅς, attracted into the gender of φόβος : moreover, such an explanation would prove inapplicable to many analogous passages, e.g. Ion 572, τοῦτο κἄμ' ἔχει πόθος, where κἄμ' ἔχει πόθος = καὶ ἐγὼ ποθῶ and governs τοῦτο : so μάντις ἦσθα = ἐμαντεύου governs τάδε, Heracl. 65 ; φόβος (ἐστὶ) = φοβοῦμαι governs τοῦτο, Heracl. 730 ; and μομφὴν ἔχω = μέμφομαι governs ἕν, Or. 1068. For the attraction which δ would suffer if it were in apposition to φόβος, cp. Hel. 282, δ δ' ἀγλάϊσμα δωμάτων ἐμοῦ τ' ἔφυ | θυγάτηρ ἄνανδρος πολιὰ παρθενεύεται. The last words of the verses just quoted offer a good example of the adverbial use of the neut. plur. of an adj. ; πολιά, of course, could not be nom. fem. for an obvious reason ; the last syllable of πολιὰ would then be long, and thus we should have a spondee in the fourth place. See also on 348 below.

242. **Καδμείας.** This word, which ought to mean *Theban*, must be used to mean *Boeotian* here, because the legend tells that of all the Boeotians the Thebans only did not go to Troy, being hard pressed by the Argives. So the Thebans could not claim any of the captives ; cp. 993, where *Argos* is used for the whole Peloponnesus.

250. **Λακεδαιμονίᾳ,** 'Clytaemnestra.' This form is rare in tragedy : ἡ Λάκαινα is the name given usually to Helen, but here to her sister Clytaemnestra. The metre too shows a probable corruption. The verse, which probably consisted of three dochmiacs, may have run, as Dind. suggests, thus : τί φής ; ἢ Λακαίνᾳ νύμφᾳ δούλαν ; ἰώ, ἰώ μοί μοι.

251. **σκότια.** See 44 *supr.*

257. **κλάδας,** 'suppliant boughs,' a heteroclite accusative plural of κλάδος found in a fragment of Nicander, quoted in Athenaeus 684 B. Other heteroclite forms from the same subst. are κλαδὶ in the celebrated scholion in honour of Harmodius and Aristogiton, ἐν μύρτου κλαδὶ τὸ ξίφος φορήσω : also κλάδα in Poet. ap. Drac. 103. 13, and κλάδεσι in Ar. Av 239. The word is restored here with great probability by Mr. Stanley, who justly objects, as against κλῆδας of the MSS. and Vulg. (*C. R.* x. 1. 35), "If κλῆδες means *keys*, what keys are meant ? Were they those of an ὀπισθόδομος of a temple of Apollo ? If so, is it probable that the captive Cassandra had been allowed to retain them until

now?" It was a sense of this difficulty which induced some edd. (among them myself) to catch at a gloss from Hesych., κλῆδες· παρὰ 'Εφεσίοις τῆς θεοῦ τὰ στέμματα, and to ascribe to the word the meaning of 'chaplets,' though no other example of such a meaning is found, and it does not in itself seem capable of such. Besides, is it not quite possible that the lemma in Hesych. is corrupt, and that Mr. Stanley's *medela* should be applied there too? We should expect here the Doric form κλᾶδας, as we have τλάμονα in 247, τᾷ νύμφᾳ δούλαν 250, ἐτεκόμαν 265. No doubt κλάδας was first changed to κλᾷδας, then to κλῆδας. "It is to be noticed," adds Mr. Stanley, "that Cassandra is represented σὺν κλάδοις·ἐγχειριδίοις and wearing a wreath on her head in *Pitture d'Ercolano*, ii. 18." The short anacrusis is quite regular; cp. 266, 271.

στεφέων, 'the holy livery of chaplets that deck thee.' From *Ag.* 1236 it would appear that these στέφη were worn on the neck as well as the head; ἐνδ. refers to *ornamental*, not *necessary* apparel.

264. **προσπολεῖν,** 'to minister to.' This is a euphemistic and ambiguous term, and is misunderstood by Hec.; hence her question, 'What is this ordinance of the Hellenes?' We learn from verse 40 that Hec. had not heard of the sacrifice of Polyxena on the tomb of Achilles.

271. **χαλκεομήστορος,** 'well versed in arms,' as it is usually understood. The MS. reading is χαλκεομίτορος (which cannot be right, as the word must form two dactyls, but the ῑ as coming from μίτος, 'a thread,' is short), or χαλκεομήτορος, which latter has been corrected to χαλκεομήστορος from a gloss of Hesych., χαλκεομίστωρ ἰσχυρόφορος, for which we should doubtless read χαλκεομήστορος· ἰσχυρόφρονος. It will be seen then that Hesych. understood the word to mean 'with heart of steel,' but the analogy of δοριμήστωρ, *And.* 1016, is in favour of 'well versed in arms.'

275. **τριτοβάμονος.** 'I who need in my hand a staff, as the fellow of my feet,' (lit. 'the third walker with my two feet'), because I am stricken in years,' lit. 'for (the support of) my aged head.'

285. **ὃς πάντα τἀκεῖθεν.** The construction is ὃς πάντα τἀκεῖθεν ἐνθάδε τιθέμενος, (τἀνθάδε) αὖθις ἐκεῖσε ἀντίπαλα, διπτύχῳ γλώσσᾳ, τὰ πρότερα φίλα πάντων ἄφιλα (τιθέμενος), 'who putting that which was there here, and again (that which was here) there in its turn (*i.e.* to balance the former *bouleversement*) by his subtilty of tongue, and (putting) ever enmity where love was—wail for me, dames of Troy.'

The sentence must be supposed to end in an aposiopesis ; there is no principal verb ; and aposiopesis would be suitable to the excited and impassioned utterance of Hecuba, who in almost incoherent language wails forth her dread and hatred of her future master. Accepting Bothe's needless conjecture of ἔσεισε for ἐκεῖσε, we should gain a principal verb, thus avoiding the aposiopesis, and we might explain very much as above, 'who dashed (violently put) all that was there here, and again conversely,' (i.e. put what was here there). Bothe's own interpretation of the passage is plainly unsatisfactory. Ἀντίπαλα is used as in *Bacch.* 275 ff., when Ceres is said to have provided food, while Dionysus devoted himself to the *corresponding, correlative* necessity of man, that is, drink ; so here 'putting what is here there' is the *converse, correlative* process to 'putting what is there here.' Of course ἄφιλα is the predicate, and the article goes with the subject, τὰ πρότερα φίλα πάντων, lit. 'the former friendly feelings of all.'

> " Alas and alas ! now smite on thy close-shorn head ;
> Now with thy rending nails be thy cheeks furrowed red !
> Woe's me, whom the doom of the lots hath led
> To be thrall to a foul wretch treacherous-hearted,
> To the lawless monster, the foe of the right,
> Whose double-tongued juggling, whose cursed sleight
> Putteth light for darkness, and darkness for light,
> By whose whisperings veriest friends are parted !—
> Wail for me, daughters of Troy ! I am ended
>   In utter calamity.
> O wretch, who by doom of the lot have descended
>   To abysses of misery !"—W.

294. ἔχει, 'holds in his hand,' not 'knows.' There is some-times held to be a double interrogation in passages like this, ἄρα being pleonastic after τίς, as in τίνος ποτ' ἄρ' ἔπραξε χειρὶ δύσμορος, Soph. *Aj.* 905 ; the double interrogation, it is said, makes the question a little less definite and direct ; e.g. in *Aj.* 905, the question asked is, 'Did he seek the hand of some one to do the deed, and then, whose?' So in the present passage, 'Are we allotted, and, if so, to whom?' For other examples, see L. and S. under ἄρα 4. It is, however, far more probable that ἄρα may be written ἆρα when the metre requires the first syllable to be long, just as ὑμῖν, ἡμῖν in Soph. for metrical purposes became ὑμῖν, ἡμῖν, and as the enclitic νυν is long or short as the metre requires in tragedy. There are many places where nothing but violent alteration of the text can dispense with ἆρα used in the same sense as ἄρα, and if this once be granted, it is unscientific to put forward

the theory of a double interrogation ; we should rather hold ἆρα in passages like this to be simply ἄρα, a particle of inference or transition. A good instance of a passage where ἆρα = ἄρα is Ar. *Nub.* 1301, ἔμελλον σ' ἄρα κινήσειν, where the sense would require ἆρ' οὔ, *nonne*, instead of ἆρα, *an*, if the passage were treated as interrogative.

297. εἰληγμένας, from λαγχάνω.

300. πιμπρᾶσιν, cp. σπείρουσιν ἢ τῷ ζῶσι Δήμητρος στάχυν, *Cycl.* 121. For examples of *hyperbaton*, see on *Bacch.* 860.

305. τὸ ταῖσδε πρόσφορον, sc. θανεῖν : the word πρόσφορον conveys not only that it would be 'expedient,' but also that it would be 'decorous' for the Trojan dames to die rather than go into captivity, but this would be most 'untow-- for the Achaeans.'

308. The frenzied maiden fancies she is in Apollo's temp which she lights up by wildly waving her nuptial torch, wl Apollo himself leads the choir. Subjoined is the spirited a. most felicitous translation of this ode, which appeared in *Kottabos*, vol. I., p. 54, by Judge Webb, formerly Fellow of Trinity College, Dublin, afterwards Regius Professor of Laws, translator of *Faust*, etc.:

> " Lift ye and lend ye—bring ye light !
>   'Tis a holy rite ! Behold, behold !
> Through the fane with a thousand torches bright
>   How the eddies of fire are roll'd !
> Hail Hymen ! Hail, King Hymenaean !
> Full blest is the bridegroom, and I too am blest,
> That am soon on the couch of a monarch to rest,
>   O Hymen, O King Hymenaean !
> While thou, O my Mother, with wail and with tear,
> Dost lament o'er my Father and Fatherland's bier,
>   For my bridal, behold, I am raising
>   The torch that so fiercely is blazing !
>   It glanceth, it gleameth, ah ! see,
>   Hymen, O Hymenaeus, for thee !
> Lend, lend me thy torches, O Hekat,
>   For the couch of the virgin, to deck it !
> Airily poise ye the twinkling feet !
>   On with the dance ! Ho ! Euoe ! ho !
> On with the dance, as 'twere to greet
>   The happiest lot that my sire could know
>   The dance it is sacred to Hymen !
> The dance, be its leader, O Phoebus, thou !
> In whose fane, 'mid the laurels, I worship now.
>   Hymen ! Hymenaeus ! O Hymen !

Come trip it, my Mother, come trip it with me,
And share in the dancing, and share in the glee !
As it were for the battle a Paean,
Shout, shout ye the great Hymenaean !
Pour forth with your voices a tide
Of melodious song for the bride,
Sing, ye maids, for the maid that is fated
With the king of the foe to be mated ! "

309. ἄνεχε, πάρεχε. These words are addressed to the fancied acolytes officiating in the temple.

315. ἐπεί. It was the duty of the mother εὐνὰς ἀγῆλαι λαμπάδας τ' ἀνασχεθεῖν.

ἐπί, 'with tears,' a rare use of ἐπί with dative ; cp. ἐπὶ συννοίᾳ, Or. 632, though that may be explained 'for the purpose of (to gain time for) reflection.' We have ἐπὶ δάκρυσι again, Hel. 176, Phoen. 1500 ; cp. also Phoen. 786, ἐπὶ καλλιχόροις στεφάνοισι. In Med. 928, we have ἐπὶ δακρύοις in a different sense, 'made for tears,' with which compare ἔρως γὰρ ἀργὸν κἀπὶ τοῖς ἀργοῖς ἔφυ, 'made for the idle,' Frag. 324. Mr. Stanley well observes that the harshness of ἐπὶ δάκρυσι is mitigated by the fact that it seems to be opposed to ἐπὶ γάμοις in 319.

317. καταστένουσ' ἔχεις, 'keepest wailing for '; cp. ληρεῖς ἔχων, 'keepest prating.' This connection of ἔχω with the part. is common with the aorist, more rare with the perfect (Soph. O. R. 701, Phil. 600), and very rare with the present as here. See on 1122.

324. ἃ νόμος ἔχει, 'as the ritual ordains.' ἅ, acc. plur., is in apposition to the preceding sentences. She calls for all the observances due to the solemnization of a regular union.

325. πάλλε, 'airily poise the foot'; cp. ἵυζε δ' ὀμφὰν οὐρανίαν, Aesch. Suppl. 788, and ῥίπτειν σκέλος οὐράνιον, Ar. Vesp. 1492. We find ἔρρε αἰθέριον ... φάρος in Antl. 830, and οὐράνια βρέμοντα below 520.

332. ἀναγέλασον. This is the reading of V, which quite corresponds to the antistrophic verse 315, if we there omit καί after δάκρυσι, a conjunction which would far more probably have been inserted than omitted erroneously between two substantives. P has ἄναγε πόδα σόν, which looks as if it had been vamped up from v. 325. The reading of P is defended by Mr. A. C. Pearson, in C. R. iv. 9, p. 425, on the theory that V dropped the syllable πο-, and then confounded Δ with the closely-resembling Λ. V drops a syllable -κο- in giving ἐξαντίζω

or ἐξανθίζω in v. 444, where the trochaic metre demands ἐξακοντίζω.

335. βοᾶτε τὸν Ὑμ. This phrase is treated as a single transitive verb, and governs νύμφαν on the principle explained and illustrated above on 59.

339. γάμων ... εὐνᾷ. Cp. Phoen. 58, τἀμὰ λέκτρα μητρῴων γάμων.

345. ἔξω, 'far from what my high hopes pictured'; cp. ἔξω γνώμης, Ion 926; ἔξω τοῦ φυτεύσαντος, Soph. Phil. 904, 'alien to your father's strain'; ἔξω νομίσεως, Thuc. v. 105.

348. ὀρθά. For adjs. in neut. plur. used as adverbs, cp. Hel. 283 (see note on 239), and ἄλεκτρα γηράσκουσαν ἀνυμέναιά τε, Soph. El. 962, and see Madv. Greek Syntax, § 88.

351. ἐσφέρετε, usually explained 'take away' (into the tent); but ἐσφέρειν always means to 'bring in,' not to 'take in': in other words Hec. could properly say ἐσφέρετε πεύκας, 'bring in the torches,' only if she were herself in the tent. I think we should read ἐκφέρετε, 'take away'; ἐκ- would be easily changed to εἰσ-: it is well known that the ancient copyists often confounded IC with K, see crit. note on Bacch. 1156.

353. νικηφόρον, used proleptically; see above on 227.

355. τἀμὰ = τὰ ἐμά, 'my part,' a common periphrase for ἐγώ. So τὸ σὸν and τὰ σά for σύ or σέ.

356. ἔστι. Observe the accent, 'as sure as Loxias lives.'

357. γαμεῖ με ... γάμον. For the cognate accus. see Madv. Greek Syntax, § 26 a; and for the cognate accus. standing, as here, beside a proper object-accus. see ibid. § 26 b; and note, as an exact parallel, Pl. Apol. 39, τιμωρία ... χαλεπωτέρα ἢ οἵαν ἐμὲ ἀπεκτόνατε.

361. πέλεκυν. There is here probably a covert criticism on the bloody details of Aeschylus in his Oresteia. In his later plays we find in Eur. a tendency to introduce in some slight measure that literary criticism which formed a feature in the middle comedy. This characteristic is especially observable in his Electra, insomuch that M. Patin describes the play as a feuilleton spirituel. In 254 ff. he adverts to many points in the handling of the story of Electra, in which he believes his illustrious predecessors, Aesch. and Soph., to have erred. So also in Suppl. 846, Phoen. 751, there are pointed allusions to supposed artistic defects in Aesch. Theb.

370. ἐχθίστων, sc. Ἑλένης.

371. ἡδονάς, 'resigning for his brother the home joys that his children might have given him'; ἡδονὰς is sometimes used very objectively, as in Soph. El. 873, Ar. Nub. 1072.

373. **λελησμένης.** This is distinctly passive, and therefore implies λήξω, but λήξομαι is the much more usual form, as in ἐλήσατο, 866 below. In *Hel.* 475 we have λελήσμεθα ... λέχος, 'I have had my wife carried off.' Obs. epic form ἤλυθον in 374.

375. **ἔθνησκον,** 'fell' (day after day); the imperfect represents the *continuance* (or *repetition*) of the same action or state, while the aorist denotes a momentary occurrence ; *veni, vidi, vici* is in Greek ἦλθον, εἶδον, ἐνίκησα, because, though the action was of course a continued action, yet the point of the despatch was that it viewed the victory as a momentary event in past time. See Goodwin, § 19, notes 1 and 2.

376. **ἕλοι.** Opt. because the relative refers to an *indefinite* antecedent, 'whomsoever the battle chanced to slay'; οὓς Αρης εἷλε would be used if the antecedents were definite ; so in Lat. *quoscunque occidisset* and *quoscunque occiderat*.

377. **ἐν χεροῖν,** 'by the hands'; so ἐν λιταῖς, 'by prayers '; ἐν δόλῳ, 'by deceit ' ; ἐν λόγοις, ' by words.'

378. **ξυνεστάλησαν,** ' were shrouded in their cerements.'

380. **οἱ δ',** 'others,' that is, the fathers, who were too old to join the expedition, but who were obliged to send their sons. ' Wife without mate, sire without seed, they died away ; vain was their rearing of children, and none shall seek their tombs with a propitiatory blood-offering.' See *El.* 90 ff. αἱ μὲν must be supplied before χῆραι, being implied in the subsequent οἱ δέ. The verse would be thus written accurately καὶ αἱ μὲν χῆραι ἔθνησκον, οἱ δ' ἄπαιδες : from this it appears that χῆραι is not the subject, but a predicate, not 'widows died,' but 'they died widows.'

382. **δωρήσεται,** 'shall give to the earth,' *i.e.* 'shall pour out upon the earth '; the ' blood-offering' was an offering to propitiate the departed heroes ; we cannot interpret 'shall offer blood-offerings to mother earth,' for we find from the enumeration in Aesch. *Pers.* 612 ff. that blood was not a part of the offering to earth ; and again, *Cho.* 120 ff. tells us that the offerings to earth consisted only of her own produce restored to her again. For the blood-offerings to dead heroes, see the eleventh book of the *Odyssey.*

384. **τἀσχρά.** The murder of Agamemnon and adultery of Clytaemnestra and Aegisthus. There should be no iota subscript in τἀσχρά, the rule being that the iota is subscribed only when *both* words fused by the crasis contain an ι ; thus καὶ εἶτα becomes κᾆτα, but καὶ ἐπὶ becomes κἀπί, τὰ αἰσχρά becomes τἀσχρά.

385. ἀοιδός, adjective, cp. *Hel.* 1109, ὄρνις ἀοιδοτάτα: so κερκίδος ἀοιδοῦ μελέτας, Frag. 527, an expression ridiculed by Ar. *Ran.* 1315.

386. τὸ κάλλιστον κλέος. This is probably the accusative, for the accusative in apposition to the sentence is the more idiomatic construction ; it may, however, of course be the nominative, like θριγκός, 489.

389. περιβολάς, 'in their fatherland came unto the vesture of clay,' cp. χθονὸς τρίμοιρον χλαῖναν, *Agam.* 872 ; γᾶν ἐπιεσσόμενος, Pind. *Nem.* xi. 21.

390. ὧν ἐχρῆν ὕπο, 'hands which owed this office to the dead' = ὑπὸ τούτων ὑφ' ὧν ἐχρῆν. The words ἐχρῆν, οὐκ ἐχρῆν, are much used in Greek when we should employ a far stronger expression ; for instance, 'having committed a most unnatural murder,' would be ὃν οὐκ ἐχρῆν φονεύσας.

392. δάμαρτι. For sing. instead of plur. see on *Bacch.* 724.

393. ὧν ... ἡδοναί, 'the sweets of whom were lost to the Greeks,' see on 372, literally, 'the joys from whom for the Achaeans (*i.e.* which might have been felt by the Achaeans) were wanting.' It is safer not to take Ἀχαιοῖς as directly governed by ἀπῆσαν, which ought to take the gen., and indeed does always take it, for the places in which it appears to take the dat. may be otherwise construed ; *e.g.* in *Med.* 179, μήτοι τό γ' ἐμὸν πρόθυμον | φίλοισιν ἀπέστω, we may take φίλοισιν with πρόθυμον, 'my zeal for my friends,' and in Thuc. ii. 61, τῆς δὲ ὠφελίας ἄπεστιν ἔτι ἡ δήλωσις ἅπασι, the dat. is a *dat. commodi*, as in the foregoing clause, τὸ μὲν λυποῦν ἔχει ἤδη τὴν αἴσθησιν ἑκάστῳ, 'an individual sense of the bitterness of war possesses each one, while the general sense of its advisability has yet to come.'

394. τὰ Ἕκτορος λυπρά, 'Hector's sad fate' (as it is generally regarded) ; she then proceeds to show that it is not a sad fate. τὰ δ' Ἕκτορός σοι λυπρὰ is, as it were, in inverted commas. Such seems to be occasionally the force of the article ; in other words, it marks a citation or quotation from the language of others, and this explains why (contrary to the usual rule) we sometimes find *the article with the predicate, e.g. Her. Fur.* 581, οὐκ ἄρ' Ἡρακλῆς | ὁ καλλίνικος ... λέξομαι : cp. *Heracl.* 978, *Or.* 1140. *Iph. Aul.* 1354.

396. ἕξις = ἥξις, 'the coming of the Greeks.' The form in the text has the authority of Hesych.

397. P and *Christus Patiens* have ἐλάνθανεν, and in 399 εἶχεν. But the imperf. without ἂν *in apodosi* cannot be defended

here, and is not parallel to the cases cited in Goodwin, § 49, 2, note 2, or in Madv. *Greek Syntax*, § 118, *a*, *b*. Elmsley's observation, that the Attic writers avoided eliding ε of the 3rd pers., really only applies to cases where confusion between 1st and 3rd pers. might arise, as in ἔπραξ' ἄν. See the excellent note of Prof. Jebb, who reads ἐλάνθαν' ἄν in Soph. *El.* 914. In *Ion* 354 the MSS. give εἶχ' ἄν, and no change there is at all plausible.

399. κῆδος, 'he would have entered into some obscure alliance,' 'the marriage made by him would never have been talked about.' It is to be observed that there is far more MSS. authority for κῦδος, which the schol. understood in a neutral sense like κλέος, 'his name would never have been in men's mouths.' But κῦδος is a *positive* word in all Greek, and ἐν δόμοις seems distinctly to point to κῆδος. σιγώμενον is the *predicate* of the sentence.

408. ἐξεβάκχευσεν governs σε, and then φρένας as part of the person addressed; see on 59.

410. ἐξέπεμπες ἄν, 'should'st have been attending their departure with such ill-boding words.'

412. τῶν τὸ μηδέν, sc. ὄντων. There are three forms of this phrase, ὁ μηδείς, ὁ μηδέν (ὤν), and ὁ τὸ μηδὲν (ὤν): cp. οὐδὲν ἦτ' ἄρα, 1161. μηδὲν and οὐδὲν are in this usage indeclinable. There is a pretty phrase in Eur. Frag. 536, which illustrates well the distinction between μηδείς as subjective and οὐδεὶς as objective; the phrase is τὸ μηδὲν εἰς οὐδὲν ῥέπει, which I would render 'naughtiness (or 'that which is naught') cometh to nought.'

415. ὑπέστη, 'is saddled with a passion for,' cp. ὑποστῆναι πόνον, *Suppl.* 189; the verb means 'to undergo unwillingly.'

416. ἄν οὐκ. For the displacement of ἄν in obedience to the metre, cp. οὐκ οἶδ' ἄν εἰ πείσαιμι, *Med.* 941. See Goodwin, § 42, 2, note.

418. 'Αργεῖα, 'invectives against the Greeks'; cp. εὐνοίᾳ τῇ σῇ, 'friendliness for you,' Pl. *Gorg.* 486; φόβῳ τῷ ὑμετέρῳ, 'fear of you,' Thuc. i. 33. For *adjectives* used, as here, to represent not a subjective, but an objective, genitive, cp. Ἕλλην ... φόνος, *Iph. T.* 72; ἀλκὴν ... Μυκηνίδα, *Phoen.* 862.

422. ἕπεσθαι, for imper.; see Goodwin, § 101.

σώφρονος, *i.e.* Penelope.

424. τοὔνομα, 'the name which they bear,' 'Why do they bear this name when they are really but menials?'

428. ποῦ δέ: cp. τί δ' ἔστι, 1050 ; the more usual phrase would have been καὶ ποῦ, for καὶ is especially employed in introducing an objection. It is frequently strengthened with εἶτα, ἔπειτα, e.g. below 1010.

430. τἄλλα, 'the rest of her woes,' especially referring to the transformation of Hecuba ; or possibly the meaning is, 'the rest of my words shall not be Ἀργεῖ' ὀνείδη, but prophecies of the sufferings of Odysseus, the future master of Hecuba.'

432. χρυσός, 'one day my woes and Troy's will be to him more to be desired than gold,' ('will be as gold'). See L. and S. under χρυσός 2.

435. ᾤκισται, 'has made herself a habitation in the strait' (between Italy and Sicily). Charybdis was the fabled daughter of Poseidon and Gaea. Cic. *Phil.* ii. 27 says, "*Charybdin dico* quae si fuit, fuit animal unum." Cp. πύργον οἰκιούμεθα, Heracl. 46. Some verses are supposed to have fallen out here, on account of the extreme abruptness of 435. Paley remarks that this is the earliest summary of the story of Odysseus ; Ar. *Vesp.* 180 ff. refers to the episode of Οὖτις. The whole passage, 435-443, has the appearance of an interpolation, and I have marked it as such ; 440 looks like an Alexandrine attempt at vigour, and the following verse is strangely frigid. Mr. A. C. Pearson, in *C. R.* iv. 9. 425, points out additional reasons for regarding this passage as spurious : (1) the feebleness of the whole passage, and especially of ὡς δὲ συντέμω in 441 ; (2) οὖ has no meaning unless we mark a *lacuna* ; (3) δίαυλος does not mean 'a strait' ; (4) πέτρας is without construction ; (5) ἐπιστάτης, which Dind. reads for ὀρειβάτης on the faith of Stephens' *codices*, does not mean 'a shepherd' ; (6) μορφώτρια σύων is a very eccentric expression ; (7) σάρκα φων. ἦσ. is impossible ; (8) κακὰ μυρία is miserably weak. Cp. a similar interpolation in *Or.* 588-590.

436. ὠμοβρώς τ' ὀρειβάτης. I have retained the reading of P and the Aldine (which give ὠμοβροστορειβάτης), with Scaliger's obvious correction. Dind. gives ὠμόφρων τ' ἐπιστάτης ('shepherd'), which rests on the questionable authority of Stephens' *codices*. The words in the text are a much better description of the Cyclops ; ὠμοβρώς is found in *Il. F.* 887.

440. σάρκα φων. ἤσουσιν. The legend was that when the sacred kine of the sun were roasted by the followers of Odysseus, 'the meat lowed on the spits,' μ. 395. But the expression in the text is, I think, not by Eur., and savours far more of Lycophron : ἰέναι σάρκα φωνήεσσαν could not mean ἰέναι φωνὴν ἐκ σαρκός. The words are probably not corrupt. Alexandrine boldness generally degenerates into unintelligibility. I cannot believe in the possibility of such an expression as σάρκα φων. ἥσουσιν, especially as it occurs in a passage highly suspicious for other reasons. [I am inclined to defend this expression, remarkable though it is. Consider the boldness of what Jelf calls the interchange of attributive forms, e.g. 564, καράτομος ἐρημία νεανιῶν, which Kühner, p. 225, renders, ' die vom Haupte abgeschnittene Oede der Jünglinge, das ist, Todesöde.' Cp. Soph. Ocd. R. 1376, Aj. 8, Phil. 952, 1123, 1131, El. 158. Here either of two analyses will reduce the expression to tolerable exactitude : (a) ἥσουσιν should strictly have φωνὴν as its object, which then might be qualified by τὴν ἐκ σαρκὸς or the like. But we have the adjective and substantive reversed, so that what ought strictly to be the logical object of the verb is to be looked for in the adjective. Usually, however, in the cases cited by the grammars, it is the transference of an attributive from one noun to another which forms the peculiarity, like Barry Cornwall's "Hear the waters their white music weave " for ' Hear the white waters weave their music.' Sometimes again, instead of two nouns of distinct reference, we have an adjective and a noun, which is the account of Carlyle's expression (Rem. E. Irving) "the hot noises of middle life " = ' the heat and noises.' Neither of these groups of cases offers an exact parallel to σάρκα φων. ἥσουσιν, but they may throw some light on the process by which such expressions arise. (b) the other 'reduction' would be to substitute (mentally) some such word as δύσονται for ἥσουσιν, 'shall clothe themselves with vocal flesh.' It might be said that ἥσουσιν is written by a sort of attraction of the expression to the neighbouring word, φωνήεσσαν. Wolff, on Ajax 738 (Teubner's Schulausgabe), recognizes this principle, saying there, "βραδεῖαν ist wegen des folgenden βραδὺς gewählt, um bei Gleichheit der Sache die Personen entgegen zu stellen," and again, on Aj. 758, he says σώματα is the word chosen, on account of the following πίπτειν. This principle helps, to my mind, to explain ἔπος in Or. 1 ; a prosateur might have said, οὐδέν ἐστι δεινόν, ὧδ' εἰπεῖν, χρῆμα, but to the poet εἰπεῖν suggested ἔπος.—H. C.]

445. στεῖχε … γημώμεθα, 'go (to Talthybius), that straightway I may marry me into the house of Death '; the expression is the same as ἐς τύρανν' ἐγημάμην, 474, ' I married into a royal line '; though it is slightly complicated by the addition of νυμφίῳ. For such pregnant constructions, cp. Or. 474, πρὸς δεξιὰν στάς, and ib. 1330; Aj. 80, ἐς δόμους μένειν : Phoen. 380, 1150, and especially 588 d below. Observe that ὅπως is in

relation with γημώμεθα, not with τάχιστα, with which it would naturally be taken in the sense of *quam primum*.

450. δάσασθαι, fr. δατέομαι. cp. δώσειν κυσὶν ὠμὰ δάσασθαι, Ψ. 21.

453. σπαραγμοῖς, 'as I tear you off'; she tears off her sacred symbols, as in *Agam*. 1235 ff. The words ἔτ' οὖσ' ἁγνὴ mean *virum nondum experta*.

455. ποῦ σκάφος, Cic. *Epp. ad Att*. vii. 35, quotes these words in the form ποῦ σκάφος τὸ τῶν 'Ατρειδῶν. ποῖ = ἐς ποτέραν ναῦν.

457. 'Ερινῦν = 'Ερινύων, gen. plur. 'Ερινύν, which is sometimes read, would be accus. sing.

460. οὐ μακράν, '*brevi*'; cp. *Or.* 858, ἔοικε δ' οὐ μακρὰν ὅδ' ἄγγελος λέξειν τὰ κεῖθεν, more usually οὐκ ἐς μακράν.

466. The whole of this very fine passage may be rendered somehow thus:

'O damsels, let me lie where I have fallen;
Service unwelcome but disservice seems;
To lie so low doth well beseem my lot,
Present, and past, and that which is to come.
Ye gods—ye will not minister to me.
Yet it is seemly to invoke your names
If any one fall on calamity.
First let my dying swan-note be of joy,
Thus shall I put more pity in my woes.
I was a queen, into a kingly house
Wed, and the mother of a princely line,
No ciphers, men of leading in the land.
No Trojan, Argive, or outlandish dame
Could boast herself of such a progeny,
All these I saw fall by the Argive spear,
To grace their sepulchres these locks I shore.
And with these eyes I saw their kingly sire,
I heard it not from others' lips, but saw him
Weltering in his life-blood at the altar,
And the town sacked. And all the girls I bore,
Fit to be jewels in the crown of wifehood,
I bore for foemen's usance: I am reft
Of all my damsels: never more, I wis,
Shall I behold them or be seen of them.'

τὰ μὴ φίλ', 'the undesired service' of helping her to rise from the ground. For the sentiment, cp. "Invitum qui servat idem facit occidenti," Hor. *A. P.* 467.

472. ἐξᾶσαι. The word is used by Plat. *Phaed*. 35 of the 'last song' of the dying swan; and Polybius xxxi. 20. 1 has the phrase, ἐξάσας τὸ κύκνειον : so it seems nearly certain that here there is an allusion to the last note of the dying swan.

474. ἦμεν τύραννοι. Most edd. read ἦ μὲν τύραννος or ἤμην τύραννος, a form which is also introduced in *Hel*. 931 ; this is held by Cobet to be a Macedonian form of the imperfect of εἰμί. The form ἤμην is found in *Chr. Pat.* 537. There is, however, no reason to change the MS. reading. It is the habit of the Attic writers, when they use plur. for sing., to recur to the sing. as soon as possible, and to use sing. and plur. in close juxtaposition, as in ἣν θάνω θανούμεθα, 904 below. τύραννοι is masc. A woman speaking of herself uses the masc. (1) when she uses the plural, as here ; (2) when she speaks *generally* of her own sex, as *El*. 775, οὐδὲ γὰρ κακῶς πάσχοντι μῖσος ὧν τέκῃ προσγίγνεται : (3) when a chorus of women speaks of itself in the sing., the masc. is sometimes used, *e.g. Hipp*. 1103, λείπομαι ἔν τε τύχαις θνατῶν καὶ ἐν ἔργμασι λεύσσων.

ἐς τύραννα. See on 445.

476. ἀριθμόν, similarly used in Ar. *Nub*. 1203, Soph. *O. C.* 381, and of one man in *Heracl*. 997. [To what is the adverb attached? Does it qualify the noun? If so, cp. Dem. *Cor*. 245. 62, ἐν τοιαύτῃ καταστάσει καὶ ἔτι ἀγνοίᾳ τοῦ ... κακοῦ : Thuc. vii. 34, τὴν οὐκέτι ... ἐπαναγωγήν. In that case, however, the article is present, and they are both *time*-adverbs ; but see Thuc. ii. 4. 3, ἣν ἄντικρυς δίοδος : Krüger quotes Dem. 19. 141, γέγονε τῶν ἐχθρῶν ἄρδην ὄλεθρος.—H. C.].

477, 478. These verses are most probably spurious ; as they stand they have no meaning ; Stephens conjectured οὓς for οὐ before Τρῳάς, and I have translated that reading ; the sentence would then be like Ar. *Av*. 659, γῆ δ' οὐδ' ἀὴρ οὐδ' οὐρανὸς ἦν : Dind. says οἴους, not οὓς, would be required. See, however, 499, where ὧν seems to be quite synonymous with οἴων.

485. εἰς ... ἐξαίρετον, lit. 'for the choice dignity of husbands,' for espousals however distinguished.

486. ἄλλοισι. In 381 the MSS. give us ἄλλοις, but there ἄλλοις must be changed to ἄλλως.

489. τὸ λοίσθιον, used as adverb. θριγκὸς is nom. in apposition to the sentence.

495. ἐκ, 'after,' cp. κάλλιστον ἦμαρ εἰσιδεῖν ἐκ χείματος, Aesch. *Agam*. 873 ; ἐξ ὀλβίων ἄζηλον εὑροῦσαι βίον, Soph. *Trach*. 284.

497. ἀδόκιμ' ὀλβίοις ἔχειν, ' unseemly for the prosperous to wear.' Her garments would betray how completely. her former ὄλβος had fled ; ὄλβος is here used in its Homeric sense of 'material prosperity.'

498. μιᾶς γυναικός, sc. Helen ; γάμων (γάμον P) μιᾶς ἕνα is the MS. reading. Dind. reads διὰ γάμω μιᾶς δύο, but μιᾶς ἕνα is surely right ; this pleonasm is much sought after by the tragics ; cp. Or. 613, Soph. El. 617, Aj. 20, Ant. 443, 492. See also 776 below.

499. οἵων ... ὦν : the rel. ὦν is here used as synonymous with οἵων, as in 477, if Stephens' conjecture there is right. See Jebb on Soph. Aj. 125, who quotes Eur. Alc. 640, ἔδειξας εἰς ἔλεγχον ἐξελθὼν ὅς εἶ. Of course ὦν τεύξομαι could not possibly by itself mean, 'what I shall have to meet !'; the relative could not be exclamatory; but here it attracts to itself the interjectional quality of οἵων, which immediately precedes.

506. δῆποτ', ' that once went delicately in Troy.'

507. στιβάδα ... ἀποφθαρῶ, 'take me away to some lowly lair, to some precipice's crest, so that I may weep my heart away, and then cast me down and perish.' She longs for a lonely place where to weep and then slay herself. The commentators, puzzled by an apparent inconsistency in the aspirations of the 'mobled queen,' have made various conjectures, e.g. χαμαιριφῆ (a word found in Chr. Pat. 1430) for χαμαιπετῆ (Nauck) ; and for δακρύοις, ἄκραις or πέτροις (Musgrave), ὄκρισι (Hartung) ; but the text is quite sound : it is a fine touch of psychological analysis to make the queen long to weep her fill before she slays herself. There is, no doubt, an allusion to the death of Niobe.

511. ἀμφί μοι, 'lift, Muse, for me the lay of Troy.' This is the traditional epic exordium of a hymn, e.g. ἀμφί μοι Ἑρμείαο φίλον γόνον ἔννεπε, Μοῦσα, is the first verse of the Homeric hymn to Pan ; so ἀμφὶ Ποσειδάωνα, ἀμφὶ Διώνυσον, ἀμφὶ Διὸς κούρους : so also ἀμφί μοι αὖ σε, Φοῖβ' ἄναξ, Ar. Nub. 595 ; hence ἀμφιανακτίζειν is 'to write dithyrambic hymns,' like that of Terpander, which began ἀμφί μοι αὖτε ἄναχθ' ἑκαταβόλον ἀειδέτω φρήν : hence, too, dithyrambic poets were called ἀμφιάνακτες.

512. ὕμνων ᾠδάν. Cp. θρήνων ... ᾠδάς, Soph. El. 88 ; δακρύων ... μέλος, Eur. Hipp. 1178 ; μέλος ... τύχης, Iph. Aul. 1280.

513. ἐν. See L. and S., ἐν, II. 1, 2.

516. τετραβάμονος ἀπήνας, 'the horse that conveyed him,' that is, the ecus durateus, 'wooden horse' ; ἀπήνη is simply a 'vehicle,' as in Med. 1123, ναίαν ἀπήνην : the adj. τετρα-

βάμονος tells the nature of the vehicle, *i.e.* that it was a horse; τετρ. is 'a horse,' like *quadrupes* in Latin, and qualifies χηλαί, ψάλια in *Phoen.* 792, 808. The horse was moved on wheels; cp. Virg. *Aen.* ii. 235, "pedibusque rotarum | subiciunt lapsus"; and Q. Smyrn. xii. 424, ἐσθλὸς Ἐπειὸς | ποσσὶν ὑπὸ βριαροῖσιν εὔτροχα δούρατ' ἔθηκεν.

520. βρέμοντα, 'rattling loudly,' 'ringing with the clash of arms within it.' βρέμειν is applied to the sound of the λωτοί in *Bacch.* 161, and to the clash of arms in *Heracl.* 832. For οὐράνια, see on 325, 1301. Cp. Virg. *Aen.* ii. 243, "atque utero sonitum quater arma dedere."

521. ἔνοπλον, '*equum fetum armis*'; so ἔνθεος is 'inspired,' ἔνθηρος is 'infested with wild beasts,' and ἔγκαρπος is 'fruity.'

522. ἀπό, 'standing on the rock and crying out from it,' cp. *Phoen.* 1223, Soph. *El.* 137, where τόν γ' ἐξ Ἀΐδα ἀναστάσεις = τὸν ἐν ᾅδου ἐξ ᾅδου ἀναστήσεις : so Soph. καθήμεθ' ἄκρων ἐκ πάγων, *Ant.* 411; and τῶν παρὰ βασιλέως, Xen. *An.* i. 1; τοὺς ἐκεῖθεν ἐπιβοηθεῖν, Thuc. i. 62; Eur. *Hel.* 1591, *Phoen.* 1223, Thuc. iii. 21, Ξ. 153, φ. 420.

526. Ἰλιάδι, κόρᾳ, sc. Pallas.

530. See note on 550.

531. γέννα, this word is followed by δώσων, which agrees with λαὸς implied in γέννα, a construction πρὸς τὸ σημαινόμενον.

534. ξεστὸν λόχον, 'the Argives ambushed in the cunningly wrought mountain pine, Troy's doom.' ξεστὸν refers in grammar to λόχον, but in sense to πεύκᾳ : for though λόχος might, and often does, indicate the '*place* of ambush,' yet the words πεύκᾳ ἐν οὐρείᾳ here force us to take λόχον as referring to the 'men that form the ambush,' and so, of course, ξεστὸν cannot be literally predicated of it. This application of an adj. to a subst., to which in sense it only mediately refers, is a frequent device whereby the Greek poets achieve dignity of language, and avoid a commonplace style. It is a marked feature in the style of Pindar. It is called by Jelf "the interchange of attributive forms." But 'the smooth-planed ambush' for 'men ambushed in a horse of smooth-planed wood' is certainly a too daring use of this figure. Hdt. iii. 8 has ξύλινον λόχον. I have slightly changed the form of both the strophic and antistrophic verse in the interests of the metre. The MS. reading is ἄεισον ἐν δακρύοις and πεύκᾳ ἐν οὐρείᾳ. The metrical form is now ‒ ⏑ ‒ ‒ ⏑ ⏑ ‒. A spondee may correspond to a trochee in this form of verse. For the prodelision cp. σθένει 'πινικείῳ, Soph. *O. C.* 1086. Dr. Heinsch would read πευκᾶν οὐρεῖᾶν,

comparing Q. Smyrn. xii. 124, οἱ δ᾽ ἐλάτῃσιν ἐπιβρίσαντες ἀν᾽ ὕλην | τάμνον δένδρεα μακρά.

535. For θεᾷ B and C give θέᾳ, and the schol. has καὶ ὁ Πρίαμος ἐξῆλθε τὴν βλάβην θεασόμενος. But θέᾳ δώσων = θεασόμενος is impossible, and is not defended by the usage of θέᾳ διδόντες in *Andr.* 1087; of πόνοις διδοῦσα, *Or.* 1663; or of φιλήμασιν ἔδωκε, *inf.* 1176. Weil (*Revue de Philologie*, Nouv. Sér. i., Paris 1877, p. 195) infers from the schol. that Priam must have been mentioned, and suggests

ἂν Δαρδανίδας ἄταν θεᾷ δώσων.

He urges that δώσοντες would have been used, not δώσων, if the part. agreed, according to the constr. πρὸς τὸ σημαινόμενον, with γέννα. He thinks that the schol. thought Δαρδανίδας meant 'Priam,' but he himself refers it to 'the people of Troy,' comparing Ἐρεχθείδης, Κεκροπίδης, Αἰγείδης for 'the Athenians' in Aristophanes, *Knights.*

536. χάριν, 'as an acceptable oblation to the virgin with coursers of immortal strain,' *i.e.* Παλλὰς Ἱππία : others take ἀμβροτόπωλος as meaning simply 'virgin goddess,' πῶλος being *virgo*, and the word being formed on the analogy of ὀρθόμαντις = ὀρθὸς μάντις : so ἀριστόμαντιν, αἰνολέοντα, αἰνογιγάντων, αἰνόπαρις, αἰνοπάτηρ, αἰνοτύραννος. Cp. "Pars stupet innuptae donum exitiale Minervae," Virg. *Aen.* ii. 31. But Herm. interprets quite differently. Instead of taking χάριν in apposition to the sentence, he takes it in apposition to ξεστὸν λόχον, and renders 'the gift of a divine steed that never felt the yoke.' This seems at first sight to give a more natural meaning to χάριν with gen. ; but in defence of the other interpretation we have, *e.g.* Aesch. *Agam.* 182, δαιμόνων χάρις = ' homage due *to* the gods.'

537. κλωστοῦ, 'with encircling hawsers of spun flax'; κλωστοῦ is from κλωστής = κλωστήρ, 'yarn.' Kirch. reads κλωστοῦ ... λίνοιο, which reading he draws from the note of the schol., καθάπερ ναὸς σκάφος κλωστοῦ λίνου ἀμφιβόλοις, ὅ ἐστι σχοινίοις, οὕτως ἐπὶ τὸν ἵππον ἐπέβαλον. The schol. seems, therefore, to take ἀμφιβόλοις as a subst. ; from the same note Matthiae drew ὡσεὶ for ὡς εἰς of the MSS. The allusion might be to the Greek custom of conveying ships over an isthmus by means of ropes and rollers. But Q. Smyrn. xii. 428, compares the drawing in of the wooden horse to the *launching* of a ship :

εἷλκον ἐπιβρίσαντες ἀολλέες, ἠύτε νῆα
ἕλκωσιν μογέοντες ἔσω ἁλὸς ἠχηέσσης
αἰζηοί.

F

As his description and that of Eur. may have been (and probably were) founded on the same now lost cyclic epic, the passage quoted from him affords good reason for our understanding the passage before us as referring to the launching of a ship, not to its conveyance over an isthmus.

539. φόνια, 'they put it in the shrine of the goddess Pallas, on the floor fateful to fatherland.'

541. ἐπί ... παρῆν: the verb and preposition are separated by *tmesis*. [There is probably a reminiscence of the Homeric ἐπὶ κνέφας ἦλθε. Cp. πολύτλας ἀνήρ, *Aj.* 958, as an echo of πολύτλας δῖος Ὀδυσσεύς, so *ib.* 175, βοῦς ἀγελαίας: and perhaps *Phoen.* 210, ἀκαρπίστων πεδίων Σικελίας (*sc.* ἁλός), is an echo of ἁλὸς ἀτρύγετοιο in Homer, as well as κυβιστῆρες, *ib.* 1131, of ὡς ῥεῖα κυβιστᾷ, Il. 745.—H. C.]

544. ἀνά. ἀνά is sometimes explained as = ἀνήειρον: but this explanation can by no means be accepted in the absence of examples to justify such a usage; neither can ἀνά mean *comitante pedum strepitu*, an employment of this preposition which cannot be defended. I believe that ἀνά is separated by *tmesis* from ἔμελπον : we have ἀναμέλπω with acc. of cogn. sign. ἀοιδάν, in *Theocr.* xvii. 113. I have retained the τ' of the MSS. after βοάν, which Dind. strikes out ; ἀνέμελπον governs both βοάν and (by a slight zeugma) κρότον, 'plied featly the rhythmic footfall, featly the jocund lay.' It must be remembered that μολπή refers, not to singing only, but to 'song and dance,' or any 'rhythmic measured movement,' being applied even to Nausicaa's game at ball (ζ. 100).

550. ἔδωκεν ὕπνῳ. The metre shows this to be faulty, the antistrophic verse being δόλιον ἔσχον ἄταν. Herm. suggests ἀπεδίωκεν ὕπνῳ: Reiske, παρ' ἴπνῳ, '*apud caminum.*' Perhaps we should read

πυρὸς μέλαιναν αἴγλαν
πυρὸς ἔδωκεν ὕπνῳ,

'the lamps alight shed a gloomy glare on the sleepers. Euripides' proneness to iteration of words, especially in choral odes, is a familiar feature in his style, and is often parodied by Aristophanes. Dr. Maguire would read, ἔπορε τοῖς ἐν ὕπνῳ. The schol. is τὸ σέλας τοῦ πυρὸς τὴν μέλαιναν αἴγλαν δέδωκε τῷ ὕπνῳ, ὅ ἐστι τὴν μέλαιναν κατάστασιν. He takes μέλαιναν αἴγλαν to mean 'darkness,' and the sense of the passage to be διεδέξατο ἡ νὺξ τὸ πῦρ, σβεσθέντος γὰρ αὐτοῦ ἐκοιμήθησαν, 'and in the houses the bright light [extinguished] gave to the sleepers but a darksome glimmer,' such as would prevail all night without any artificial light in the countries with which Eur. was familiar. The note of the schol. suggests that we might read ἀντέδωκεν ὕπνῳ, which would sufficiently correspond with the antistrophic verse. Perhaps the poet wrote ἀντιδέδωκεν (the schol. writes δέδωκεν). We could then read in the antistrophe, δούλιον ἔσχον ἄταν, 'in their joyance they gat for themselves chains and slavery.' For ἔσχον, 'gat them,' cp. Pind. N. x. 24, Οὐλία παῖς ἔνθα νικάσαις δὶς ἔσχεν ... εὐφόρων λάθαν πόνων, and the commentary thereon. I own I do not understand δόλιον ἔσχον ἄταν, which cannot mean 'they grasped the steed that betrayed them,' and is very feebly expressed if it merely signifies 'they were betrayed.' However we take the passage, ὕπνῳ means 'to sleep,' in the sense of 'to such as slept.' for, as the context shows, many watched.

551. ὀρεστέραν, Ar. Lys. 1262 calls her ἀγροτέρα ...Ἄρταμι σηροοκτόνε ... παρσένε σιά ... κυναγέ.

554. κόραν, sc. Ἄρτεμιν, which word indeed the MSS. supply, but the metre shows it to be a gloss.

557. βρέφη, 'the sweet infants clung with scared hands to their mothers' skirts.' Cp. 745, 1090. For the sing. ματρί, cp. σῶμα δ' ἐς ἥβην ἦλθεν τέκνων, Med. 1008 ; ἐκίνουν θύρσον, Bacch. 724, where see note.

560. λόχου. Here λόχου is 'the place of ambush,' the horse ; ἔργα is in apposition to the foregoing clause, "quae quidem omnia Minervae consilio facta sunt."

564. καράτομος. This extremely bold expression can by no means be rendered literally in English. The meaning is 'the young men butchered, alone and defenceless, added laurels to the crown of Hellas, nursing mother of brave boys.' The adj. καράτομος refers in sense rather to νεανιῶν than to ἐρημία. Cp. 533. The MSS. give νεανίδων, but this must be wrong. The young women would be carried away as captives; the young men who were butchered would be such as were surprised alone, and so could not offer any successful resistance.

570. εἰρεσίᾳ μαστῶν. This again is a very bold expression. It has been explained absurdly in many ways. Musgrave holds that as Andr. is said πορθμεύεσθαι, which is an allusion to a ship, so Ast. is said to follow behind like a boat towed after a ship, impelled mammarum desiderio. Others, supposing Ast. to be in the carriage with Andr., render, 'close to his mother's breasts, shaken with the motion of the carriage.' It need hardly be said that Eur. would not have written anything so absurd as this ; and against Musgrave's explanation, among other considerations, it may be urged that Ast. was

certainly not a suckling at this period. I fancy that in this
bold expression there must be a reminiscence of the use of
ἐρέσσειν in the sense of the 'measured rhythmical *planctus* or
beating of the breast,' by which Greek women expressed their
grief; cp. γόων ... ἐρέσσετε ... χεροῖν πίτυλον, Aesch. *Theb.* 855;
ἔρεσσ' ἔρεσσε καὶ στέναζε, *Pers.* 1046. So here παρὰ εἰρεσίᾳ
μαστῶν must (by a very bold use of language) mean παρὰ
μητρὶ μαστοὺς ἐρεσσούσῃ, 'beside his mother, who is beating
her breasts' as the car advances. παρὰ εἰρεσίᾳ μαστῶν = παρὰ
μητρὶ μαστοὺς ἐρεσσούσῃ is not more bold than καράτομος ἐρημία
νεανιῶν = νεανίαι καράτομοι ἐν ἐρημίᾳ. Matth. understands
εἰρεσίᾳ μαστῶν to mean 'her heaving breasts'; but this is as
daring an expression as is implied in my explanation, and is
not in accordance with the almost *technical* usage of ἐρέσσειν =
plangere. Cp. διερέσσειν of wild impassioned waving of torches,
1258. We might, however, take παρὰ as an adverb, and
understand εἰρεσίᾳ μαστῶν to mean 'borne on the breast.'
The Greek poets are fond of figures taken from rowing, as in
πτερύγων ἐρετμοῖσιν, *Ag.* 52; and (a still closer parallel) a poet
quoted by Athenaeus, xv. 699 A, has εἰρεσίῃ γλώσσης ἀπο-
πέμψομεν εἰς μέγαν αἶνον: so here εἰρεσίᾳ μαστῶν might mean
literally, 'by the oarage, conveyance, of her breast,' *i.e.* 'borne
on his mother's breast.' But the chief objection to this view
seems to be that Ast. is not described as a child of such
very tender age throughout the play. Verse 1171 clearly
shows that Ast. was not an infant; for how could he observe
and perceive the royal attributes of his father's state? (This
difficulty, however, would be avoided by accepting Prof.
Crossley's view of 1171, that the οὐκ is *drawn back*, and
qualifies γνούς and ἰδών as well as οἶσθα: see note on 1171.)
But ἕπεται seems a strange word to describe an infant borne
on his mother's breast. The version of L. and S., 'clasped
close to her throbbing breasts,' is hardly to be found in the
Greek words. Mr. E. G. Butler of Ennis College takes ἕπεται
as meaning 'keeps time with,' 'follows the motions of,' a sense
somewhat supported by ἑσπόμενος δουρί, M. 395. Ast. might
be borne on her throbbing breasts, though not a suckling,
and with them he would rise and fall. Mr. Stanley would
read παρὰ δ' εἰρεσίαις ἀστῶν. He conceives that Andr. is
brought on the stage in an ἐκκύκλημα, like Euripides in *The
Acharnians*. The men pushing it along are compared to rowers.
The young Ast. walks beside them. For the plur. of εἰρεσία
he compares Orph. *Arg.* 374, 1039; and for the concrete
meaning and defining genitive, Soph. *Phil.* 936, Aesch. *Pers.*
914. He notices that there is no allusion to horses or mules
yoked to the car, as there is in the *Electra* when Clytae-

mnestra comes on the stage. Dr. Joseph Heinsch (*Comment.
Eurip. Specimen*, Glatz. 1886) conjectures παρ' ἀπειρέσια κλαίων
ἕπεται, comparing Soph. *Aj.* 927, ἀπειρεσίων πόνων, and Q.
Smyrn. ἀπειρέστον κεχάροντο. He also suggests παρὰ δ' ἀπτό-
μενος μαστῶν, comparing ἧψω δὲ γονάτων, *Her.* 245 ; ἅψαι μητρός,
439 ; ποδῶν ἐφηπτόμην, ἅψασθαι, *Chr. Pat.* 2104, 2453 ; χρωτὸς
ἅψασθαι, *ibid.* 464 ; ποδῶν ἐφάπτομαι, *ibid.* 773, all of which
references have their weight, as the *Troades* is one of the
plays of which the *cento* is composed. If I ventured to
ascribe to Eur. epic diction at all, I would borrow from it
more largely, and read πὰρ δ' ἀπερείσι' ἀλαστῶν ἕπεται, 'beside
her follows sore distraught,' thus avoiding the asyndeton and
adhering closely to the MSS. For ἀλαστῶν, cp. Leaf on M. 163,
not L. and S., who give a meaning incompatible with the
usage of the word and with its presumed etymology.

572. νώτοισι. So νῶτον is applied to any flat surface, the
sea, the land, a rock, an altar, and (with a metaphorical allusion to a horse) it is used of a tree in *Bacch.* 1074.

576. ἀπό, sc. λελησμένοις ἀπὸ Τροίας.

577-601. This beautiful antiphony may be compared with
the solemn litanies of the *Persae.*

578. ἐμόν, 'Why keenest thou this coronach ; 'tis mine.'
Andr. says that her case is so piteous that ὤμοι belongs to her
as of right ; τῶνδ' ἀλγέων is the gen. after an interjection, as in
οἱ 'γὼ θανάτου τοῦ σοῦ μελέα, *Iph. A.* 1287 ; οἴμοι τῶν ἐμῶν ἐγὼ
κακῶν, *Phoen.* 384 ; φεῦ τοῦ ἀνδρός, 'ah, what a man,' Xen.
Cyr. iii. 1. 39. I have preserved ἐμὸν and τῶνδ' of the MSS.
against Hermann's ἐμῶν and τόνδ', which Dind. accepts.

583. ἐμῶν τ' εὐγ. παίδων = ἐμοί τ' εὐγενεῖς παῖδες, the abstract
noun being used for the concrete.

584. ἐμᾶς agrees with πόλεος in next verse but one.

585. λαμπρά, 'too evident is the ruin.'

588 a. λῦμ', 'thou that wert mutilated by the Achaeans,'
i.e. Hector. Such would be the natural meaning of λῦμα.
But it is perhaps better to take the word in the sense of
λύμη, 'scourge of the Achaeans.' Cp. *pernicies* in "pernicies
tempestas barathrumque macelli," Hor. *Ep.* i. 15. 31.

588 b. κοίμισαι, 'take me to Hades to sleep,' *constructio
praegnans.* See on 445.

589. πόθοι, 'deep are these yearnings of us who have to
dree this weird.'

"Sore are our yearnings, sharp anguish is come on us,
O sorrow-stricken :
Ruined our city is; cloud over cloud do our miseries
thicken,
Sent by the hate of the Gods, since thy son was from
Hades delivered,
He for whose bridal accurst were the bulwarks of Ilium
shivered.
Pallas the Goddess is left amid corpses blood-boultered
that crowd her,
Spoil for the vultures, and Troy 'neath the yoke-band of
thraldom hath bowed her."—W.

592. ὁ δὲ σὸς γόνος. Andr. has not heard of the death of
Paris by the arrow of Philoctetes (Soph. *Phil.* 1425). Paris
had already been slain : see v. 952.

595. ἤνυσε. See on 232.

597. ἐλοχεύθην, 'where I was in travail,' lit. 'was delivered';
cp. *Bacch.* 3.

598. ἐρημόπολις. This is Seidler's emendation for ἔρημος
πόλις : exactly similar is Porson's μετωποσωφρόνων for μετώπων
σωφρόνων (which violates the pause) in Aesch. *Suppl.* 194.

603. ἀδάκρυτ', used as an adv., 'without tears,' 'yea, even
the dead remembereth with wet eyes'; cp. Byron, "And
thou who tell'st me to forget, Thy looks are wan, thine eyes
are wet."

604. ἡδύ, 'what a sweet thing tears are,' a very common
idiom.

605. μοῦσα. See 120, "the chant with sorrow fraught."—W.

609. τὸ μηδέν. See on 412 ; for the aor. expressing what is
wont to happen, see Madv. *Syn.* § iii., Rem. *a* ; Goodwin,
§ 30, 1.

612. δεινόν, 'strange,' 'mighty,' not 'terrible,' so δεινὸν τὸ
τίκτειν, 'strange is the power of motherhood.'

614. ἄλλος τις, *Ajax alter ;* see 70. 'Such a one as Ajax,'
i.e. 'a ravisher.' The plural is more usual when a proper
name is used to denote the type or class to which the indi-
vidual belonged : cp. Χρυσηΐδων μείλιγμα, *Ag.* 1439 ; Λαμάχων
ἀπαλλαγείς, Ar. *Ach.* 270 ; but for the sing. cp. Aesch. *Prom.*
86, αὐτὸν γάρ σε δεῖ Προμηθέως.

615. χἄτερα, 'you are hapless even in your other daughter,'
Polyxena, lit. 'on the other side,' two only being contem-
plated, Polyxena and Cassandra. Hec. replies, 'Ay, hapless
beyond measure and beyond count.' The construction is,

νοσῶ γε ταῦτα ὧν ἐστί μοι οὔτε μ. οὔτε ἀρ. Observe ἕτερος sometimes = ἄλλος : of this a good example is in *Hec.* 361, τὸν "Ἑκτορός τε χάτερων πολλῶν κάσιν. See also 362.

621. **σαφές**, 'here is plainly told the riddle which Tal. but now obscurely shadowed forth'; πάλαι often refers to the quite recent past in the Attic writers, just as *procul* in Latin comedy means 'hard by.'

622. **νιν αὐτή.** Kirch. reads νιν αὐτήν, a common pleonasm in the tragics.

623. **ἀπεκοψάμην**, 'I smote my breast for the dead.'

624. **προσφαγμάτων**, 'how heinous was the sacrifice of thee.' For gen., see on 578.

627. **ζώσης**, 'she was more blessed in her death than I who live'; βλέπειν is, as often, quite synonymous with ζῆν.

629. **ὦ τεκοῦσα**, 'O mother' (of the sacrificed Polyxena). Musgr. reads οὐ τεκοῦσα, 'O mother, that barest me not,' *i.e.* mother-in-law ; so *Ion* 1324, χαῖρ' ὦ φίλη μοι μῆτερ οὐ τεκοῦσά περ, but there the final words only explain that μῆτερ is used as a term of respect, as in 1182, 1228, below, and so I would understand οὐ τεκοῦσα if read here; I do not think Eur. would have expressed in those terms the relation of a mother-in-law. Musgr. might have quoted in support of his conjecture, τίκτουσαν οὐ τίκτουσαν, *Chr. Pat.* 62. But the whole conception of a mother-in-law as a mother is foreign to Greek thought.

633. **ἀλγεῖ**, the dead man 'has not the pain of feeling his woes.' There is no need to supply a second οὐδέν. See on 172 above, 1171 below. Mr. A. C. Pearson, finding an objection in the tense of ἠσθημένος, proposed to read τῶν κακῶν δ' ἔσβη μένος. But ἠσθημένος does not necessarily imply any more than αἰσθανόμενος, and if it did we could understand, 'having known what the ills of life are.'

635. **ἀλᾶται**, 'wanders away from,' *i.e.* 'loses,' 'is bereft of,' cp. εὐφροσύνας ἀλᾶται, Pind. *O.* i. 94 ; but the addition of ψυχὴν makes the phrase a little difficult, 'in thought he loses his happiness,' *i.e.* 'he reflects on his lost happiness,' 'he misses his former happiness,' so Dante's well-known "nessun maggior dolore Che ricordarsi del tempo felice Nella miseria," and Tennyson's "This is truth the poet sings, That a sorrow's crown of sorrow is remembering happier things."

636. **ὥσπερ οὐκ ἰδοῦσα φῶς.** It was probably this passage which suggested to Seneca the reflections on a future life which he puts into the mouth of his chorus in his *Troades*, "Quaeris quo iaceas post obitum loco | quo non nata iacent," *Tro.* 410 ff.

638. ἐγὼ δέ, 'I aimed at high repute, and having gained much of it, yet I was balked of success,' that is, all my plans were frustrated by this great calamity, which has made me a slave instead of living a pattern to wives. τῆς εὐδ. depends on τοξεύσασα. Paley shows that τύχη means 'the hitting the mark,' aptly comparing μὴ 'κ τύχης ὡρμισμένους, 'anchored not out of bow-shot,' H. F. 203.

641. ἐξεμόχθουν, see 873, 'whatsoever things have been devised that are of good repute for women, all these I attained unto in the house of Hector.' So below, 873, ἐξεμόχθησαν = 'achieved (the recapture of) Helen.'

642. πρῶτον μέν, Dind. has bracketed 642-651 and 656-657. I formerly followed him, bracketing even 652-655. I now believe that Eur. wrote the whole passage, if he ever wrote a line. It is exactly in his vein, and the difficulties are just such as his style presents, but which an imitator would be afraid to introduce. The sentence is very confused. As ἔνθα in 642 cannot mean 'whereas' (though edd. have carelessly assumed that it could), but must mean 'where,' we must suppose that the writer of these lines was going to say, 'In the first place I used to remain in the house, where a woman ought to remain, for not to stay at home ever carries in its train ill-repute, whether a woman's fame be otherwise be-smirched or not'; but he subsequently modified the form of the sentence in such a way as to leave ἔνθα without any ante-cedent ; αὐτὸ τοῦτο in 643 is τὸ μὴ ἔνδον μένειν, and τούτου in 645 is τοῦ μὴ ἔνδον μένειν : so too ἥτις οὐκ ἔνδον μένει, 644 = τὸ μὴ ἔνδον μένειν, according to a familiar idiom whereby the Attic writers, instead of saying ἀγαθοῦ ἐστιν ἀνδρὸς μὴ ἀδικεῖν, often write ἀγαθοῦ ἐστιν ἀνδρὸς ὅστις οὐκ ἀδικεῖ. The passage may be analyzed, δόμοις being antecedent to ἔνθα, thus : πρῶτον μὲν παρεῖσα πόθον τούτου [i.e. τοῦ μὴ ἔνδον μένειν] ἔμιμνον ἐν δόμοις, ἔνθα ἥτις οὐκ ἔνδον μένει, [ταύτῃ] αὐτὸ τοῦτ' ἐφέλκεται κακῶς ἀκούειν, 'First, I used to stay in the house, where whoso stays not [to her] this very thing [her gadding abroad] bringeth disrepute.' The sentence in prose would have run thus, πρῶτον μὲν παρεῖσα πόθον τοῦ μὴ ἔνδον μένειν ἔμιμνον ἐν δόμοις ἔνθα ἐχρῆν, ἐπεὶ αὐτὸ τὸ μὴ ἔνδον μένειν ἐφέλκεται κακῶς ἀκούειν γυναιξί, κἂν προσῇ ψόγος κἂν μή. Cp. π. 294. αὐτὸς γὰρ ἐφέλκεται ἄνδρα σίδηρος. The whole passage, 642-651, is found in Chr. Pat. ; the difficulty of construction is there avoided by reading οὖν γε for ἔνθα. The omission of the article before κακῶς ἀκούειν is irregular (Goodwin, § 92-93, Madv. § 154). Cp. 1056 below.

646. κομψά, 'the tinsel-talk of women.'—W.

647. εἰσεφρούμην. See L. and S. under εἰσφρέω.

648. οἴκοθεν, 'having *by nature* a sound reason to guide me';
οἴκοθεν, like *domi*, means, 'having about me,' 'having a store of';
we find *domi est* in Cic.; and Cat. has (xxxi. 14) "gaudete
quidquid est *domi* cachinnorum," 'laugh all the laughs ye
have' (lit. 'have about you,' 'keep stock of'). See 963.

650. ἀμέ = ἇ ('in what matters') ἐχρῆν με νικᾶν πόσιν: so νικᾶν
καὶ δίκαια κἄδικα = 'in both good cases and bad,' Ar. *Nub.* 99;
ἤδη is the Attic form of ἤδειν, plup. of οἶδα.

655. αὐθεντῶν. This word always means 'murderer' in
Eur. We have only the authority of Suidas and grammarians
for αὐθεντής = δεσπότης, which sense is more natural here. In
Suppl. 442, where δῆμος αὐθεντής χθονὸς would also require the
sense of δεσπότης, Dind. accepts Markland's conjecture, εὐθυντής.
It would be easy to read εὐθυντῶν here, but the word may be
explained as meaning, 'murderess of my kin.' Hector's
murderers were her murderers. Orestes calls Clytaemnestra
his murderess because she slew his father. See 920, 921.

659. μισήσομαι, fut. mid. in semi-passive sense, 'I shall
get myself hated'; so in *Ion* 597, 611.

663. καινοῖσι, 'by means of a new marriage.'

664. Cp. Virg. *G.* iii. 517, "maerentem abiungens fraterna
morte iuvencum."

666. καίτοι, 'yet the brute-kind is dumb, unreasoning,
lower than man.' Observe the subject has the article, the
predicates have not.

677. κλέπτομαι, 'and I am not beguiled by the phantasy
that it will e'er be well with me—sweet were even such a
phantasy.' Cp. κρεῖσσον δὲ τὸ δοκεῖν κἂν ἀληθείας ἀπῇ, *Or.* 230;
cp. also Sen. *Tro.* 432, "prosperis rebus locus | ereptus omnis,
dira qua veniant habent; | miserrimum est timere cum speres
nihil."

681-700. I give Mr. Way's rendering of this fine passage:

"Though never yet I stepped aboard a ship,
From pictures seen and hearsay know I this,
That, if there lie a storm not passing great
On mariners, for deliverance all bestir them:
This standeth by the helm, that by the sail;
That baleth ship: but if the sea's full flood
In turmoil overwhelm them, cowed by fate
To the waves' driving they commit themselves.
So I withal, though many a woe is mine,
Am dumb, and I refrain my lips from speech,

For the gods' misery-surge o'ermastereth me.
But, dear my daughter, let be Hector's fate,
Seeing no tears of thine shall ransom him ;
But honour him that is to-day thy lord,
Tendering the sweet lure of thy winsomeness.
If this thou do, thy friends shall share thy joy,
And this my son's son shalt thou rear to man,
To Troy a mighty aid, that children born
Of him hereafter may in days to come
Build her, and yet again our city rise."

686. ἄντλον, 'keeping out the sea water'; this word in the tragic poets always means the inimicum imbrem, the sea water which makes its way into the ship through leaks and chinks ; cp. ἄντλον οὐκ ἐδέξατο in Aesch. Theb. 796, and the well-known passage, ἀλίμενόν τις ὡς εἰς ἄντλον πεσών, Hec. 1025, where ἄντλον does not mean the vessel's hold, but the inimicum imbrem of the sea. For εἴργων, cp. κλῆθρον εἰργέτω στέγης, Frag. 364. 20.

687. τύχη. Nauck reads φορᾷ, with Chr. Pat. 628.

695. δέλεαρ, 'allurement'; τρόπων is the descriptive gen., see Madv. Syntax, § 54 b, Rems. 1 and 2.

697. παῖδα τόνδε παιδός. Astyanax, son of Hector.

700. κατοικίσειαν. I have given Nauck's correction of ἵν' εἴποτε | ἐκ σοῦ of the MSS.; Ald. reads ἵν' οἵ ποτε | ἐκ σοῦ. A. C. Pearson conjectures μεγίστην ὠφέλησιν, εἴποτε|ἐκ σοῦ. The opt. is attracted into the mood of ἐκθρέψειας ἄν. For this attraction of the opt., see on Bacch. 1255.

709. μῶν οὐ, sc. ἔδοξε, 'is it that he is to have a different master from me ?' οὐ goes with τὸν αὐτόν.

713. ἐπῄνεσ', 'I commend your reserve, unless your tidings are fair'; αἰδῶ is the 'respect for her feelings,' which seems to make his tale so hard to tell ; but if his tidings be good, she does not commend his withholding them so long.

716. λέγων : observe the change of tense in λέξας, 718 ; cp. ἐμόχθουν and κατεξάνθην, 755 ; γαμεῖ and ἐδούλευσ', 962 ; βαῖνε and ἀπόδος, 1039.

719. νικήσειε, 'may such a vote be carried about his flesh and blood,' an impers. use of the verb which is common enough, see L. and S., νικάω 3.

722. εὐγενῶς, 'let your grief be a noble grief, nor deem you are strong when you are helpless.'

725. κρατεῖ, 2nd pers. sing. pass.

726. ἡμεῖς, 'we are strong enough to contend with one woman.' There is certainly an ironical bitterness about these words which does not harmonize with the tone of the rest of the speech. Hence Nauck proposes ἡμῖν τε πῶς γυναῖκα μάρνασθαι μίαν | οἷόν τε.

729. 'Αχαιοῖς, Nauck and Kirch. read 'Αχαιῶν with V, comparing 638 above, and *Bacch.* 1100, ἵεσαν ... Πενθέως.

735. τιμηθείς. For the construction πρὸς τὸ σημαινόμενον, cp. 531, 852, and *Bacch.* 1307, ἔρνος ... κατθανόντα.

737. εὐγένεια ἀπώλεσεν, cp. Sen. *Tro.* 500, "grave pondus illum magna nobilitas premit."

737-755. I append Mr. Way's version :

" Thy father's heroism ruineth thee,
Which unto others was deliverance.
Ill-timed thy father's prowess was for thee !
O bridal mine and union evil-starred,
Whereby I came, time was, to Hector's hall,
Not as to bear a babe for Greeks to slay,
Nay, but a king for Asia's fruitful land !
Child, dost thou weep?—dost comprehend thy doom?
Why with thine hands clutch, clinging to my robe,
Like fledgling fleeing to nestle 'neath my wings?
No Hector, glorious spear in grip, shall rise
From earth, and bringing thee deliverance come,
No kinsman of thy sire, no might of Phrygians ;
But, falling from on high with horrible plunge,
Unpitied shalt thou dash away thy breath.
O tender nursling, sweet to mother, sweet !
O balmy breath !—in vain and all in vain
This breast in swaddling-bands hath nurtured thee.
Vainly I travailed and was spent with toils ! "

742. σφαγεῖον is 'a vessel for holding blood,' not 'a victim,' which is σφάγιον. Hence Nauck, οὐ σφάγιον υἱόν : Kirch., οὐ σφάγιον ἶνιν : but the verse labours under another defect, for τέξομαι, not τέξω, is the Attic future of τίκτω : moreover 'Ασιάδος with an adj. is strange in next verse ; we have πᾶσαν 'Ασιάδα in *Ion* 1355, but that is not so strong a case as here, for γῆν would easily be understood with πᾶσαν 'Ασιάδα, just as in 'Ασιάδος κρούματα, Frag. 371, κιθάρας must be supplied. These defects in diction, as well as the weakness of the two lines. seem to betray the hand of the interpolator.

745. ἀντέχει, cp. Sen. *Tro.* 802, "quid meos retines sinus | manusque matris? cassa praesidia occupas." See note on 1090.

749. συγγένεια, 'kin,' used here collectively, but of a single kinsman in *Or.* 1233.

753. διὰ κενῆς, 'in vain,' see L. and S., κενός 2.

755. This verse occurs in *Med.* 1026.

756. οὔποτ' αὖθις, 'for you will never embrace me more.' Observe, it should be μήποτ' αὖθις, if the meaning were 'now for the last time embrace me.'

759. βάρβαρα, 'un-Greek,' as Mr. Way renders it. The word could not, of course, mean 'barbarous' in the modern sense of 'cruel,' though it sometimes comes near it, as in *Hel.* 501, ἀνὴρ γὰρ οὐδεὶς ὧδε βάρβαρος φρένας.

779. στεφάνας, 'the highest parapet,' 'battlement of the ramparts.' In a different sense is στεφ. used in *Hec.* 910, ἀπὸ στεφάναν κέκαρσαι πύργων, 'thou art shorn of thy coronal of towers,' where πύργων is the *descriptive* gen., or gen. describing the material of which the coronal was composed.

782. κηρυκεύειν, 'such tragical announcements ought to be left to him who is pitiless, and more prone than is my spirit to heartlessness.' τῆς ἡμ. γνώμης = ἐμοῦ, as "sententia Catonis" stands for 'Cato' in Hor.

786. συλώμεθα, 'we are reft of thee,' lit. 'of thy life'; Eur. uses ψυχὴν Ὀρέστου as a periphrasis for Ὀρέστην.

790. ἄρχομεν, 'this is all I am mistress of'; Hec. says that she has nothing now in her power to give Ast., but πλήγματα κρατὸς στέρνων τε κόπους, she can but smite her head and beat her breast in mourning for him. For the former gesture of grief, cp. Cic. *Brut.* 278, "nulla perturbatio animi, nulla corporis, frons non percussa, non femur, pedis, quod minimum est, nulla supplosio."

791. τί γὰρ οὐκ ἔχομεν, 'what evil are we spared, what woe do we want, to fulfil the sum of our utter ruin?' χωρεῖν διὰ ὀλέθρου = ὄλλυσθαι, and must be distinguished from χωρεῖν εἰς ὄλεθρον.

794. This very exquisite ode is quite Pindaric in the skill with which the mythical glories of Ilium are interwoven and connected with its fall. It is this extraordinary literary skill on the part of Pindar to which Mr. Matthew Arnold has paid a just tribute when he says, "Pindar is literally saturated with the spirit of style." I do not know of any ode in the tragic poets which illustrates better than this the matchless mastery of execution, which is the glory of Greek poetry, and the wonder and despair of all subsequent art. It will be needful to give a sketch of the mythological story, omitting all details unnecessary for the present purpose :—

Laomedon had a daughter Hesione, and sons Priam, Tithonus, and Ganymede,* which latter were beloved of the gods. Tithonus became the consort of Aurora, and was at last (in that his old age was immortal) carried up in a celestial car to the presence of the gods. Ganymede was the cup-bearer of Zeus. Apollo and Poseidon, being under the wrath of Zeus, were made to be in bondage to Laomedon, in the which they built the walls of Troy; but Laomedon cozened them of the covenanted reward, and Poseidon sent a sea monster to ravage the land, to appease the which Laomedon was constrained to sacrifice even his daughter Hesione, to be devoured by him. But Hercules, returning from the Amazons, and seeing Hesione exposed for death, covenanted to slay the monster and save the maiden, for the magic mares which Zeus had given to Laomedon in restitution for Ganymede. Yet Laomedon again forswore his oath, and would not give the mares, albeit Hercules slew the monster and rescued the maid. So Hercules invaded Troy and utterly destroyed it, and Telamon, king of Salamis, was with him, and helped him; to whom he gave Hesione as the meed of victory.

The key-note of the ode is, that Ganymede and Tithonus availed not to avert ruin from Troy, notwithstanding their influence with the gods. Subjoined is a prose version of the ode, which needs a poetical garb to do it justice :—

"King Telamon of bee-haunted Salamis, thou that madest thee a habitation in the sea-girt land, over against the sacred hill [the Athenian Acropolis] where Athenè showed the first sprout of the dark-green olive—a crown and glory heaven-high to Athens fat with oil—of old to the sack of Troy, Troy our town, thou marchedst, fellow-captain with the son of Alcmena, lord of the bow, when first he led forth the flower of Hellas, being wroth for the mares, and at Simois' stream stopped his good ship, and made fast the cables from the poops, and took from his barks that which was the cunning of his hand, even death to Laomedon : and the walls chiselled according to the plumb-line of Phoebus with the red breath of fire he brought to nought, and laid waste the land ; yea, twice with two succeeding blows the spear of the foeman laid low the bulwarks round about Dardania. All for nought then, thou son of Laomedon, thou that walkest delicately with the golden goblets, thou bearest the wine that filleth the cup of Zeus—a high ministry—and thy mother-land is burning with fire. On the shores of the deep there is a

---

* Ganymede is sometimes made the son of Tros, Ilus, or Assaracus.

voice and lamentation, women shrieking, as the bird for her brood, shrieking for their mates and their children and their mothers ; foredone are the pools where thou wast wont to bathe, and the courses wherein thou didst exercise thee ; yet is thy young face beautiful in the calm of its loveliness beside the throne of Zeus ; and the land of Priam hath the Grecian spear brought to ruin.

" Love, Love, that didst come into the abodes of Dardanus, touching the hearts of the heavenly ones, how mightily didst thou exalt Troy, when thou didst ally her with the gods—no blame shall I speak of Zeus, but the light of white-winged Aurora balefully, balefully looked on the downfall of the land, and its high places, albeit she had in her bowers from this land a lord the father of her brood, whom the celestial car of gold rapt on high, to be a great hope to his fatherland—but brought to nought are all the ties that bound the gods to Troy."

796. ἐπικεκλιμένας, cp. λίμνῃ κεκλιμένος Κηφισίδι, E. 709.

800. λιπαραῖσι, not 'fertile,' for Thuc. expressly tells us that Athens was λεπτόγεως, but 'rich in olive oil'; hence Aristophanes says that those who give Athens this traditional epithet praise her in terms more fitting for *sardines à l'huile*, ἀφύων τιμὴν περιάψας, *A ch.* 639.

810. ἔσχασε. See L. and S., σχάζω, II. 3.

811. εὐστοχίαν = 'his well-aimed shafts,' abstract for concrete, as εὐγένεια, 583. Nauck escapes the difficulty, or rather mitigates the boldness of the expression, by reading ἐξεῖλεν ἰόν.

812. κανόνων, see 6 above.

814. πίτυλος, any regular, recurring sounds, as (1) of oars (hence νεὼς πίτυλος, 'a bark with its plashing oars,' 1123); (2) the plash of falling tears, or of wine into the cup ; (3) of rhythmically recurring blows, 'thuds,' whether (*a*) of mourners beating the breast (1236) or (*b*) of pugilists boxing, whence the metaphor here ; (4) of recurring attacks, as of madness, terror, etc.

815. Δαρδανίας, gen. governed by περί.

816. ἐν οἰνοχόαις, small vessels for ladling the wine from the κρατήρ into the cups ; ἐν = 'with '; cp. ἐν κλάδοις, *Bacch.* 110 and note.

824. πλήρωμα, not = πλήρωσις, 'task of filling,' a usage which it would be hard to defend, and which certainly is not paralleled in Soph. *Trach.* 1213 ; πλήρωμα κυλ. is naturally ' that which fills the cups,' and so the word is used in *Ion*

1051, 1412, *Cycl.* 209. καλλίσταν λατρείαν is accus. in apposition to the sentence.

825. ἁ: the ellipse of γᾶ might be urged in confirmation of the soundness of my conjecture on *Bacch.* 406, Πάφον θ' ἂν θ' ἑκατόστομοι for ἂν ἑκατόστομοι which defies explanation. The weak point of my reading was, of course, the ellipse of γᾶν, which I could defend by adducing this parallel passage. However, I now adopt Dr. Verrall's view, which does not entail the ellipse of γᾶ, but of νᾶσος, which occurs among the preceding words.

829. ὑπέρ: observe the *hyperbaton* of the preposition; βοῶσι must be supplied in the principal sentence from βοᾷ in the dependent.

831. εὐνάτορας. This is the reading of the MSS., but it can be reconciled with the antistrophe only by iterating ὀλοόν, a course which I have adopted, following the suggestion of Bothe. The usual reading is εὐνάς, but that makes — — in strophe = ⌣ ⌣ ⌣ in antistrophe, and, moreover, εὐνᾶς applied to *persons* = 'husbands,' would be hard to defend. Herm. suggested ἄορας, which exactly suits the antistrophe, without even postulating the resolution of long syllables which is required by the reading in the text. Hermann's reading is accepted by Dind., but the word, tempting as it is, has no authority. We have in Suidas, ἄορες· αἱ γυναῖκες, on which the note of Kust. is "*imo* ὄαρες· *vid. Schol. Hom. ad. Il. l.* 327." Hesych. has ἄορες· γυναῖκες λέγονται καὶ τρίποδες, and in *Etym. Magn.* we find ἄωροι αἱ γυναῖκες· γίνεται ὄαροι· κατὰ μεταπλασμὸν ὄαρες, καὶ κατὰ ὑπέρθεσιν καὶ ἔκτασιν ἄωρες. Hesych. also has ὄαρας· γάμους· οἱ δὲ γυναῖκας. But how could such a word be corrupted into εὐνάτορας? The word used in 1309 below, is ἀκοίτας. Besides, the word here must mean 'husbands' not 'wives,' and for this there is no authority.

836. χάρισι, this might also mean 'through delight in your office'; cp. ἔνοπτρα, παρθένων χάριτας, 1109 below; in favour of my rendering is *Bacch.* 236, ὅσσοις χάριτας 'Αφροδίτης ἔχων.

842. μέλων, lit. 'being a cure to'; Way renders 'Thrilling the hearts of abiders in heavens.' But see *Hel.* 197, *Andr.* 850, where μέλειν means little more than 'to be familiar with' or 'known to.'

844. ἐπύργωσας. This word is metaphorical, as in 508; there is no allusion to the building of the walls of Troy.

846. ὄνειδος. The meaning is: I will not dwell on the fact that Ganymede failed to procure the interposition of

Zeus, for this might seem to be an aspersion on Zeus; but I will tell how Tithonus could not influence Aurora to help the city.

850. **όλοόν.** It is more poetical, and more in accordance with the usage of the word, to connect όλοὸν with φέγγος rather than with ὄλεθρον. I fancy, moreover, that Sen. had this passage in his mind when he wrote, "Memnon cuius ob luctum parens | pallente maestum protulit voltu diem." *Tro.* 248.

852. **ἔχουσα**, construction πρὸς τὸ σημαινόμενον, inasmuch as Ἡμέρας φέγγος is merely a paraphrase for Ἡμέρα. See on 735.

856. **ἀστέρων**, 'a starry car'; this is perhaps the gen. of material, like ἄστρων εὐφρόνη, Soph. *El.* 19, 'a starry night'; χιόνος πτέρυγι, 'a snowy wing,' *Ant.* 114; σῶμα σποδοῦ, *El.* 758; τραύματα αἵματος, *Phoen.* 1616. Or should we rather take ἀστέρων as gen. of *source, origin*, 'a car sent from the starry skies'?

859. **φίλτρα**='influences towards producing affection.' I think the correlative word μίσηθρον, 'an influence for producing hatred,' should be introduced in Frag. 495, the whole point of the passage being that the female sex are a great *instrument for disseminating hatred* against themselves, the false bringing censure on the true, until men have no faith in their wives; μισηθὲν is the reading of the MSS. The Frag. runs as follows:

> ἄλγιστόν ἐστι θῆλυ μίσηθρον γένος·
> αἱ γὰρ σφαλεῖσαι ταῖσιν οὐκ ἐσφαλμέναις
> αἶσχος γυναιξὶ καὶ κεκοίνωνται ψόγον
> ταῖς οὐ κακαῖσιν αἱ κακαί· τὰ δ' εἰς γάμους
> οὐδὲν δοκοῦσιν ὑγιὲς ἀνδράσιν φρονεῖν.

863. **καὶ στράτ. 'Αχ.**, sc. σὺν ἐμοὶ ἐμόχθησε, 'I am he who underwent so much, and with me (toiled) the Achaean host.' Cp. 868, which is just the same, the participle agreeing with the nearest subst.

864. **ὅσον δοκοῦσί με**, 'not so much as men deem by reason of my wife, but rather to meet the man who, false to his host, filched away my spouse.' Perhaps another covert criticism on Aesch. *Ag.* 400 ff. ὅσον is accusative of measure.

869. **Λάκαιναν.** He cannot bear to utter the name *Helen*, a very Euripidean touch of nature; 891 ff. are also very characteristic.

873. **ἐξεμόχθησαν.** See 641.

874. κτανεῖν. When the infin. expresses a purpose it is generally active or middle, even when the passive would seem more natural, as here. (Goodwin, § 97.)

876. ἐᾶσαι μόρον, 'to give up (the design of) slaying her in Troy.'

879. ποινάς, accus. in apposition to foregoing clause, 'as a retribution for those whose friends fell in Troy.'

884. ὄχημα. This is the nom. ; Zeus is called, 'thou stay of the earth, and thou that restest on it.' The doctrine that the supreme godhead was the Air (which supports the earth and rests on it) is distinctly recognized in Frag. 869, 935 (Nauck), the latter passage being referred to by Cic. N. D. ii. 65. In N. D. i. 29, Cic. ascribes this doctrine to Diogenes of Apollonia ; the following words of his (Frag. 6, Mullach) at all events imply this view, καί μοι δοκέει τὸ τὴν νόησιν ἔχον εἶναι ὁ ἀήρ, καὶ ὑπὸ τούτου πάντα καὶ κυβερνάεσθαι, καὶ πάντων κρατέειν, καὶ οὐκ ἔστιν οὐδὲ ἕν ὅ τι μὴ μετέχοι τούτου. So Democritus (Frag. 5, Mullach) says, οὐκ ἀπεικότως τῶν λογίων ἀνθρώπων ὀλίγους ὃν νῦν ἠέρα καλέομεν Δία μυθέεσθαι καὶ πάντα οὗτος οἶδε καὶ διδοῖ καὶ ἀπαιρέεται. This hypothesis, that the earth is supported by the air, is ascribed by Plut. (Mor. 896 E) to Anaximenes, and by Aristotle (De Caelo, 2. 13) to Anaximenes, Anaxagoras, and Democritus ; the very phrase τῆς γῆς ὄχημα is applied by Hippocrates to the air. After apparently identifying Zeus with Air, Eur. puts aside the question whether the law of his action is to be found in Necessity or in the Anaxagorean Νοῦς, but ends by finally expressing his adoration for a mysterious Principle of good which carries on the moral government of the world. Eur. appears to make an opportunity here for himself to give utterance to his religious views, for it is hard to see how this sudden and subtle apostrophe befits dramatically the circumstances of the Trojan queen. Indeed the subject is at once dismissed after a passing exclamation from Menelaus. But it is quite in the manner of Eur., who aimed at elevating the popular views on religious dogma, and purging the latter of its frivolities and deformities. The fine phrase, δι' ἀψόφου βαίνων κελεύθου, reminds one of Cowper's hymn, "God moves in a mysterious way, His wonders to perform." For νοῦς as a god, cp. Cic. N. D. i. 11, "Ergo animus, ut ego dico, divinus est, ut Eur. audet dicere, Deus."

889. τί δ' ἔστιν ; 'What? How strange are these adjurations !' So must we render with the above punctuation, which is usually adopted. Perhaps, however, a better punctuation is, τί δ' ἔστιν εὐχὰς ὡς ἐκαίνισας θεῶν ; 'what mean

these new-fangled adjurations ?' lit. 'what is the reason that
(ὡς = quod) you have so revolutionized the (the customary)
appeals to the gods?'

892. αἱρεῖ, an allusion to the name 'Ελένη, as Aesch. *Ag.*
761, ἑλέναυς ἕλανδρος ἑλέπτολις, and the (prob. spurious) pas-
sage, *Hec.* 442, 'Ελένην ἴδοιμι, διὰ καλῶν γὰρ ὀμμάτων | αἴσχιστα
Τροίαν εἷλε.

899. τίνες : the ellipse of the 3rd pers. plur. of the subst.
verb is rare, especially in a dependent question.

901. ἦλθες, ' you (that is, your case) did not come to any
formal discussion ; the host unanimously gave your life to me
whom you wronged.' Most edd. give ἦλθεν, the reading of
the schol., but ἦλθες of the MSS. is really more idiomatic ;
cp. 218, and note there. A somewhat similar usage is illustrated in note on 930.

904. θανούμεθα. For the plur. immediately following the
sing. applied to the same person, see above **474.**

906. τοῦδ', sc. τοῦ λόγου τυχεῖν, 'lest she die without a hearing.'

910. κτενεῖ, not *interficiet* but *interficiendam probabit*, 'will
justify her death and ensure it.' ὥστε μ. φ. ' so as not to leave
a loop-hole for her escape.'

911. σχολῆς, 'this concession will require time,' lit. 'this
concession, it is the part of leisure (to make),' *i.e.* should be
made only by one who is not pressed for time.

916. ἐγὼ δ'. ' Yet (taking up) those charges which I deem
you would bring against me if you did begin an argument
with me, I will reply to your pleas, setting against each other
your charges against me and mine against you' (*i.e.* against
Hecuba, Priam, and Aphrodite to whom you will appeal);
ἅ σ' οἶμαι κατ. is 'as regards the charges which I think you
will make '; ἅ is not relative to τοῖς σοῖσι as an antecedent.
We must supply τοῖς ἐμοῖς after τὰ σά. For a similar and
equally natural ellipse, cp. note on 285.

919. ἀρχάς, plur. though referring to Paris only ; cp. ἅρπαις,
the sword of Perseus, *Ion* 192 ; ξίφεσι, sword of Ajax, Soph.
Aj. 231. So also 'Ιππόλυτος ... Πιτθέως παιδεύματα, *Hipp.* 11 ;
'Ελένην ... τάφῳ προσφάγματα, *Hec.* 265 ; and γάμοι passim.

922. δαλοῦ. Hec., when pregnant with Paris, dreamed
that she brought forth a lighted torch which burned the
city ; hence she was warned to expose the child she bore,
and Priam gave him to a servant to expose on Mount Ida ;
but the child escaped, and lived to fulfil the weird and
bring about the burning of the town.

925. δόσις, ·what she offered,' 'promised to him'; so ἐδίδου = 'offered.'

926. ἐξανιστάναι = ἀνάστατον ποιεῖν, 'to destroy.'

928. κρίνειεν = προκρίνειεν, 'prefer,'see L. and S. κρίνω, II. 7.

929. ἐκπαγλουμένη. Here ἐκπαγλέομαι means 'to express admiration,' generally 'to *feel* admiration.'

930. ὑπερδράμοι, 'should (be pronounced to) surpass,' so σὺ δ' ἦσθα ... ἄναξ, 'you (he used to say) are to be king,' *H. F.* 467; πλουτεῖς ἐν οἷ πλουτοῦσι, 'you talk of your riches and his poverty,' *And.* 212. So Cic. *Att.* ix. 2 B, "*Eripiebat* Hispanias: *tenebat* Asiam ... *persequebatur*," 'he *talked* of wresting the Spains from Pompeius, occupying Asia, pursuing him into Greece.'

931. τὸν ἔνθεν, 'the rest of the argument.' I have corrected the reading of all the edd., τὸν ἐνθένδ', which would introduce a very unpleasant *asyndeton* ; ἔνθεν is here, as often, a demonstrative adverb of time.

932. γάμοι, plural in same sense as singular ; see 919 ; γάμοι is here used of her illicit union with Paris : so in Πανὸς ἀναβοᾷ γάμους, *Hel.* 190. the word is applied to 'rape,' 'violence.'

934. οὔτ' ἐς δόρυ. The meaning is, 'neither have you on the one hand, being brave enough to fight, been worsted in battle ; nor on the other hand have you tamely submitted, and acquiesced in subjugation without a struggle ; no, you faced the barbarians and conquered them.' Literally, 'you are not subjected to the barbarians, either through facing them in battle (and failing therein) or by (accepting) their rule (without a struggle).' Cp. *Andr.* 680, *Iph. Aul.* 1400.

935. ἃ δ' ηὔτ., 'what was goodhap to Hellas was ruin to me, and I am taunted when I deserve only to be praised.' For the accusative, see Madv. *Syn.* § 27 a.

936. πραθεῖσα, 'betrayed,' 'undone,' lit. 'sold,' see L. and S. πιπράσκω, II.

937. ἐξ ὧν = ἐκ τούτων ἐξ ὧν, 'by those at whose hands I ought to have received a crown for my head.'

938. αὐτὰ τὰν ποσίν, 'you will say I am evading the very point at issue,' my clandestine flight from your house.

941. ἀλάστωρ. Paris is called 'the evil genius' of Hecuba. Nauck reads ὁ τῆσδε ληστήρ, and in 942, εἴτ' ἀλάστορα for εἴτε καὶ Πάριν.

944. Κρησίαν. Paris took advantage of the absence of Men. in Crete.

946. **φρονήσασ'** ἐκ δόμων, Nauck ; φρονοῦσα (or φρονοῦσά γ'), MSS. ; φρονοῦσ' ἐκ δωμάτων, Dind.

948. **τὴν θεόν.** Aphrodite. Paley would omit τήν, but see *H. F.* 1129, τὴν θεὸν ἐάσας, where the metre demands the article.

951. **ἔνθεν δ'.** ἔνθεν is here a relative adverb of place = ὅθεν, *unde*; 'but (to advert to a point) *from whence* you might draw a specious argument against me.' The point is that when Paris died she should have returned to the Greeks, for then she could plead no union brought about by divine agency (θεοπόνητα), as was her union with Paris brought about by Aphrodite; her subsequent union with Deiphobus was not θεοπόνητος. She pleads in her defence violence and constraint on the part of Deiphobus.

958. **σῶμα κλέπτουσαν**, 'trying to escape by stealth.' The pres. part. is also used as an imperf. part.; she would have said, σῶμ' ἔκλεπτον, 'I tried to escape,' and the part. means the same thing ; see Goodwin, § 16. 2, οἶδα δὲ κἀκείνω σωφρονοῦντε, ἔστε συνήστην, 'I know that these *were*,' etc., Xen. *Mem.* i. 2. 18.

961. **ἐνδίκως.** This passage can hardly be sound. Eur. would not have written ἐνδίκως ... δικαίως. It has been attempted to explain ἐνδίκως as referring to the abstract justice of Helen's death, while δικαίως refers especially to the question whether Men. was the fit agent to inflict it ; but no such distinction can be made out. The best conjecture hitherto put forward is that of Seidler and Hermann, δίκαιος for δικαίως, 'how then, justified as I am, could I justly be slain by thee, my husband?' δίκαιος, fem., is common enough in Eur. But none of the conjectures are even probable. I have obelized the passage. But I am strongly disposed to believe that Eur. wrote as follows :

πῶς οὖν ἔτ' ἂν θνήσκοιμ' ἂν ἐνδίκως, πόσι,
πρὸς σοῦ ; δικαίοις ἦν ὁ μὲν βία γαμεῖ.

δικαίοις is the ind. pres. 2nd pers. of δικαιόω, and the meaning is, 'dost thou punish her whom,' etc., or 'thou punishest her whom,' etc. ; for this use of δικαιόω, cp. εἴ τινα πυνθάνοιτο ὑβρίζοντα τοῦτον ... κατ' ἀξίην ἑκάστου ἀδικήματος ἐδικαίευ, Hdt. i. 100. It may be added that *Chr. Pat.* 2594 has the word δικαιοῦσα. Mr. A. C. Pearson would read, θνήσκοιμ' ἐναισίμως, πόσι,| πρὸς σοῦ δικαίως θ', comparing for ἐναισίμως *Alc.* 1077.

963. **τὰ δ' οἴκοθεν κεῖν'.** These words are usually explained as meaning 'that natural gift,' viz. 'beauty,' οἴκοθεν in 648 above being compared ; but this makes it very hard to give a ˍ

good sense to ἐδούλευσ', of which τὰ οἴκοθεν is supposed to be the subject. It seems to me much better to take ἐδούλευσ' for ἐδούλευσα, and explain, 'and as regards my domestic life in his (Deiphobus') house, I was in bitter servitude instead of being the prize of victory.' We are told by a schol. on Homer, that on the death of Paris, Πρίαμος τὸν Ἑλένης γάμον ἔπαθλον ἔθηκε τῷ ἀριστεύσαντι κατὰ τὴν μάχην· Δηΐφοβος δὲ γενναίως ἀγωνισάμενος ἔγημεν αὐτήν : Helen therefore was actually 'the prize of victory' (νικητήρια), but instead of being treated as such she was forced to live a life of constraint and slavery. It would seem impossible that Eur. would make Helen say, 'My natural gifts (i.e. beauty) lived in slavery instead of (gaining) the prize of victory'; what prize of victory? Moreover, a passage of Seneca, Tro. 920, written apparently with reminiscence of the passage now under consideration, seems to me to show that ἐδούλευσ' is 1st pers. Helen, in comparing her sufferings with those of the Greeks, says : "Durum et invisum et grave est | Servitia ferre ; patior hoc olim iugum | Annis decem captiva." Busche conjectures καίν' for κεῖν', 'I suffered a new slavery.'

965. τὸ χρῄζειν. χρῄζειν would have been more natural ; but we find the article with the infin. even in much stronger cases than this, e.g. μακρὸς τὸ κρῖναι ... χρόνος, Soph. El. 1030 ; τὸ ... δρᾶν ... ἀμήχανος, Ant. 79 ; καρδίας δ' ἐξίσταμαι τὸ δρᾶν, 1105 ; so Trach. 1115, Thuc. ii. 53, Eur. Frag. 901. 6.

967. πειθώ, 'showing the rottenness of her specious plea.

973. ἀπημπόλα, 'was ready to barter away' (as a bribe to Paris to adjudge her the victory). The imperfect, as Mr. Stanley remarks, refers to what the agent was ready to do, as ἐδίδου, 'he offered to give,' Aesch. 3. 83. See Madv. Greek Syntax, § 113, Rem. 1 ; and Goodwin, M. and T. § 11, note 2. A very good example is Ar. Nub. 63, προσετίθει, 'she wanted to add.' The meaning is, 'Here and Pallas would never have sacrificed Greece, and with it their favourite cities, for victory in a trial which was merely a freak and a whim (παιδιαῖσι καὶ χλιδῇ).'

980. ἐξῃτήσατο, 'asked as a boon from her sire,' not gained as a boon ; ἐξαιτεῖσθαι can mean 'to gain as a boon' when followed by accus. with infin., as in Her. 49 ; but with accus. rei it means either (1) 'to crave a boon,' as here, Heracl. 476 etc., or (2) 'to avert by begging,' deprecari, as in τὰ πρόσθεν σφάλματ' ἐξ., And. 54.

981. μὴ μαθεῖς ποίει = μὴ ἀμαθεῖς ποίει, 'do not assume them to be irrational' ; see L. and S., ποιέω, A. vi. Cp. faciamus,

'assume,' 'make out,' in Cic. ἀμαθία sometimes means 'brutishness,' as in *And.* 170, but does not mean 'lewdness,' like μωρία, ἀφροσύνη.

982. μὴ οὐ πείσῃς, take care 'lest you fail to convince the judicious'; οὐ was inserted by Seidler, and is to be taken closely with πείσῃς : some word like ὅρα is to be understood ; cp. ἄθρει, μὴ τοῦτο ᾖ τὸ ἀγαθόν, Plat. *Gorg.* 495 B ; μὴ οὐ θεμιτὸν ᾖ, Plat. *Phaed.* 67 B, where the antecedent verb is omitted, as here.

984. Μενέλεω, gen.

985. ἄν, often found twice in a verse ; three times below, 1244.

986. αὐταῖς 'Αμ., 'Amyclae and all'; Amyclae, a city of Laconia, was the kingdom of Tyndarus, the father of Helen, and therefore the dwelling-place of Helen in her maidenhood. The idea of the power of the goddess to transport Helen with the whole town in which she dwelt to Ilium, was probably suggested by the boast of Zeus, Θ. 20 ff., as Paley suggests.

988. ἐποιήθη, 'transformed itself into,' 'constituted itself a goddess of desire.' Helen had pleaded that Aphrodite had come with Paris to Sparta, and that it was in vain to try to resist the goddess who inspired her with passion ; Hec. replies, 'she never came or inspired you ; it was your own passions which you allowed to exercise on you the influence of Aphrodite : all lewd desires do in us the work of Aphrodite ' The verb ἐποιήθη might also be explained, ' was assumed to be,' as ποίει, 981.   Matth. renders "fecit id quod tu Veneri tribuis, locum Veneris apud te tenuit," thus halting between the two explanations which I have offered.

990. ἄρχει, 'and rightly the name of the goddess *Aphrodite* has in it the beginning of the word ἀφρο-σύνη.'   The fact that the first two syllables of ἀφρο-σύνη, 'lewdness,' are found in 'Αφρο-δίτη is made the theme of an etymologizing passage which reminds us of *Bacch.* 286 ff.   It will be seen at once that ἄφρο- (ἀφρός, ' foam ') in 'Αφροδίτη has no affinity whatever with ἀφρο- (ἄφρων, 'lewd') in ἀφροσύνη. On the etymologizing vein in Eur. see *Bacch.* p. xxxviii. To this verse is prefixed in Cod. Havn. the word ὡραῖον. This is the word which the scholiasts used to express their admiration of a line ; so also γν. = γνώμη or γνωμικόν, and κ. = καλόν.   These marginal expressions of admiration often lead to corruption. With the present passage cp. Aesch. *Theb.* 578, δίς τ' ἐν τελευτῇ τοὔνομ' ἐνδατούμενος, where the prophet must be supposed to have said some such words as ὦ Πολύνεικες νεῖκος ἔφυς, as in *Phoen.*

1495, ὦ Πολύνεικες ἔφυς ἄρ' ἐπώνυμος : thus the meaning of the Aeschylean passage would be that the seer divided the name into Πολύ- and -νεικες, and repeated the latter half. So here *Aphrodite* is said to have the first half of ἀφροσύνη in her name; the words could not mean, ' begins with ἀφροσύνη,' nor indeed would this be a true statement.

991. ὄν, rel. to νιν 988.

993. Ἄργει = Peloponnesus ; see 242. ' In Argos didst thou sojourn with scant means, and thoughtest that, escaped from Sparta, thou couldst deluge with thy extravagances the city of the Trojans, though overflowing with gold.' But perhaps κατακλύσειν ῥέουσαν is proleptic, 'to deluge it till it flowed with gold' (squandered by thee). The sentiment would be more natural if πόλιν could be taken as subject of κατακλύσειν, ' that it would deluge you with gold ' ; but with the nom. partic. preceding, and the ellipse of σε, this would be out of the question.

997. ἐγκαθυβρίζειν, epexegetic, ' large enough for thy luxury to revel in.'

1001. κατ' ἄστρα, ' not yet translated to the skies.'

1003. ἀγωνία. "ἀγωνία, παλαίστρα· 'Εὐριπίδης δὲ Τρῴασι, πόλεμον."—Hesych.

1004. τοῦδε, ' if the cause of Men was reported to you to be triumphing.'

1009. τἀρετῇ δ' οὐκ ἤθελες. Sc. ἄμ' ἔπεσθαι.

1010. κλέπτειν, imperf. infin. ; see on 958, and Goodwin, § 15, 3, 'You say you used to try to flee by stealth, letting yourself down with ropes from the ramparts.'

1012. ἐλήφθης. The meaning is, 'why did you not destroy yourself ?'

1017. γαμοῦσι, future.

1020. γάρ, for γάρ standing fourth word in sentence, see on *Bacch.* 451.

1022. ἐπὶ τοῖσδε, ' after all this,' "sic re se habente, his a te commissis sceleribus." as the old Comm. explain ; cp. 1028.

1024 τὸν αὐτὸν πόσει, 'lookedst on the same heaven as thy husband' ; ὁ αὐτός often takes a dat. to denote agreement, like ὅμοιος, παραπλήσιος : cp. 1049 below and τὸν αὐτὸν χῶρον ἐκλιπὼν ἐμοί, Aesch. *Cho.* 543. So "idem facit occidenti," 'as if he killed,' Hor. *A. P.* 467 ; "eadem facit omnia turpi," ' same as an ugly woman,' Lucr. iv. 1168.

1025. **ἐρειπίοις**, 'in tattered weeds,' usually of 'wrecks' or 'ruins,' used of 'carcases' of slaughtered sheep in Soph. *Aj.* 308, and as here in *Niobe* of Soph., λεπτοσπαθήτων χλανιδίων ἐρειπίοις (Frag. 400, Dind.).

1026. **ἀπεσκ.** Properly 'scalped'; here, as in *El.* 241, ἐσκυθισμένον, 'shorn bare.' Hdt. iv. 64, describes how the Scythians scalped their slain.

1032. **θνήσκειν**, 'that she *shall* die,' the pres. infin. is found instead of the fut. when it follows verbs of *commanding*, such as θὲς νόμον here ; as εἰπὼν μηδένα παριέναι εἰς τὴν ἀκρόπολιν, 'having given orders that no one *should pass* into the citadel,' Xen. *Hell.* v. 2. 29 ; Goodwin, § 15, 2, note 3.

1034. **πρὸς Ἑλ. ψόγον,** 'save yourself from a charge of unmanliness on the part of Hellas'; ψόγον πρὸς Ἑλλ. is 'blame from Greece,' and τὸ θῆλυ is added to specify the nature of the charge to be brought against Men. Cp. *Med.* 218, δύσκλειαν ἐκτήσαντο καὶ ῥᾳθυμίαν, where the meaning is δύσκλειαν ῥᾳθυμίας, as here the meaning is ψόγον θηλύτητος.

1036. **ἐμοί,** 'you have come to the same judgment as I, that she, of free will, left my house for a stranger's bed, and the Cyprian goddess has been brought into her plea but for the sake of speciousness.' ἐνεῖται, perf. pass. of ἐνίημι. The point in the whole case regarded as most cardinal by Helen, Hecuba, and Menelaus, is the question whether agency of Aphrodite can be proved in extenuation—a strong contrast to the modern point of view. Helen has recourse to it again in 1042.

1040. **ἀπόδος,** 'atone for,' as in I. 387, πρίν γ' ἀπὸ πᾶσαν ἐμοὶ δόμεναι θυμαλγέα λώβην. The word really means only *reddere.*

1044. **μὴ προδῷς.** For μὴ with aor. subj. in prohibitions, see Goodwin, § 86.

1046. **δ',** 'for I at once declare my indifference to her.' See on 53 above. δέ sometimes connects two clauses which stand to each other in the relation of cause and effect, and to some extent = γάρ : cp. Z. 160, τῷ δὲ γυνὴ Προίτου ἐπεμήνατο. '*for* the wife of P.'

1049. **σοὶ ταὐτόν,** see on 1024. This passage is extremely skilful. Hec. still fears the influence of Helen's fascinations, and says, 'let her not embark on the same ship with thee.' Men. replies with scornful confidence in his resolution, 'What, is she then heavier than of yore ! will she sink the vessel?' Hec. 'He is no lover who loves not for ever.' Men. 'That is as the heart of the loved one may have proved.' Cp. for the sentiment Andromeda (Frag. 140), ὅσοι γὰρ εἰς ἔρωτα πίπτουσιν βροτῶν | ἐσθλῶν ὅταν τύχωσι τῶν ἐρωμένων | οὐκ ἔσθ' ὁποίας λείπεται τόθ' ἡδονῆς. Very like 105 in expression is Moore's "The heart that once truly loved never forgets, But fondly loves on to the close"; but the meaning of the Greek verse is rather that when a man is once strongly enamoured, the feeling can always be aroused again. It is more like "They sin who tell us love can die," Southey, *Curse of Kehama*, a. 10.

1057. θήσει. τιθέναι, with dat. without prep. is a poetical usage, *e.g.* χέρσῳ ... θεῖναι, *Hel.* 1064; ἔθηκε ... ξυγάστρῳ δῶρον, Soph. *Trach.* 691; 'she will put in all women continence,' *e.g.* 'she will inspire them with a regard for continence.' He adds, 'This is no easy task; yet her downfall will alarm their incontinence, even though they be yet more hateful than she is.' But certainly σωφρονεῖν πάσαισι θήσει is a very harsh expression, especially as there is no article before σωφρονεῖν. To read πάσαις ἐνήσει would be an improvement; but a word is needed which would mean ' to warn,' 'to enjoin on'; perhaps we might read φήσει for θήσει, 'she will (by her fate) *tell* all women to be chaste.'

1060. Mr. Way's spirited version is as follows:

"So then thy temple in Troy fair-gleaming,
And thine altar of incense heavenward steaming,
    Hast thou rendered up to our foes Achaean,
O Zeus, and the flame of our sacrificing,
And the holy burg with its myrrh-smoke rising,
    And the ivy-mantled glens Idaean
Overstreamed with the wan snow riverward-rushing,
And the haunted bowers of the World's Wall, flushing
    With the first shafts flashed through the empyrean!

"Thine altars are cold; and the blithesome calling
Of the dancers is hushed; nor at twilight's falling
    To the night-long vigils of gods cometh waking.
They are vanished, thy carven images golden,
And the twelve moon-feasts of the Phrygians holden.
    Dost thou care, O King, I muse, heart-aching,—
Thou who sittest on high in the far blue heaven
Enthroned,—that my city to ruin is given,
    That the bands of her strength is the fire-blast break-
        ing?

"O my belovèd, O husband mine,
    Thou art dead, and unburied thou wanderest yonder,
Unwashen!—but me shall the keel thro' the brine
Waft, onward sped by its pinions of pine,

To the horse-land Argos, where that stone wonder
The Cyclop walls cleave the clouds asunder.
And our babes at the gates, in a long, long line,
Cling to their mothers with wail and with weeping that
    cannot avail—
'O mother,' they moan, 'alone, alone, woe's me! the
    Achaeans hale
Me from thy sight—from thine—
To the dark ship, soon o'er the surge to be riding,
    To Salamis gliding,
    To the hallowed strand,
Or the Isthmian hill 'twixt the two seas swelling,
    Where the gates of the dwelling
    Of Pelops stand!'

"Oh that, when, far o'er the mid-sea sped,
    Menelaus' galley is onward sailing,
On the midst of her oars might the thunderbolt dread
    Crash down, the Aegean's wildfire red,
Since from Ilium me with weeping and wailing
Unto thraldom in Hellas hence is he haling :
And lo, Zeus' daughter, like maid unwed,
Hath joy of her mirrors of gold, and her state as of right
    doth she hold !
Nevermore may he come to Laconia, home of his sires :
    be his hearth aye cold !
    Never Pitanè's streets may he tread,
Nor the Goddess's temple brazen-gated,
    With the evil-fated
    For his prize, who for shame
Unto all wide Hellas's sons and daughters,
    And for woe to the waters
    Of Simoïs, came !

    "Woe's me, woe's me !
Afflictions new, ere the old be past,
On our land are falling !   Behold and see,
Ye wives of the Trojans, horror-aghast,
Dead Astyanax, by the Danaans cast
From the towers, slain pitilessly."

1064. αἰθερίας, 'the smoke of the myrrh as it (when burnt)
mounts high into air,' cp. 325, and αἰθερία δ' ἀνέπτα, *Med.* 440.

1069. πρωτόβολον, 'and that limit of the land, the holy
abode that brightens under the first shafts of the rising sun.'
There was an ancient opinion that Mount Ida received the
first rays of sun, which it collected and formed into an orb ;

and hence it was supposed to be the boundary of the world
on the east; Lucr. v. 662, says, 'Thus they tell that from the
high mountains of Ida scattered fires are seen at day-break,
that these then unite as it were into a single ball, and make
up an orb ' (Munro's trans.). So Pomponius Mela, whom Musgrave quotes : " Pene a media nocte spargi ignes passimque
micare, et, ut lux appropinquat, ita coire ac se coniungere
videntur," ii. 18. Hence Musgrave suggested νύχα λαμπομέναν,
and certainly καταλαμπομέναν is weak, unless taken, as in the
above rendering, close with πρωτόβολον ἁλίῳ.

1073. παννυχίδες, 'night festivals,' *pervigilia.*

1074. ξοάνων τύποι, periphrasis for ξόανα='statues,' 'images '
of the gods.

1075. σελᾶναι, the recurring festivals, twelve in all, held
on the νουμηνία, or first of each month, which was sacred to
Apollo. σελήνη often means ' month ' in Eur.; here ' monthly
festivals ' at the full moon, according to some, but more probably on the νουμηνία. In the *Erechtheus* (Frag. 352) σελῆναι are
round (full-moon-shaped) cakes, ὁμοίως δὲ καὶ αἱ σελῆναι
πέμματα πλατέα κυκλοτερῆ, Suid., and again ἐν 'Ερεχθεῖ τὰς
σελήνας πελάνους εἴρηκεν Εὔρ., *i.e.* the πέλανοι, or 'sacrificial
cakes,' mentioned in 1063.

1077. μέλει, ' on my soul weighs the thought, whether thou
mindest thee of these things mounted on thy heavenly throne,
even the air.' μέλει is also followed by ὅπως, ὡς, μή : ἐπιβεβὼς
with accus. usually means 'lighting upon ' or ' going to,' or
' attacking,' but we find the phrase νῶθ' ἵππων ἐπιβάντες, and
there is here a hinted metaphor from mounting a steed. Eur.
affects this metaphor, cp. ἀναχαιτίσειε and νώτοις of a tree,
Bacch. 1070. 2.

1078. οὐράνιον, perhaps for the metre we should read
ὀράνιον, the Aeolic form, as Dind. does in Soph. *O. C.* 1466.

1084. ἀλαίνεις, 'wanderest forlorn.' "Secus inferorum ripas
animae vagantur, quorum corpora sepultura carebant," Barnes.

1085. ἄνυδρος. ' without the lustral water,' which formed
part of the rite of sepulture. See 1152.

1088. νέμονται, '(men) inhabit,' τείχη being accus.; but it
is quite possible that τείχη is nom., and the subject of the verb
νέμονται, though τείχη is neut. and νέμονται plur.; for τείχη
implies and really means πόλεις. We have already had many
instances of this constr. πρὸς τὸ σημαινόμενον in this play. See
on 119, 531, 735, 852, 1090, 1209, 1223. Neut. plur. with
plur. verb is a common epic usage, as in καὶ δὴ δοῦρα σέσηπε
νεῶν καὶ σπάρτα λέλυνται, B. 135.

1090. **κατ**ά**ορα** agrees with τέκνα implied in τέκνων πλῆθος. κατήορα (ἀείρω) is 'hanging from their mothers' clothes,' cp. ἄλοχον ... ὑποσειραίους ... ἕλκουσαν, *H. F.* 445; ἐκκρήμνασθε πατρῴων πέπλων, *H. F.* 520; μέθεσθ' ἐμῶν πέπλων, *H. F.* 627. The rest of the strophe is the cry of the children.

1094. **ναῦν :** after this word some words like ὥστε με πέμπειν must be understood ; 'they are bearing me to the dark hulk to take me to Salamis or Corinth.'

1097. **δίπορον κορ.** "**Ισθ.** = the peak of Acrocorinthus on the isthmus, commanding two straits ; δίπορον = *bimarem*.

1098. **πύλας,** 'where the holds of Pelops have their gate '; the isthmus is the gate of Peloponnesus.

1100-1105. **Μενέλα,** gen.; the nom. has three forms, Μενέλαος, Μενέλεως, Μενέλας. ἀκάτου ἰούσας is the gen. absolute ; 'would that, while the bark of Men. was walking the midmost main, an awful levin bolt of the Aegaean, hurled with both hands (by Zeus) would fall in the midst of the oars.' ἰέναι, with accus. = 'to traverse,' is common in Attic ; Homer uses the gen., not accus. πλατᾶν (gen. plur.) is Seidler's correction of πλάταν of the MSS.; but the passage still labours under difficulties, some reference to Zeus as the hurler of the lightning seems required ; hence Reiske thought that δίπαλτον might mean διϊ-παλτον, but there is no analogy for such a word. Musgrave again conjectured Ἰδαίου (sc. Διός) for Αἰγαίου, which last word indeed is far from satisfactory : if sound, Αἰγαίου πῦρ must be 'a bolt such as often descends on the Aegaean,' which is noted for its thunder-storms. In favour of Musgrave's conjecture it may be urged that Zeus is described in the *Iliad* as Ἰδηθεν μεδέων, and we have ὅς Διὸς ἱρεὺς | Ἰδαίου ἐτέτυκτο, II. 606. We have in *Hel.* 130. μέσον περῶσι πέλαγος Αἰγαίου πόρου, but the order of the words here quite precludes the possibility of connecting πέλαγος Αἰγαίου (πόρου being understood).

1104. **ὅτε,** 'now that,' with a semi-causal sense, as in Ar. *Nub.* 34, *Ach.* 647, Soph. *Aj.* 1095, etc. See 1162 below.

1105. **γᾶθεν,** 'from my country Ilium '; cp. "Thebis indidem," 'from the same Thebes,' Nep. *Epam.* v. 2.

1107. **χάριτας,** see on 836, 'the delight of girls '; cp. *Or.* 1112. Διὸς κόρα is, of course, Helen, who is supposed by the chorus to be in the enjoyment of her wonted luxuries. They have no faith in Menelaus' intention of putting her to death. χρύσεα ... κορᾶ is parenthetical. The subject of ἔλθοι in next verse is Μενέλεως.

1111. **Πιτάνας,** one of the divisions of the city of Sparta.

1112. χαλκόπυλόν τε θεάν, Athenè Chalcioecus, who had a temple in the acropolis of Lacedaemon.

1114. ἑλών, 'having captured her who by her adultery brought scathe and scorn on mighty Hellas, and bitter woe on the waters of Simois.' Again, ἑλών is used with a play on the name Ἑλένη.

1118. καινῶν, gen. after μεταβάλλουσαι, 'here are new mishaps coming in exchange for (i.e. in succession to) others still new'; μετ. is intrans.

1122. ἔχουσιν, see on 317; the connection of the aor. part. with ἔχω, to denote at once the preceding action and the present state, is almost a periphrasis of the perfect; the usage is mostly confined to the poets, but is found not unfrequently in Xenophon, where however it is the perf. part. not the aor. that is joined with ἔχω. The aor. in this phrase has that *present* signification which is commented on in note on 53 above.

1123. πίτυλος, 'the steady sweep of one ship's oarage that was left behind is to take the rest of the spoils of Neoptolemus to Phthia'; see 816. λελ. refers in grammar to πίτυλος and in sense to νεώς: see 533, 564.

1126. ἀνῆκται, 'has set sail'; ἀνάγειν ναῦν and ἀνάγειν absol. are used in the sense of 'to put a ship to sea,' lit. 'to lead up'; the ship at sea, appearing to be raised toward the horizon line, is said to be μετέωρος. The anapaest in the fourth foot is quite justifiable in the case of a proper name, the first two syllables of Νεοπτόλεμος are pronounced as one.

1129. οὐ θᾶσσον οὕνεκ', lit. 'being influenced by which consideration more than (by) having any pleasure in staying, he is gone,' (i.e. 'more than any convenience he might have found in waiting to see all his prizes put on board'). The phrase is somewhat contorted, and many conjectures have been made, especially οὐ for ἤ (Seidler), ἔχειν for ἔχω (Hermann), i.e. 'too quickly to feel any pleasure in staying.' But there is no occasion for change. Cp. Soph. O. C. 890, οὗ χάριν | δεῦρ' ᾖξα θᾶσσον ἢ καθ' ἡδονὴν ποδός.

1131. ἀγωγός, 'drawing from me many a tear'; we have ἄγειν δάκρυ in this sense in Alc. 1081.

1134. θάψαι, sc. τινά, 'she asked of Neopt. that Ast. might be buried,' cp. παῖδας δὲ μεῖναι τοὺς ἐμοὺς αἰτήσομαι, Med. 780, 'I will pray that they may remain.' Barnes proposed σ' for σφ', and Nauck κἄμ' ᾐτήσατο, but without reason.

1138. νιν is added because the verb πορεῦσαι stands at some distance from its object, 'the shield of brass, the terror of the Greek.'

1140. λύπας ὁρᾶν, in apposition to the foregoing clause, μή νιν πορεῦσαι, 'that he should not bring to the chamber, where Andromache is to meet her new lord, the shield of Hector to be a pain to her eyes.'

1141. κέδρου ... λαΐνων. The words refer to the modes of burial customary at Athens. "Recent investigations of numerous graves in the Attic plain seem to prove that the burial of unburnt bodies in earthen or wooden coffins or in grave-chambers cut from the living rock, was at least as prevalent (as cremation); according to Cic. (Legg. ii. 22), the burying in grave-chambers cut from the rock was even the older of the two. The rocky soil of Attica, bare of trees, made this sort of burial, rather than cremation, convenient for the majority of the inhabitants."—Guhl and Koner, p. 292.

1142. θάψαι, sc. τινά, as above 1134, and τινὰ is again understood with δοῦναι in next verse. In all these cases in translation the passive voice might be used, the construction having been explained in a note, 'she prayed that he might be buried in this, and might be given into your arms,' etc.

1144. στεφάνοις. "An obolus, being the ferriage for Charon, was put into the mouth of the corpse; the body was then washed and anointed by the women and placed in a white shroud (πέπλοισιν, 143). It was crowned with flowers and wreaths, and thus prepared for the lying in state (πρόθεσις)." —Guhl and Koner, p. 289.

1145. 'Since she has now left the country, and the hurried departure of her lord Neopt. has prevented her from consigning the child to the tomb.' For ἀφείλετο μή, see Madv. Syn., § 210.

1148. ἀροῦμεν, so Elmsley for αἰροῦμεν of the MSS., see Heracl. 322. This word must come from ἀείρω (fut. ἀρῶ [ᾰ] contracted from ἀερῶ, which never occurs), for the fut. of αἴρω is ἀρῶ [ᾰ]. Now ἀείρειν δόρυ certainly does not mean 'to set sail.' We might possibly follow the ingenious explanation of Seidler (reading, however, ἐπαμπισχόντες, 2nd aor. part., not ἐπαμπίσχοντες, pres.) and understand 'having buried him we shall raise the spear over his tomb.' This Seidler shows to have been a custom in the case of those who met a violent death, the spear being a sign that the relatives of the dead bound themselves to take vengeance on the murderers. This ingenious view, which quite removes all difficulties in the language of the passage, he defends by these quotations from Harpocration: 'ἐπενεγκεῖν δόρυ ἐπὶ τῇ ἐκφορᾷ καὶ προαγορεύειν ἐπὶ τῷ μνήματι·' Δημοσθένης κατ' Εὐέργου καὶ Μνησιβούλου ταῦτά φησιν ἐπὶ τοῦ βιαίως ἀποθανόντος, i.e. Dem. in the case of a violent death uses the words 'to set up a spear at the burial and (thus) give warning at the tomb'; again (to translate in an abridged form, without giving the Greek, except where requisite), 'Istrius tells us, that in the case of Procris and Cephalus there is a tradition that Erechtheus stuck a spear in the ground at the grave, ἐπὶ τοῦ τάφου δόρυ καταπεπηγότα, διὰ τὸ νόμιμον εἶναι τοῖς προσήκουσι τοῦτον τὸν τρόπον μετέρχεσθαι τοὺς φονέας.' If δόρυ could mean 'a mast,' there would be no difficulty, for ancient Greek mariners are described frequently in Homer as lowering the mast into the ἱστοδόκη on coming into port, and raising it again by the πρότονοι when about to sail. But there is no warrant for δόρυ = 'a mast.' However, as αἴρειν τὰς ναῦς, αἴρειν στόλον, are good expressions for 'setting sail,' and as δόρυ certainly can mean 'a ship,' perhaps we may assume that αἴρειν δόρυ might mean 'to set sail.' In that case we ought to read here αἴρωμεν δόρυ, as Mr. Stanley suggests. It must be owned that the Greeks would hardly erect, or allow to be erected, a monument of vengeance against themselves.

1153. ἀναρρήξων, probably means 'to dig in the ground,' not 'to hew out of the rock,' for though the word would rather convey the latter sense, the phrase γῆν τῷδ' ἐπαμπισχόντες is in favour of the former.

1154. ὡς ξύντομ': the meaning is 'that your efforts and mine concurring and therefore abridged for us (in their duration) may start our oar on its homeward voyage.'

τἀπ' ἐμοῦ. The regular construction would have been τὰ ἀπὸ ἐμοῦ καὶ τὰ ἀπὸ σοῦ, because ἐμοῦ and σοῦ denote separate and contrasted sources of action; τἀπ' ἐμοῦ τε κἀπὸ σοῦ ought in strictness to mean the one indivisible act which you and I together perform. Eur. could here have written τἀπ' ἐμοῦ καὶ τἀπὸ σοῦ without any violation of the metre. But the poets allow themselves some latitude in cases like this; cp. τῶν ἄνω τε καὶ κάτω, Aesch. Cho. 116; τῶν ἁλόντων καὶ κρατησάντων, Agam. 315.

1156. θέσθε, addressed to the attendants of Tal., who had brought the body laid out on a shield.

1158. ὄγκον. We find ὄγκον τύχης, 'dignity of estate' in Frag. 81; ὄγκον absol. = 'repute,' Phoen. 717; ὄγκον ὀνόματος, 'high-sounding name,' Soph. Trach. 817; but none of these

is quite parallel to the present use, 'more renown for war
than for wisdom.' Yet we can hardly understand ὄγκον in a
sense which would be at least semi-physical, 'O ye whose
reasons are not so weighty as your spears.' ὄγκος is 'high-
blown pride' above 108.

1160. μὴ Τροίαν ποτέ, cp. Sen. *Tro.* 750, "hae manus Troiam
erigent?"

1161. οὐδὲν ἦτ' ἄρα, 'so you prove to have been after all
but cowards,' cp. ὅδ' ἦν ἄρα | ὁ ξυλλαβών με, 'this *is* then the
one that seized me,' Soph. *Phil.* 978 ; οὐκ ἦσαν, 'they turn out
not to be,' 'they are not after all,' *v.* 209. For this use of
the imperf. see Goodwin, § 11, note 6.

1162. ὅτε has the same sense as in 1105, 'so ye are after all
but cowards, *since* we used to fall beneath your arms, when
Hector was victorious in the fray, and many a doughty hand
besides ; yet, now ye are so greatly afraid of a child, though
the town is sacked and the Phrygians put to the sword.' The
passage might be taken thus : 'so ye were but cowards when
we used to fall before you, though Hector and many another
were victorious in the fray ; and now when the city is taken
ye are so afraid of a child.' But this would rather require
πόλεως θ' ἁλούσης. Moreover, the usage of ὅτε implied in the
first reading is quite common, see L. and S. ; the words
διωλλύμεσθα μὲν ἐδείσατε δὲ = διολλυμένων ἡμῶν ἐδείσατε, and ὅτε
goes with ἐδείσατε as well as with διωλλύμεσθα. Cp. "Occidis
parvus quidem | sed iam timendus," Sen. *Tro.* 800.

1166. ὅστις, *i.e.* οὐκ αἰνῶ φόβον τούτου ὅστις φοβεῖται μὴ διεξ.
λόγῳ, 'I commend not the fear of him who fears without
probing its grounds by reason.' Cp. *Med.* 220.

1171. νῦν δ' αὖτ'. This is an extremely obscure passage,
and there is no reason why we should suppose it to be corrupt.
αὖτ' = αὐτὸ seems to refer to τὸ τυραννεύειν implied in τυραννίδα
(or perhaps rather it = αὐτὰ and refers to all the foregoing
substantives), but we can hardly explain with Paley and
others that 'Ast. had seen with his eyes and known in his
mind only (*i.e.* not in practice and reality) what it was to be
a king, but had not had the opportunity to enjoy the honours
which he possessed by right in his own house.' We can
hardly explain thus, for ψυχή does not mean the 'reason,' thus
sharply contrasted with experience, in Eur., and even if it
did, γνοὺς σῇ ψυχῇ is incompatible with οὐκ οἶσθα. Now ψυχή
in Eur. means 'the life' or 'the feelings,' or it is a periphrasis
for a person, e.g. ψυχὴν Ὀρέστου = Ὀρέστην (cp. 786). It might
perhaps be taken here in the last sense : 'You have seen and

known what it is to be a king, but you do not know it in your
own person, and you never at all (οὐδὲν) experienced that rule
which was your heritage' (ἐν δόμοις ἔχων); σῇ ψυχῇ being supposed to be the same as ἐν σοί, 'in your own case.' Cp. 1252.
Herm. explains: "Vidisti quidem ista, sed nescis te vidisse, neque
iis usus es, quum tamen domi haberes." But this version slurs
the difficulty in σῇ ψυχῇ: does he take these words with γνούς
or with οἶσθα? in either case they are otiose, and (more
broadly) what would be the point in such a reflection as
'sovereignty, etc., thou sawest and didst understand *though
thou now knowest not that thou didst'*? The late Dr. Kennedy on
the appearance of this ed. in 1882 favoured me with the following communication : " I would place ἰδὼν μὲν γνούς τε between commas, construing σῇ ψυχῇ with οἶσθα, and taking it
to mean the soul, or departed spirit, of the child, which will
go down to Hades with no more than a child's knowledge, and
so abide there. Cp. ψυχὰς Ἄϊδι προΐαψεν | ἡρώων. This explains
the present tense, οἶσθα, otherwise, I think, inexplicable. The
sentiment μακάριος ἦσθ' ἂν is virtually the same as that ascribed
to Hector by Schiller in his *Hektor's Abschied*. But Christ-
ianity felicitates the child who dies free from human stains.
Paganism condoled with the child who died without human
glories and memories of human joys. Of course the μὲν ... δὲ
(in 1171, 1172) stand as they do, because the 'non-using' is
antithetic to the 'seeing and recognizing.' I send a translation of the context from 1167, which will show clearly my
interpretation of the lines ; οὐδὲν is, of course, adverbial :

'O dearest one, how sad thy fate in death !
For, in the city's front if thou hadst died
It's champion, having gained thy manhood's prime
And wedlock, and a monarch's godlike state,
Blest thou hadst been, if aught of these is blest.
But now—though thou didst see and recognize
These things, my child, thy spirit knows them not ;
None didst thou use, when thou wast housed with all.'

The maintenance of the life-state in Hades is well known as
the Greek creed. See the Νέκυια of Homer and of Virgil, and
the motives assigned by Oedipus for blinding himself." [We
might make the οὐκ before οἶσθα negative the whole sentence,
as οὐδὲν does in 633. The difficulty here would be that the
participles ἰδὼν and γνούς *precede* the οὐ which, according to
this theory, should negative them, but displacement of οὐ by
hyperbaton is not uncommon, e.g. Soph. *El.* 1062, δαρὸν οὐ for
οὐ δαρόν : *Phoen.* 877, τί δρῶν οὐ : *Hipp.* 587, χρῆν μὲν οὔ σ'
ἁμαρτάνειν.—H. C.]

1173. **κρατός** : βόστρυχον κρατὸs is the accus. of closer speci-
fication, σ' being directly governed by ἔκειρεν, 'ah, sad it is
that the walls of your country, the ramparts of Loxias, have
shorn you of the curling tresses that your mother tended so
oft.' The construction is ὡς ἀθλίωs τείχη πατρῷα, Λοξίου πυργώματα, ἔκειρέ σε κρατὸs βόστρυχον ὃν πόλλ' ἐκήπευσε κ.τ.λ.

1176. **φιλήμασίν τ' ἔδωκεν**, 'gave up to kisses'; cp. λουτροῖs
χρόα ἔδωκε, Hel. 1383.

1177. **ἵν' αἰσχρὰ μὴ λέγω**. This passage is generally explained by edd. as if Eur. had used the words ἔνθεν ἐκγελᾷ
ὀστέων ῥαγέντων φόνοs to avoid employing ἐκκέχυται ἐγκέφαλοs,
and they have inferred that ἐγκέφαλοs was regarded as a
coarse and disgusting word by the Greeks. This is quite
wrong. Homer often uses ἐγκέφαλοs, and so does Eur. himself, and no reflecting person could deny that the expression
in the text is absolutely shocking, if ἐκκέχυται ἐγκέφαλοs is
coarse. The fact is, neither expression is shocking, but the
phrase in the text is so vigorous that Eur. adds, 'not to say
anything shocking.' This phrase always introduces an
apology *for something said or about to be said*, and does not
refer to a phrase suppressed lest it should prove offensive; it
does not explain the reason why the phrase used is employed
and another avoided, but asks the indulgence of the hearers
for the phrase used : the words ἵνα μηδὲν ἐπαχθὲs εἴπω in Dem.
always *introduce* some phrase which he fears may possibly for
some reason offend some of his audience. ἔνθεν refers to βόστρυχον, 'from which spirts out the gore through the shattered
skull.' Cp. "caput | ruptum cerebro penitus expresso," Sen.
Tro. 1125. The metaphor of the 'exploding wave' in Plat.
Rep. 473 C, is a sufficient comment on the use of the word
ἐκγελᾷ. Cp. Frag. 388, κάρα τε γάρ σου συγχεῶ κόμαιs ὁμοῦ |
ῥανῶ δὲ πεδόσ' ἐγκέφαλον, also ·Cycl. 402, and a very similar
passage in Soph. *Trach.* 781.

1178. **εἰκούs**, 'resemblances,' 'how sweetly you remind me
of your father'; εἰκοὺs is acc. plur. of εἰκώ, a poetical form of
εἰκών implied in gen. εἰκοῦs (which is the MS. reading here),
acc. sing. εἰκώ, acc. plur. εἰκούs, but not found in nom. This
is a most beautiful and natural sentiment, as also are the
reflections which follow ; the conception of making Hecuba
see in the hands of her grandson something to remind her of
Hector, is very touching. The thought is expanded and
spoiled by Sen. *Tro.* 470 ff. and 655 ; but delicately used by
Virg. *Aen.* iii. 490, "Sic oculos, sic ille manus, sic ora ferebat";
Cp. also δ. 149.

1182. μῆτερ, used here simply as a term of respect to an old woman ; so in 629, 1228.

1184. κώμους, properly of a 'revelling band.' but also of any company, *e.g.* of hunters, and even of a flock of doves in the *Ion* 1197 ; hence Nauck's κομμούς is needless.

1188. ἄϋπνοί τε κλῖναι, I have here introduced a conjecture of my own for ὕπνοι τ᾽ ἐκεῖνοι of the MSS., which is explained, 'those broken or anxious sleeps,' but where are we to get 'broken' or 'anxious,' and this is the whole point of the phrase? The change is very slight ; ἄϋπνοι at the beginning of a verse would be very easily changed to ὕπνοι, and then ΤΕΚΛΙΝΑΙ having been changed to ΤΕΚΕΙΝΑΙ by an error in one letter, ἐκεῖναι would, of course, have been assimilated in gender to ὕπνοι. Cp. τροφαί τε ματρὸς ἄϋπνά τ᾽ ὀμμάτων τέλη, *Suppl.* 1138 ; ὕμνοι and πόνοι have been conjectured for ὕπνοι, but how could such a corruption be accounted for? Here the sense is most natural, 'all my kisses. all my fostering care, all my sleepless nights for thee, all have come to nought.' For κλῖναι, cp. κλισίας, 113 above. The late Prof. H. A. J. Munro suggested ὕπνοι τε κοινοί, comparing 54, 58, 706.

1189. γράψειεν, observe the two accusatives, like λέγειν τινά τι.

1193. ἰτέαν, properly 'a targe made of willow wicker-work'; cp. Virgil's "salignas umbonum crates."

1195. σώζουσ᾽, imperf. part.

1196. τύπος, the mark made by Hector's arm.

1197. περιδρόμοις, subst.

1199. προστιθεὶς γενειάδι, putting the arm with the shield on it to his chin.

1201. ἐς κάλλος, 'God gives us not such fortunes as to aim at adornment' ; cp. ἐς κάλλος ἀσκεῖ, *El.* 1073 : ἐς παρασκευήν, *Bacch.* 457 ; εἰς ἔριν θυμούμενος, Soph. *Aj.* 1018, and below 1211.

1204. τοῖς τρόποις. 'life' (or perhaps 'mischance,' see on verse 104 above), 'like an idiot in its haviour, leaps now this way. now that.' ἔμπληκτος ὡς ἄνθρωπος reminds one of Macbeth's terrible description of life, "It is a tale Told by an idiot, full of sound and fury Signifying nothing" ; or Tennyson's "Time a Maniac scattering dust And Life a Fury slinging flame." αὐτὸς εὐτ. = 'is uniformly happy' ; the MSS. give αὐτός, which may be explained 'of himself,' 'independent of the chances and changes of this mortal life.' With the whole passage cp. the opening lines of Seneca's *Troades*, and *ib.* 270 ff.

1207. πρὸ χειρῶν, 'in front of them,' *Rhes.* 374, Soph. *Ant.* 1279.

1209. νικήσαντά σε. Another example of the construction πρὸς τὸ σημαινόμενον, see on 119. The accus. is governed by some such word as στεφανοῖ implied in σοὶ προστίθησι ἀγάλματα, 1212.

1211. ἐς πλ. θηρώμενοι, 'not pursuing these public competitions to excess'; for ἐς, see 1201 ; the poet hints that the competition for success in the public games was pushed too far by the Greeks of his time, who in this respect contrasted unfavourably with eastern nations.

1213. τῶν σῶν ποτ' ὄντων, partitive gen.

1217. ἔθιγες. This is addressed to the dead Hector ; 'your death went to my heart.'

1221. καλλίνικε. This ought regularly to be the nom., but it is attracted into the case of μῆτερ as in ὄλβιε κῶρε γένοιο, Theocr. xvii. 66 ; cp. *Pers.* iii. 28, "stemmate quod Tusco ramum millesime ducis." Conversely nom. sometimes stands for vocative, as δύστηνος, ἀντὶ τοῦ ; Soph. *O. T.* 1155. οὖσα is the imperf. participle.

1223. οὐ θανοῦσα, 'thou must go to the grave with the dead, though thou diedst not.' θανοῦσα, is fem. because it refers to μῆτερ, of which σάκος is merely explanatory ; ἐπεὶ gives the reason why she has said στεφανοῦ, 'receive this garland' to the shield.

1227. ὄδυρμα, elsewhere 'a wailing,' is found only in plur., here 'an object of lamentation.' *Chr. Pat.* 1518 has ὄδυρμα in the same sense as here.

1228. μᾶτερ. See on 1182.

1231. τελαμῶσιν, 'bandages,' probably strips of the πέπλοι mentioned above : it was the custom of the ancients to wash and bind the wounds of the dead, and even to apply fomentations to them.

1232. τἄργα δ'. οὐ Though acting like a physician, 'having the name of one,' yet she cannot bring about τὰ ἔργα, the results of the healing art on her dead grandson.

1236. πιτύλους. See on 814.

1239. Herm. would fill the lacuna by θαρσήσασ', Musgr. by Ἑκάβη, σάφ'.

1240. οὐκ ... πόνοι. The reading of the MSS. is πλὴν οὑμοὶ πόνοι | Τροία τε ... μισουμένη, which Seidler has endeavoured to explain as follows, "nihil igitur actum est in concilio deorum

nisi ut me infelicem redderent et Troiam ante alias urbes
odissent," 'so it turns out (see on 1161) that the gods have
had but one concern, my woes, and Troy eminently abhorred
by them ; that their only business was (the inflicting of) woes
on me, and the (sating of) their hatred against Troy.' Before
πόνοι some word meaning 'vindictively inflicted' would be
taken out of μισουμένη. However, by very slight changes,
ἐμοὶ and Τροίᾳ and' μισουμένῃ, Bothe explains, 'so then the
gods have nothing but woe in store for me, and the eminently
hated Troy.' In Bothe's arrangement of the verse, ἐμοὶ would
be in a slightly unnatural position, but not more unnatural
than the exigencies of metre could well excuse. I feel sure
that Bothe's emendation should be accepted, and that the
verse cannot be satisfactorily explained in the way suggested
by Seidler. Mr. Stanley suggests οὐκ ἦν ἀρεστὸν θεοῖσι or οὐκ
ἤραρεν θεοῖσι, but ἄρα is quite requisite, and Bothe's correction
of the passage is simpler.

οὐκ ἦν ἐν θεοῖσι = ' the gods have nothing in store for me,'
is not a very normal expression, but is helped out by the well-
known epic tag, θεῶν ἐν γούνασι κεῖται.

1243. ⏑ — ⏑ — — The words of Eur. are here hopelessly
lost. V gives as the first words of next verse, ἀφανεῖς ἂν
ὄντες, and an obvious interpolator in P gives ἔστρεψέ τ' ἄνω,
meaning, of course, ἔστρεψε τἄνω. Many phrases could be
supplied here which would satisfy the metre and give sense,
but this would be merely an idle exercise of ingenuity in the
absence of all evidence. Still more idle is it to endeavour to
elicit some meaning from the guess of the interpolator of P,
and foist on Eur. some such grotesque reflection as ' had the
god swallowed us up by turning the surface of the earth
downwards, we should have vanished quite, and not been a
theme for poetry.' Equally absurd is the sentiment which
emerges if we accept the reading of Stephens, εἰ δὲ μὴ for εἰ δ'
ἡμᾶς in 1242, 'only for the utter destruction which the god
has inflicted on us we should never have been heard of.'

1244. ὑμνηθεῖμεν = ὑμνηθείημεν, 1st aor. pass. opt. Observe
ἂν thrice.

1252. ἐν σοὶ κατέκναψε, 'wretched mother who in your
person (i.e. by your death) has torn to tatters all the hopes of
her life.' ἐν for ἐπὶ and κατέκναψε for κατέγναψε (which violates
the metre) are the conjectures of Porson. For κατέκναψε is
usually read κατέκαμψε, the obvious conjecture of Burges,
' has brought to its goal' (metaphor from the δίαυλος). But
this is unnecessary. Recent edd. now invariably restore
κνάπτω for γνάπτω when the metre requires it, e.g. ἀλλ κναπτό-

μενοι, Aesch. *Pers.* 576. κνάπτω is properly to 'card' wool, then generally to 'mangle' or 'tear'; κατέκναψε is ἅπαξ εἰρημένον, but that is no reason for rejecting it. There are several ἅπαξ εἰρημένα in the *Bacchae* alone.

1253. ὡς depends on ὀλβισθείς, 'thou that wert deemed so blest for being the son of such a noble line, by a dread fate hast thou fallen.'
.

1256. κορυφαῖς, the 'heights' on which stood the acropolis.

1258. διερέσσοντας, διασείοντας, Hesych., 'wildly tossing their arms with their torches'; cp. use of ἐρέσσειν noted on 570.

1261. ἀργοῦσαν, not to keep the fire 'idle,' to let it *do its work*.

1265. μορφάς, 'two phases'; it is impossible to decide whether these two phases of the one command refer to (*a*) the directions to the λοχαγοί, (*b*) those to Hec. and the other Trojan dames, or to (*a'*) the rest of the captives who are to depart at the sound of the trump, (*b'*) Hec. who is to go at once. In *Iph. Aul.* 196 Eur. speaks of the πεσσῶν μορφαὶ πολύπλοκοι, and in Frag. 210 μορφαὶ is used of the various *phases* of human sorrow. Seidler reads μοίρας, Herm. μομφάς.

1272-1283.
   "Ah wretched I !—the uttermost is this,
   The deepest depth of all my miseries ;
   I leave my land ; my city is aflame !
   O aged foot, sore-striving press thou on
   That I may bid mine hapless town farewell.
   O Troy, midst burgs barbaric erst so proud,
   Soon of thy glorious name shalt thou be spoiled.
   They fire thee, and they hale us forth the land,
   Thralls !   O ye Gods !—why call I on the Gods ?
   For called on heretofore they hearkened not.
   Come, rush we on her pyre, for gloriously
   So with my blazing country should I die."—W.

1277. ἐμπνέουσ', imperf. part. δήποτ', 'once.'

1278. ἀφαιρήσει, future middle of ἀφαιρέω with passive meaning.   Dind. gives a 3rd future form, ἀφῃρήσει.

1287-1302.

HEC.   " Woe is me ! ah for the woes that be mine !
   Kronion, O Phrygian Lord, our begetter, our father,
   Dost thou see how calamity's tempests around us gather,
      Unmerited doom of Dardanus' line ?

CHO.   He hath seen : yet is Troy, the stately city,
   A city no more, destroyed without pity.

Hec.   Woe is me, woe, and a threefold woe !
Ilios is blazing, the ramparts of Pergamus crashing
Down, with the homes of our city, 'mid flames far-
        flashing
Over their ruins a furnace-glow !
With its wide-winged blackness the heaven's face
        covering,
O'er our spear-stricken land is the smoke-cloud
        hovering.
In madness of ruin-rush earthward they reel,
Our halls, 'neath the fire and the foemen's steel."
                                        —W.

1290. ἀνάξια. Zeus as the ancestor of Troy, being the father of Dardanus by Electra, daughter of Atlas, is called on to witness the sufferings of his people. The words ἀνάξια τᾶς Δαρδάνου γονᾶς probably mean 'things unworthy of (casting a slur on) the divine origin of Dardanus,' 'sufferings unworthy of our boast that we have Zeus to our father'; but the words may also mean 'undeserved by the race (descendants) of Dardanus.'

1292. ἁ δὲ μεγ., 'fallen, city no more, is the strong city; Troy is down.'

1297. ἄκρα. It can hardly be doubted that these verses, 1287-1293, 1294-1301, were antistrophic as written by Eur., but it is impossible to restore the antistrophic correspondence without resorting largely to conjecture. This verse, for instance, obviously does not correspond with the strophic verse 1289; hence we cannot pronounce whether ἄκρα is ἄκρᾱ, nom. fem. sing., or ἄκρᾰ, nom. neut. plur. from ἄκρον: in either case it refers to the 'peaks,' 'summits,' culmina, of the ramparts.

1300. πτέρυγι. This is usually taken to mean a 'fan'; cp. Or. 1426 ff., where feather-fans (ῥιπίδες) are spoken of as a Phrygian institution, and such a fan is described in the words εὐπᾶγι κύκλῳ πτερίνῳ: such an allusion then would be fitting in the mouth of the chorus here, 'the land is come to nought even as smoke before a fan' πτέρυγι might, however, refer to the wing of the wind. See 1320, and Jebb on Soph. O. C. 381.

1301. οὐράνια, 'having suffered a terrible fall'; cp. 519, οὐράνια βρέμοντα.

1303. ὦ τέκνα. Hec. calls on her children; the chorus cry, 'it is on the dead that thou callest in thy wailing.' Hec. 'Yes, I call on them, laying my old limbs on the ground, and beating the earth with my hands.' *Cho.* 'And we too in turn kneel on the ground and call on our lords in the under world.' διάδοχα is neut. plur. used adverbially. The chorus speaks of itself in the sing., though the words τοὺς ἐμοὺς ἀκοίτας imply its plurality.

1313. ἄϊστος, 'unconscious' here, as in 1321; the word often means 'unseen.' Unburied and friendless as he is, dead Priam is spared the consciousness of the present woe. This is a reflection to which Eur. is prone, e.g. κέρδος δ' ἐν κακοῖς ἀγνωσία, Frag. 204; cp. Gray's "No more! where ignorance is bliss, 'tis folly to be wise."

1318. ἔχετε. See above on φιλήμασίν τ' ἔδωκε, 1176; so here it would have been more natural to say, 'the deadly fire and the battle spear have you in their power,' than 'ye have in you the deadly fire,' etc.

1320. ἴσα, nom. fem. sing., as the antistrophic verse 1305 shows; 'and (soon) the dust (of the falling towers) like smoke shall rob me of the sight of my home, with its wings spread out on the air.' Some word like πετασθεῖσα must be supplied with πτέρυγι. The dust of the falling towers is *expressly* compared to smoke, and *covertly* to a huge wing which shut out the view of the town. Cp. Sen. *Tro.* 20, "Nec coelum patet | undante fumo; nube ceu densa obsitus | ater favilla squalet Iliaca dies."

1322. εἴσιν, 'will vanish,' lit. 'will go away so as not to be seen.' ἀφανὲς is proleptic.

1326. ἔνοσις, 'soon shall ruin engulf the whole town.' The falling towers are heard within.

1330. δούλειον. This word, like φόνιος above 1318, is oftener an adjective of three terminations, than of two, as here.

DESCRIPTION OF THE METRES.

I HAVE in the following pages given a description of all the metres in the play, omitting iambic trimeters, except when they are so mingled with choral metres as to be possibly not recognized. I may observe here, that the choral senarius is broadly distinguished from the common type of senarius by its purity. The choral senarius properly consists of pure iambi ; we sometimes, however, find in choral odes a not pure senarius, but in these cases the long syllable is resolved, and thus is avoided that weightiness which characterizes the senarius of dialogue and narration.

This play is unusually abundant in lyrical passages. Where these passages are not antistrophical, I refer to each line by its number among the verses of the whole play, adding the first and last words of the verse to prevent any possible confusion. In the antistrophic parts, I refer to each verse according to its place in the strophe, and I wish the reader to number each line of the strophe and antistrophe, 1, 2, 3, etc., in his copy. When the strophic and antistrophic verse correspond exactly, I set down one scheme for the two, but if there is any divergence, however small or however legitimate, even the resolution of a long syllable, I then give the scheme both of the strophic and antistrophic verse.

I have avoided technical terms as much as possible. Dactyls and trochees form the staple of every choral ode, and for this reason I should prefer to call a cretic a trochaic dipodia catalectic, but that *cretic* is a more familiar term to schoolboys. The choral odes are formidable to junior students, because they have been so overlaid with technical language. But let the teacher, instead of lecturing about paeons and epitrites, at once tell his class that most choruses are written in dactyls and trochees, and that there are a few other normal types with which he can become quite familiar after a few days' practice, and soon the task of detecting the rhythm in a

121

lyrical passage will become a pleasant exercise of the ear and
the intelligence, instead of a despairing effort of overloaded
memory. I think it will be useful here to quote some most
instructive words of Prof. B. H. Kennedy. The passage
occurs in his *Studia Sophoclea*, and he is condemning the
vagueness of Prof. Campbell's views about the scansion of the
choral odes.

"With respect to the metres of this chorus (Soph. *Oed. R.*
150-175), Campbell says of strophe a', 'the stately dactylic
measures are only once interrupted by the more meditative
iambic rhythm (152-160), and by a trimeter with anacrusis,
giving a sort of anapaestic turn.' Again, he speaks of 'iambic
and trochaic rhythms,' and of 'interchange of anapaestic with
dactylic' in strophe β'. Again, in strophe γ', of 'one dactylic
or anapaestic line,' while 'the other rhythms are iambic and
trochaic.' But, in regard to strophe β', he also alludes to
'the union of dactyls and trochees in logaoedic lines.' Had
he taken a comprehensive view of the metrical character of
the whole ode, he would have given more decided prominence
to this last feature, which he only mentions incidentally : he
would have seen that the whole character is dactylo-trochaic
or logaoedic, with frequent anacruses, giving not only to
dactylic lines an anapaestic semblance, but also to trochaic
an iambic air.

"The same reason which exists for scanning, as Campbell
does,

$$ἰ|ήιε \ Δάλιε \ Παιάν$$

also exists for scanning, as he does not,

$$Πυθ|ῶνος \ ἀγλαὰς \ ἔβας$$

and again,

$$ὦ \ | \ πόποι \ ἀνάριθμα \ γὰρ \ φέρω,$$

while the line which follows contains (whether so printed or
not), two verses :

$$πήμ|ατα \ νοσεῖ \ δέ \ μοι \ πρόπας$$
$$στόλος \ | \ οὐδ' \ ἔνι \ φροντίδος \ ἔγχος.$$

"It is of course admitted that a trochaic verse with anacrusis of one time becomes iambic, ('Mary, I believ'd thee
true,' becoming ' O Mary, I believ'd thee true '), as a dactylic
verse with anacrusis of two times becomes anapaestic, 'over
the water to Charlie,' becoming 'let us over the water to
Charlie'). What I mean is, that *whether the scansion shall
recognize anacrusis or not must depend on a general view of the
metrical character of the whole.* Thus, in the third line of an
Alcaic stanza, anacrusis must be recognized on account of the
dactylo-trochaic rhythm of the other lines."

The point to which I particularly wish to direct the attention of the student, is the principle so well expressed here by Prof. Kennedy, in the words which I have printed in italics. It was the neglect of this principle which so long obscured the character of the Alcaic and Sapphic stanzas. As an illustration of the unscientific method, let me give the metrical description of the Sapphic stanza as I was taught it at school. Here it is:

$$— \smile — — | — — \smile \smile — | \smile — — —$$

2nd epitrite, choriamb., bacchius ; the Adonic being of course recognized as dactylic $— \smile \smile — | — —$. To remember such a mode of scansion was a misdirected effort of memory. Now a general view of the metrical character of the whole teaches us that we have nothing but dactyls and trochees, and that the metre is :

$$— \smile | — \smile | — \smile \smile — | — \smile | — \smile \; (ter)$$
$$— \smile \smile | — \smile$$

a dactyl standing between two trochaic dipodies, and the Adonic being dactyl and trochee. Horace injured the effect of the metre by strengthening the first trochaic dipody (*i.e.* substituting a spondee for the second trochee), and precisely similar was his modification of the Alcaic stanza, of which I shall write down the Horatian type as an excellent illustration of the value of the doctrine of the anacrusis in giving solidarity to a stanza, which was once supposed to begin with iambi and end with dactyls and trochees. It will be seen that there is nothing in the stanza but dactyls and trochees :

$$\smile | — \smile | — — || — \smile \smile — | — \smile \smile \; (bis)$$
$$\smile | — \smile | — — | — \smile | — \smile$$
$$— \smile \smile | — \smile \smile | — \smile | — \smile$$

Here also, as in the Sapphic measure, Horace departed from the type of his Greek originals by strengthening the first dipody, in the first pair of verses and in the third verse.

METRES.

98–234. Anapaestic systems, for metrical anomalies in which see note on 98.

239–292.

239. τόδε ... πάλαι. $\smile \smile \smile | — \smile | — || \smile — | \smile \; \overline{\smile\smile} | — ||$ $\smile \smile \smile | — \smile | —$ dochmiac trimeter, two or three syllables having dropped out, perhaps πάρεσθ' or ὁ φόβος, which might be iterated after the manner of Eur.

241. αἰαῖ. ‿ —|‿ — iambic dimeter.

242. Θεσσαλίας ... χθονός. — ‿ ‿|— ‿|—||— ‿ ‿|— ‿|
— ||— —|— ‿|— dochm. trim.

245. τίνα ... μένει. ‿ ‿ ‿|‿ ‿ ‿|⌢ ||‿ ‿ ‿|— ‿|
— ||— ‿ ‿|— ‿|— dochm. trim.

247. τοὐμὸν ... Κασάνδραν. — —|‿ ‿ ‿|⌢ ||‿ ‿ ‿|
— ‿|—||— ‿ ‿|— —|— dochm. trim.

250. ἢ ... μοι, see note, where the proper form of the verse
is suggested; it probably ran somehow thus: ‿ —|— ‿|— ||
— —|— —|— ||‿ ‿ ‿|— —|— dochm. trim.

252. ἢ τὰν ... γέρας ὁ. — —|— —|— ||— ‿ ‿|— ‿|⌢
dochm. dim.

253. χρυσ....ζόαν. — ‿ ‿|— ‿|— ||‿ —|— ‿|—dochm.
dim.

256. ῥῖπτε. — ‿ ‿|— ‿ ‿|— dactyl.

257. κλάδας...στολμούς. ‿|— ‿ ‿|— ‿ ‿|— ‿|— ‿ ‿|
— ‿ ‿|— —|— dactyl. and troch. syzygies with short
anacrusis.

260. τί δ' ... τέκος. ‿ ‿ ‿|— ‿|⌢ ||‿ ‿ ‿|‿ ‿ ‿|
⌢ dochm. dim.

262. τῷ. — ‿ ‿|— —|— dochm.

265. ὤμοι ... ἐτεκόμαν. — ‿ ‿|— —|— ||— ‿ ‿|‿ ‿ ‿|
— dochm. dim.

266. ἀτὰρ ... Ἑλλάνων. ‿|— ‿ ‿|— ‿ ‿|— ‿|—·‿ ‿|
— ‿ ‿|— —|— dactyl. and troch. syzyg. with short anacr.

269. τί τόδ'...λεύσσει. This verse is incomplete as it stands.
It was probably a dochm. trim ; or possibly, ἔλακες being
repeated, it was a dochm. dim. with dactyl interposed between the dochmii, thus :
‿ ‿ ‿|‿ ‿ ‿|⌢ ||— ‿ ‿||— ‿ ‿|— —|—

271. τί δ'...δάμαρ. ‿|— —|— ‿ ‿|— ‿ ‿|— ‿|— ‿|
— dactyl. and troch. syzyg. with short anacr.

272. Ἄνδρ. ... τύχαν. — ‿ ‿|— ‿|—||‿ ‿ ‿|— ‿|—
dochm. dim.

275. ἐγώ...χερί. ‿|— ‿|—|— ‿ ‿|— ‿ ‿|— ‿|— ‿ ‿
dactyl. and troch. syzyg. with short anacr.: the first trochaic
dipody is catalectic—a very common feature in Pindar and
the Choral Odes. In fact the cretic foot is really a troch.
dip. cat.

276. δευομ. ... κάρᾳ. — ‿ ‿|— —|— ||‿ —|— ‿|—
dochm. dim.

279. ἄρασσε.   ⏑|— ⏑|— ⏑|— ⏑|-- troch. with anacr.,
the last catalectic (this feature I shall not notice again.)

280. ἔλκ'.   — ⏑ ⏑|— ⏑|— ⏑|— ⏑|—— dactyl. and
troch. syzyg.

281. ἰώ μοί μοι.   ⏑ —|—— antispast.

282. μυσαρῷ...δουλεύειν.   ⁀|— ⏑ ⏑|— ⏑ ⏑|— ⏑|— ⏑|
——|— dact. and troch. syzyg. with long anacr. resolved.

284. πολεμίῳ.   ⏑ ⏑ ⏑|—— ⏑|—‖⏑ ⏑ ⏑|— ⏑|— dochm.
dim.

285. ὃς ..ἐνθάδ'.   —|— ⏑|—|— ⏑|— ⏑ troch. with anacr.

286. ἀντίπαλ'.   — ⏑ ⏑|— ⏑ ⏑ ⏑|— ⏑|— ⏑|——|— dact.
and troch. syzyg.

287. φίλα...πάντων.   ⏑ ⏑ ⏑|⏑ ⏑ ⏑|⁀‖⏑ ⏑ ⏑|——|
— dochm. dim.

289. γοᾶσθέ μ'.   ⏑|— ⏑|—|— ⏑|— ⏑|—⏑ troch. with
anacr.

290. δύσποτμος.   — ⏑ ⏑|— ⏑|— dochm.

291. τάλαιν'.   ⏑|— ⏑|— ⏑|— ⏑|— troch. with anacr.

292. προσέπ.   ⏑ ⏑ ⏑|———|— dochm.

308-324 = 325-341.

1.   ⏑ ⏑ ⏑|⏑ ⏑ ⏑|—‖⏑ ⏑ ⏑|— ⏑|— dochm. dim. =
— ⏑ ⏑|— ⏑|⁀‖⏑ ⏑ ⏑|⏑ ⏑ ⏑⏒.

2.   ⏑ —|⏑ —| iamb. dip. = —— |—— (a license often taken
in exclamations).

3.   — ⏑ ⏑|⏑ ⏑ ⏑|— dochm.

4.   ⏑ ⏑ ⏑|— ⏑|⏑ ⏑ ⏑|— troch. dip. = ⏑ ⏑ ⏑|— ⏑|
— ⏑|—

5. lost = 329   ⏑ ⏑ ⏑|⏑ ⏑ ⏑ troch. dip.

6.   ⏑ ⏑ ⏑|— ⏑|—‖⏑ ⏑ ⏑|——|— dochm. dim.

7.   ⏑ —|⏑ —|⏑ —|⏑ — iamb. dim.

8.   ⏑ —|— ⏑ ⏑|— ⏑|— glycon.

9.   ⏑ —|⏑ —|⏑ ⏑ ⏑|⏑ ⏑ ⏑ iamb. dim.

10.   ⏑ —|⏑ —|⏑ —|⏑ ⏑ ⏑|⏑ ⏑ ⏑|— ⏒ iamb. trim. =
⏑ —|⏑ —|⏑ —|⏑ ⏑ ⏑|⏑ —|— —

11.   ⏑ —|⏑ —|⏑ —|⏑ — }iamb. dim.
12.   ⏑ —|⏑ ⏑ ⏑|⏑ —|⏑ —

13.   ⏑ ⏑ ⏑|— ⏑|—— troch.

14. ◡ — — | ◡ — — — bacchii.

15-16. ◡ — | — ◡ ◡ ◡ | — ·· ◡ | — glycon.

17. — ◡ | — ◡ ◡ ◡ | — | — ◡ | ◡ ◡ ◡ | = dact. and troch. syzyg.

444-461. troch. tetram. catal.
511-530 = 531-550.

1. — ◡ ◡ | — ◡ ◡ | — dact.

2. — ◡ | — — — | — — strong troch. dipod.

3. — ≃ | — ◡ ◡ | — troch. and dact. syzyg.

4. — | — ◡ ◡ | — — | — dact. and strong troch. dip. with long anacr.

5. — | — ◡ ◡ | — — | — ◡ | — — | — dact. and strong troch. dip. with long anacr.

6. ⌢◡ | — ◡ ◡ | — ◡ ◡ | — — dact. and troch. with resolved anacr.

7. — — | — ◡ ◡ | — — ◡ | — ·· ◡ | ⌣⌣ ◡ | — ◡ dact. and troch.

8. ◡ ⌣⌣ | ◡ — | ◡ — | ◡ ◡ ◡ iamb. dim.

9. ◡ — | ◡ — ··· | ◡ ◡ ◡ ◡ | ◡ ◡ ◡ ◡ | ◡ — | ◡ — | ◡ — | — iamb. tetram. cat. = ◡ ◡ ◡ ◡ | ◡ ◡ ◡ ◡ | ◡ ◡ ◡ ◡ | ◡ ◡ ◡ ◡ | ◡ — | ◡ — | ◡ — | — (θεᾶς is a monosyllable.)

10. ◡ | ⌢◡ ◡ — | — ◡ — two cretics with anacr.

11. ◡ ◡ ◡ | ◡ ◡ ◡ | — ◡ | — troch. dim. cat. (Τρῴάδος, ω short as in πατρῷος and other similar words.)

12. ◡ — | ◡ — | ◡ — | ◡ — iamb. dim.

13. ◡ ◡ ◡ | ◡ ◡ ◡ | ◡ — | ◡ ◡ ◡ = ◡ ◡ ◡ | ◡ ◡ ◡ | ◡ — | ◡ — iamb. dim.

14. ≃ ◡ ◡ | ◡ ◡ ◡ | ◡ — | ◡ — iamb. dim.

15. }
16. } ◡ — | ◡ — | ◡ — | ◡ — iamb. dim.

17. ◡ | — ◡ | — — | — ◡ troch. syzyg. with anacr.

18. ◡ ◡ ◡ | — ◡ | — ◡ troch. syzyg.

551-567.

551-559. iamb. dim.

560-564. ◡ — | ⫰⫰ ◡ | — ◡ | — troch. with iamb. base.

565. ◡ — | ◡ — | ◡ ◡ ◡ | ◡ ◡ ◡ iamb. dim.

566. — ◡ ◡ | — ◡ ◡ | — dact.

567. ◡ — | ◡ ◡ ◡ | — — | — iamb. dim. cat.

568-576.   Anapaestic system.

στρ. α′ 577-581 = 582-585.

1. ⏑ — — ‖ — ⏑ | — ⏑ | — ⏑ bacchius + troch. tripody.

2. ⏑ — | ⏑ — ‖ — ⏑ | — ⏑ | — ⏑ iamb. dip. + troch. trip. (this verse by its violent antispastic movement is admirably adapted to express emotion).

3. — — | — | — ⏑ | — strong troch. dip. cat. + weak troch. dip. cat.

4. ⏑ ⏑ ⏑ | — ⏑ | — ⏑ troch. trip. (ithyphallic).

στρ. β′ 586-587 b = 588 a–588 d.

1-2. ⏑ — — | ⏑ — — bacchii.

3. — ⏑ ⏑ | — ⏑ ⏑ | — dact. penthemimer.

4. — ⏑ | — ⏑ | — ⏑ troch. trip. (ithyphallic).

στρ. γ′ 590-595 = 596-601.
Dact. hexam.

794-859.
στρ. α′ 794-806.

1. ⏑ | — ⏑ ⏑ | — ⏑ ⏑ | — ⏑ | — ⏑ ⏑ | — ⏑ ⏑ | — dact. with troch. clausula and short anacr.

2. — | — ⏑ ⏑ | — ⏑ ⏑ | — — | — ⏑ | — dact. and troch. with long anacr.

3. Dact. hexam.

4. — ⏑ ⏑ | — ⏑ ⏑ | — — | — ⏑ | — — dact. strong troch. clausula.

5. Dact. hexam.

6. ⏑ — — | — ⏑ ⏑ | — ⏑ ⏑ | — — | — ⏑ | — — | — ⏑ | — bac- chius and dact. troch. claus.

7. — ⏑ ⏑ | — ⏑ ⏑ | — — | — ⏑ ⏑   ⎫
8. — ⏑ ⏑ | — ⏑ ⏑ | — ⏑ ⏑ | — ⏑ | — — ⎭ dact. troch.

στρ. β′ 820-838.

1. ⏑ | — ⏑ | — | — ⏑ | — ⏑ | — ⏑ ⏑ | — ⏑ ⏑ | — — dact. troch. with anacr., the first troch. dip. being catal.

2-3. — ⏑ ⏑ | — ⏑ ⏑ | — dact. penthem.

4. — | — ⏑ | — — | — ⏑ | — ⏑ anacr. strong and weak troch. dip.

5. — ◡ ◡ | — ◡ ◡ | — ◡ ◡ | — ◡ ◡ dact. tetr.

6. — ◡ ◡ | — ◡ ◡ | — dact. penthem.

7. ◡͡◡ | — — | — ◡ | — troch. with anacr.

8. — ◡ | — ◡ ◡ | — ◡ | — dact. troch.

9. — ◡ ◡◡ | ◡◡ ◡ ◡ | — ◡ | — ◡ dact. troch. with resolu-
tion twice (of the cretic and dactyl) in antistrophe.

10. — ◡ | — ◡ | — ◡ | — ◡ troch. dim.

11. ◡͡◡ | — ◡ ◡ | — ◡ | — ◡ dact. troch. with anacr.

12. — ◡ ◡ | — ◡ ◡ | — dact. penthem.

13. ◡ — | ◡ ◡◡ | ◡ — | ◡ ◡ ◡ ◡ | ◡ ◡ ◡ ◡ | ◡ ◡ ◡ | ◡ — |
◡ — iamb. tetram. (obs. χρυσεος in antistrophe).

14. — ◡ ◡ | — ◡ ◡ | — ◡ ◡ | — ◡ ◡ | — — dact.

15. — ◡ | — ◡ | — — troch. trip. (ithyphallic).

1060-1122.
στρ. α' 1060-1070.

1-2-4-5. ◡ — | — ◡ ◡ | — ◡ | — glycon.

3-6. — — | — ◡ ◡ | — — pherecrat.

7. ◡ — | ◡ — || — ◡ | — ◡ | ◡◡ ◡ | — iamb. dip. + troch.
dim. cat. (antispastic movement characteristic of the Aeolian
measures of Pindar as contrasted with the Dorian).

8. ◡ ◡ ◡ | ◡ ◡ ◡ | ◡ ◡ ◡ | ◡ — iamb. dim. (perhaps we
should read ὀράνιον in antistr.).

9. — ◡ ◡ | ◡ — || ◡ ◡ ◡ | ◡◡ ◡ | — iamb. dim. + dochm.

10. — ◡ ◡ | — ◡ ◡ | — ◡ ◡ | — ◡ | — ◡ dact. with troch.
claus.

στρ. β' 1081-1099.

1. — ◡ ◡ | — ◡ ◡ | — dact. penth.

2. ◡ — | ◡ ◡ ◡ | ◡ — | ◡ iamb. dim. cat.

3. ◡ — | ◡ ◡ ◡ | ◡ ◡ ◡ | ◡ — | ◡ — | ◡ — iamb. trim.

4. — — | — ◡ | — ◡ ◡ | — ◡ dact. troch.

5. — | ◡ ◡ ◡ | ◡◡ ◡ | ◡ ◡ ◡ | — — ⎫
6. — | ◡ ◡ ◡ | — ◡ | — ◡ | ◡◡ ◡ | — — ⎬ troch. with anacr.

7. ◡ ◡◡ | ◡ — | ◡ — | ◡ — iamb. dim.

8. ◡ ◡ ◡ | ◡ — | ◡ — | ◡ — | ◡ — | ◡ — iamb. trim.

9. — ◡ — | — ◡ — | ◡ — | — ◡ — | ◡ — | ◡ ◡ ◡ | — ◡ |
— cretico-troch. (i.e. a succession of troch. dipodies, the first
four dipodies being catal.)

10-14. — ⌣ ⌣| — ⌣ ⌣| — dact. penthem.
15. ⌣ ⌣ ⌣|⌣ ⹦⹦|⌣ —| ≃ iamb. dim. catal.

1216-1217.

1216. ⌣ —|⌣ — iamb. dip.
1217. ἔθιγες … πόλεως. ⌣ ⌣ ⌣|⌣ ⌣ ⌣|—‖⌣ ⌣ ⌣|— ⌣ '
— ‖ ⌣ —|— ⌣|— dochm. trim.

1226-1229.

1226. — —|⌣ — iamb. dip.
1227. ὀδύρμα. ⌣|— ⌣|— ⌣|— ⌣ —|— ⌣ —|anacr. troch.
dip. cretics.
1228-1229. ⌣ —|⌣ —|— ⌣|⌣ iamb. dim. catal.
1230. οἴμοι. — —|— ⌣|— ‖ ⌣ —|— ⌣|— dochm. dim.

1235-1239.

1235, 6, 8. ⌣ ⹦ —|⌣ —|⌣ —| ≃ iamb. dim. cat.
1237. — — —
1239. imperfect; prob. was a dochm. dim. ; may have run
as Herm. suggests θαρσήσασ' ἔνεπε τίνα θροεῖς αὐδάν — —|— ⌣|
⹁ ‖ ⌣ ⌣ ⌣|— —|—

1250-1260.
Anapaestic.

1287-1293 = 1294-1301.

1. ⌣ ⌣ ⌣|⌣ ⌣ ⌣|— dochm.
2. ⌣ —|⌣ —|⌣ — iamb.
3. imperf., the antistr. verse is — ⌣|— ⌣|⌣ ⌣ ⌣|— ⌣|
— ⌣|— ⌣|— ⌣|— troch. tetr. cat.
4. This verse does not correspond with its antistr. ἄκρα τε
τείχεων, and as this verse may be either ⌣ —|⌣ —|⌣ — or
— ⌣ ⌣|— ⌣|— it does not lend itself to any correction of
the strophic line.
5. ⹦ ⌣|⹦⌣|⹦⌣|⹦⌣ troch. dim.
6. — ⌣|— ⌣|— ≃ troch. trip.
7. ⌣ ⹦|⌣ —|⌣ ⹦ | ⌣ ⹦⹦ iamb. dim.
8. ⌣ ⌣ ⌣|— ⌣|⌣ ⹦⹦|⌣ —|⌣ —| ≃ iamb. trim. catal.

I

1301–1315 = 1316–1332.

1. ◡ — — — | ◡ ◡ ◡ ◡ | — ◡ | — ◡ | — bacchius + troch. dim. cat.

2. ◡ — iamb.

3. — ◡͞◡ | ◡ ◡ ◡ ◡ | ◡ ◡ ◡ ◡ | ◡ — | ◡ — | ≃ iamb. trim. cat.

4. ◡ — | ◡ — ‖ — ◡ | — ◡ | — ◡ | — iamb. dip. + troch. movement (cp. 578, 1067, 1307, 1310).

5. ◡ — | ◡ — | ◡ — | ◡ ◡͞◡ | ◡ ◡͞◡ | ◡ — iamb. trim.

6. ◡ — | ◡ — | — ‖ ◡ — | ◡ — | — two iamb. dip. cat.

7. ◡ ◡́ ◡ | ◡ — ‖ ◡́ ◡ ◡ | — ◡ | — — iamb. dip. and troch. movement.

8. — ◡ | — ◡ | — ◡ | — ◡ }
9. — ◡ | — ◡ | — —   } troch.

10. ◡ ◡́ ◡ | ◡ ◡ ◡ ◡ | ◡ — | ◡ — ‖ — ◡ — iamb. with troch. clausula.

11. ◡͞◡ ◡ | ◡ ◡͞◡ | ◡ ◡͞◡ | ◡ ◡͞◡ | ◡ — | ◡ — iamb. trim.

12. ◡ ◡ ◡ | ◡ ◡ ◡ ◡ | ◡ ◡ ◡ ◡ | ◡ ◡ ◡ ◡ | ◡ ◡ ◡ ◡ | ◡ ◡ ◡ iamb. trim. with all the long syllables resolved.

13. — — | ◡ — | ◡ — | ◡ — iamb. dim.

14. ◡ — | ◡ — | ◡ ◡ ◡ | ◡ — | ◡ iamb. dim. hyperm.

15. ◡́ ◡ ◡ | ◡ ◡ ◡ | ◡ ◡ ◡ | — ◡ | — ◡ troch. trim. brachycatalectic (*i.e.* wanting a foot).

INDEX TO NOTES.

I. ENGLISH.

II. GREEK.

A.

ἄγειν δάκρυ, 1131.

ἀγωγός, 1131.

αἴγλαν, 550.

αἴρειν δόρυ, 1148.

ἀίσσει, 156.

ἄκληρος, 32.

ἄκρᾰ or ἄκρᾱ, 1297.

ἀλαστῶν, 570.

ἀλάστωρ, 941.

ἀλᾶται, 635.

ἀμβροτόπωλος, 536.

ἀμφί μοι, 511.

ἂν repeated, 985, 1244.

ἀνὰ in tmesis, 544.

ἄνα = ἀνάστηθι, 98.

ἀνάγειν ναῦν, 1126.

ἀναγέλασον, 332.

ἄντλον, 686.

ἀνύειν, 595.

ἀοιδός, adj., 385.

ἄορας, 831.

ἀπειρέσια, 570.

ἀπεμπολᾶν, 973.

ἀπήνη, 516.

A.

ἀπῆσαν, not with gen., 393.

ἀπό, pregnant, 522.

ἀπόδος, 'atone for,' 1040.

ἀποσκυθίζειν, 1026.

ἀποφθαρῶ, 507.

ἄρα, 1161, 1240.

'ἀροῦμεν)('ἀροῦμεν, 1148.

ἄρχειν, 790, 990.

αὐθεντῶν, 655.

αὐλός, 126.

B.

βαίνειν with accus., 128.

βάρβαρα, 'un-Greek,' 759.

βοᾷ, 're-echoes.' 29.

βρέμειν, of clash of arms, 520.

Γ.

γᾶθεν, 1105.

Δ.

δαίμων, 'lot,' 204.

δάσασθαι, fr. δατέομαι, 45.

δέλεαρ, 695.

διὰ κενῆς, 753.

διερέσσειν, 1258.

134

δίπορον = bimarem, 1097.
διαθέντες, 'the dead,' 175.
δούλειος, two termin., 1330.
δούρειος ἵππος, 14.
δυσ-, 75.

E.

ἐγκέφαλος. 1177.
ἐκγελᾷ, 1177.
εἰκούς, 1178.
εἰληγμένας, fr. λαγχάνω, 297
εἷλκε, 70.
εἰρεσία, 570.
ἐκ, 'after,' 495.
ἐν, 377, 513, 816.
,, in composition, 521.
ἐνδίκως, 961.
ἔνθα, 642.
ἔνθεν, 931, 951.
ἔνοπλον, 521.
ἔνοσις, 1326.
ἐξαιτεῖσθαι, 980.
ἐξανιστάναι, 'to destroy,' 926.
ἐξανύειν, 232, 595.
ἐξᾶσαι, 472.
ἐξελίσσειν, 3.
ἔξω, 345.
ἐπί, 315.
ἐπικεκλιμένος, 796.
ἐπιστάτης not 'shepherd,' 435.
ἐρειπίοις, 1025.
ἐρημία, 26, 564.
ἐρημόπολις, 598.
Ἐρινῦν, gen. plur., 457.
ἐς, 1201, 1211.
ἔστι, 'lives,' 356.

ἐσφέρετε, 351.
ἔσχον, 'gat,' 550.
εὐθαλής, 217.
εὐνάτορας, 831.
εὐσεβεῖν)(εὖ σέβειν, 85.
εὔφθογγος, 127.
ἔχει, 'holds,' not 'knows,' 294.
,, with part., 317, 1122.
,, followed by dat., 1176, 1318
ἐχρῆν, 390.

H.

ἡδονάς used objectively, 372.
ἦμεν or ἦ μέν or ἤμην, 474.
ἤνυσε, 595.
ἠσθημένος = αἰσθανόμενος, 633.

Θ.

θέᾳ for θεᾷ, 535.
Θεράπνα, 211.
θήσει, with simple dat., 1057.

I.

Ἰδαίου for Αἰγαίου, 1100.
ἰέναι with acc., 1104.
Ἰλιὰς κόρα, 526.
ἵξις, 396.
ἰτέα, 1193.

K.

Καδμείας, 'Boeotian,' 242.
καί in objections, 428.
καινίζειν, 889.
κάλως ἐξιέναι, 94.
κάνων, 6, 812.
καράτομος, 564.

στάθμη, 6.
στιβάς, 507.
σφαγεῖον)(σφάγιον, 742.
σχάζω, 810.

Τ.

τάδε, 100.
τεκοῦσα, 629.
τελαμῶνες, 1231.
τετραβάμονος ἀπήνας, 516.
τιθέναι with simple dat., 1057.
τοῖχοι, of a ship, 116.
τριτοβάμων, 275.
τρόποι, 'haviour,' 1204.
τύχαι, 104.

Υ.

ὑμνηθεῖμεν = ὑμνηθείημεν, 1244.
ὑπέστη, 415.

Φ.

φίλτρα, 859.

Χ.

χαλκεομήστωρ, 271.
χάριν, 536, 836, 1107.
χρυσός, 432.

Ψ.

ψυχή, 1171.

Ω.

ὧν = οἵων, 499.

GLASGOW: PRINTED AT THE UNIVERSITY PRESS BY ROBERT MACLEHOSE AND CO.